ALL HALLOWS' MAGIC

WHITE HAVEN WITCHES (BOOK 4)

TJ GREEN

All Hallows' Magic
Mountolive Publishing

ISBN 978-0-9951163-7-5

Cover design by Fiona Jayde Media
Editing by Missed Period Editing

Other Titles by TJ Green

Tom's Arthurian Legacy Series
Excalibur Rises - Short Story Prequel
Tom's Inheritance
Twice Born
Galatine's Curse
Tom's Arthurian Legacy Box Set

White Haven Witches Series
Buried Magic
Magic Unbound
Magic Unleashed

Invite from the author -

You can get two free short stories, *Excalibur Rises* and *Jack's Encounter*, by subscribing to my newsletter. You will also receive free character sheets of all the main Whitehaven Witches.

By staying on my mailing list you'll receive free excerpts of my new books, as well as short stories, news of giveaways, and a chance to join my launch team. I'll also be sharing information about other books in this genre you might enjoy.

Details can be found at the end of *All Hallows' Magic*

Cast of Characters

Avery Hamilton - owns Happenstance Books
Alex Bonneville - owns The Wayward Son pub
Reuben Jackson - owns Greenlane Nursery
Elspeth Robinson - owns The Silver Bough
Briar Ashworth - owns Charming Balms Apothecary
Mathias Newton - DI with Cornwall Police
Caspian Faversham - CEO Kernow Shipping

1

Avery looked out of the window of Happenstance Books and sighed. Winter was on its way.

Rain lashed down and water poured along the gutters, carrying crumpled leaves and debris. The street was populated by only a few hardened individuals who scurried from shop to shop, looking windblown and miserable.

She watched a young man struggle down the road, his arms wrapped around him in an effort to keep his leather jacket sealed. He really wasn't dressed for the weather. He had a beanie pulled low over his head, and she suspected it was soaked.

He paused in front of her shop and looked up at the sign, hesitated for the briefest of seconds, and then pushed the door open, making the door chimes ring. A swirl of damp air whooshed in before he shut it behind him and shook himself like a dog. He was of average height with a slim build, and his jeans hung off his hips. He pulled his woollen hat off and wiped the rain from his face, revealing light brown hair shorn close to his scalp. He looked up and caught Avery's eye.

Avery smiled. "Welcome. You've picked a great day for shopping."

He smiled weakly in response, but it was clear that his mind wasn't on the weather. "I had no choice. I'm looking for someone."

Avery frowned, sensing she already knew what was coming. She'd been feeling unsettled for days, and tried to put it down to the change in the seasons and the coming of Samhain in a couple of weeks. Unfortunately, that didn't explain the unusual tarot readings she'd had recently. "Who are you looking for?"

He looked around nervously, noting a few customers tucked into the armchairs she had placed around the displays and in corners. The blues album playing in the background contributed to the mellow feel, and the shop smelt of old paper and incense. Nevertheless, his eyes were filled with fear.

Avery smiled again, gently. "Come and talk to me at the counter. No one will hear you." She moved around behind the till, sat on a stool, and hoped the young man would feel less threatened with something between them.

He followed her, leaning on the counter and dropping his voice. "I'm new to White Haven. I arrived here recently with my family, drawn by the magic here. We've been trying to work out where it comes from—or rather, who," he said, rushing on, "and you're one of the people I've narrowed it down to."

Up close, Avery could see his pallor under his stubble, and his fear was more obvious. Despite that, he looked her straight in the eye, as if daring her to disagree. She kept her voice low and even. "May I ask how you can detect magic?"

"I may have some ability," he said, vaguely.

Avery hesitated, casting her awareness out. She could sense something unusual about him, but he didn't feel like a witch. He was risking a lot, she could tell, and suddenly it seemed mean to be so circumspect. "Your abilities have served you well. How can I help?"

"My brother is ill. He needs a healer."

"Why don't you take him to a doctor?"

"They would ask too many questions."

"I'm not a healer. Not a good one, anyway." His face fell. "But I do know someone who is. Can you tell me more?"

"Not here. Later. Can you come to this address?" He reached into his pocket, pulled a piece of paper out, and slid it across the counter.

She glanced at it, recognising the street. It ran along the coast on the hillside. There was no way that just she and Briar were going there. She didn't sense danger, but she didn't know him or his family. "Okay. But there'll be more than two of us, is that okay? We're all trustworthy."

He swallowed. "That's fine. So are we." With that he turned and left, a blast of cold air swirling behind him.

Avery went to the window and watched him run up the street, wondering where he was from, what magic he possessed, and where this visit would lead. It seemed the relative peace of the last few months wouldn't last.

Since Lughnasadh, the night they had successfully fought off the Mermaids with the aid of the Nephilim, life in White Haven had calmed down. She and the other four witches—El, Briar, Alex, and Reuben—had been able to get on with their lives without fear of being attacked. Their magic, released from the binding spell, still hung above the town, but it had reduced in size. The unusual level of spirit activity had continued, which meant they were still casting banishing spells regularly, but the three paranormal investigators—Dylan, Ben, and Cassie—monitored most of that.

Avery was disturbed from her thoughts by movement in her peripheral vision, and she turned to see Sally, her friend and shop manager, coming back from lunch.

Sally frowned. "You look deep in thought."

"I've just had a visitor."

"Oh?" Sally raised her eyebrows.

"He's scared and needs our help."

Sally knew all about Avery and other witches' powers. "You don't know him, I presume?"

"No. He's just arrived in White Haven. I need to phone Briar and Alex."

"All good. Have your lunch and take your time. It's not like we're run off our feet."

Avery nodded and headed to the room at the back of the shop where there was a small kitchen and stock room. From here there was a door that led to her flat above the shop, and she headed through it and up the stairs.

Her flat was in its usual, chaotic state. Books were scattered everywhere, the warm woollen blanket on the sofa was rumpled and half on the floor, and the room needed a good tidying. That would have to wait. It was cool, the central heating turned low, and she adjusted it slightly so it would be warmer for the evening. She pulled her phone from the back pocket of her jeans and called Briar while she put the kettle on and heated some soup.

Out of all of the witches, Briar was the most skilled at Earth magic and healing. She ran Charming Balms Apothecary and lived alone in a cottage off one of the many lanes in White Haven. Fortunately, Briar was free that evening, and after Avery arranged to collect her at six, she called Alex, hoping he wouldn't be too busy at work.

Alex owned The Wayward Son, a pub close to the harbour, and he was Avery's boyfriend, although she always felt really weird calling him that. It sounded like they were fourteen. But what else could she call him. Her lover? That sounded too French, and somehow seedy. Her partner? Sort of, but they didn't live together. Anyway, whatever she called him, he was all hers and completely hot, and she was smitten.

They'd got together in the summer, and things were still going strong.

"Hey kitten," he said when he answered her call. "How are you?"

"Kitten! I like that. I'm good, what about you?"

"Busy. The pub is pretty full for the lunch rush. I'm not exactly sure where they're coming from in this weather, but I can't complain."

"It's quiet here," she explained, leaning against the counter and stirring her soup. "But that's okay. Look, I'll get to the point. I've had a visitor, no one we know, but he knows we're witches and needs our help. Are you free tonight?"

She could hear the concern in his voice and the background noise fade away as he moved rooms. "What do you mean? He knows about us?"

"Yes, but he wouldn't explain. I sensed some kind of magic, but he's not a witch. He said he needs a healer, so I'm picking up Briar at six. Can you come with us?"

"Yes, absolutely. And I'll stay at yours tonight, if that's okay?"

She grinned. "Of course. See you later."

***

It was dark by the time the group pulled up outside the whitewashed house on Beachside Road. It was a double-fronted Victorian villa, used for holiday rentals. A portion of the front lawn had been turned into a drive, and an old Volvo hatchback took up most of the space.

"First impressions?" Briar asked from where she sat next to Avery on the front bench of her Bedford van. She was petite and pretty, and her long dark hair was pulled back into a loose ponytail.

"I can't feel anything magical," Avery said, feeling puzzled but also relieved.

"Me, neither," Alex agreed. He sat on the end, next to the passenger window, looking at the house. Like Briar he was dark haired, but far from petite. He was tall and lean, with abs to die for, and his arms were covered in tattoos. He often wore his shoulder length hair down, but tonight it was pulled back into a top knot and his jaw was covered in stubble. "It worries me. Didn't you even get a name?"

"Nope. He didn't stick around long enough," Avery answered. "But I didn't get anything dodgy from him. He was just scared."

"Come on," Briar said, pushing Alex to move. "If someone's hurt, we need to get on with it."

The rain still lashed down, and they raced up the path and sheltered beneath the porch as Avery knocked on the door.

A young woman with long, purple hair opened the door and scowled. "Who are you?"

"Charming," Alex said, amused. "We were invited."

A voice yelled, "Piper! You bloody well know who it is. Let them in."

Piper glared at them and then turned and stomped off, leaving the witches to let themselves in.

Briar smirked and shut the door behind them. "She seems fun."

They stood in a large hallway with doors on both sides, and directly ahead stairs led to the upper level. Piper had already disappeared, but the man Avery met earlier bounded down the staircase, looking both relieved and harassed. "Thanks for coming. I wasn't sure you would. Follow me." He immediately turned to head back up the stairs.

Alex called him back. "Hold on, mate. Before we go any further, who are you, and what's going on?"

He stood for a second, speechless, and then seemed to gather his wits. "Sorry. I'm not thinking straight. I'm Josh." He shook their hands. "My brother is really ill, and I'm worried he might not survive. That's what's upsetting Piper, too. She has a weird way of showing it. Look, I get that you're worried, but I'm not a threat. It's easier if I just show you."

It seemed that was all they would get from Josh, and he ran up the stairs. Alex glanced at Briar and Avery, and followed him. Avery could already feel their combined magic gathering, but she still didn't sense any magic from elsewhere. She gave a last sweep of the hall and then followed the others up the stairs.

On the first floor, Avery detected a strange smell. She wrinkled her nose. It was odd, unpleasant, and cloying.

Josh led them into a room at the back of the house, and as soon as they stepped inside, the smell magnified and Avery tried not to heave.

They were in a large bedroom, and in the double bed in the centre of the room a man lay writhing in a disturbed sleep. A young woman sat next to him, watching with concern, and trying to hold his hand. She looked up when they entered, and a mixture of fear and relief washed over her.

What is going on here?

The man was covered in a sheen of sweat, and his hair stuck to his head. He was bare-chested, but most of his trunk and one of his arms was wrapped in soiled bandages, and it was from these wounds that the smell emanated.

Briar ran forward. "By the Great Goddess! What the hell's happened to him? His wounds are infected!"

The young woman stood, moving out of the way. "Can you help him?"

Briar barely glanced at her. "I'll try. You should have come to me sooner. What's his name?" She placed her box of herbs, balms, and potions on the floor, and started to peel the man's bandages away. He immediately cried out, his arms flailing, and Alex leapt forward to help restrain him.

Josh explained, "He's Hunter, my older brother. This is my twin sister, Holly."

Holly nodded briefly at them, and then went back to watching her brother helplessly. Avery could see the similarity between her and Josh. They both had light brown hair and hazel eyes, although Holly was shorter than her brother, and her hair fell in a wavy bob to her shoulders. The man writhing on the bed had dark, almost black hair, a light tan, and a muscular build.

Avery asked, "What happened to him?"

Josh met her eyes briefly and then watched Hunter again. "He was attacked several days ago. We've been on the road, and only got here recently. It has taken me a while to track you down."

Avery watched Briar resort to using a sharp pair of scissors to cut the bandages away. Avery recoiled as the smell hit her, and then gasped at the size of the wounds. He had long, deep claw marks across his chest, back, and left arm, and they were inflamed and oozing pus. As Briar pulled the sheet away, they saw more bandages around his legs.

Alex looked up. "What the hell did this? And why didn't you go to a doctor?"

"Because they would have involved the police," Josh explained. "We can't afford that to happen."

As they watched Hunter twist and turn, Avery scented magic, and she looked around, alarmed. Briar and Alex must have too, because they paused momentarily.

"What's causing that?" Avery asked sharply, raising her hands, ready to defend herself.

"What?" Josh asked, his eyes wide.

"Magic. We can sense it now."

"Oh no," he answered. "He's changing again."

"He's what?"

But Avery could barely finish the question when Hunter shimmered in a strange way, as if his body was melting, and then his shape changed into a huge wolf, snarling and twisting on the bed.

"Holy crap!" Alex exclaimed, leaping backwards out of the way of his snapping jaws. "He's a *Shifter*! Why the hell didn't you warn us?"

"Because we hoped you wouldn't have to know," Holly said tearfully, running forward with Josh to try and calm her brother down. In a split second, she changed into a wolf too, leaving her clothes behind as she leapt onto the bed. She yelped, and her presence seemed to calm Hunter down. Within seconds, he lay back on the bed, panting heavily. His wounds looked even worse in this form if that was possible; his fur was matted and bloodstained.

Avery dropped her hands and sighed heavily. "You're all Shifters?"

"'Fraid so," Josh said with a weak smile.

"So, I guess he was attacked by another Shifter?"

"You could say that."

Briar leaned back on her heels. "This will probably make things a bit trickier."

"But can you still help?"

"Yes! I'm a good healer, but I have limited experience with Shifters."

Like none, Avery thought, *just like the rest of them.*

Briar continued, "Does he change a lot at the moment?"

Josh nodded. "He doesn't seem to be able to control it. His change won't last long, but we think it's getting in the way of his healing. His wounds keep opening, and we can't get them clean."

She nodded and thought for a second. "I need to give him a sedative. It will calm him down, which will hopefully prevent him from shifting."

"You have a spell for that?" Josh asked.

Briar shrugged. "In theory. I'll have to make it stronger than usual. I need your kitchen to make a slight change to one of the potions I have with me."

"I presume you're all witches, then?" Josh asked. "I mean, I thought that's what I sensed, but I wasn't sure."

"Yes, we are," Avery said. "But we'll talk later. For now, let Briar work her magic."

2

Josh escorted Briar to the kitchen, leaving Avery with Alex and the two Shifters.

Alex looked across the bed at Avery. "Well, this is new."

She grinned. "Isn't it?"

"I just wish I didn't have the feeling they've brought trouble with them."

"They seem harmless—for wolves. At least they're not Mermaids," she said, referring to the summer when they'd been attacked by the Daughters of Llyr. She looked at Holly. "Can you understand me, wolfy?"

Holly thumped her tail on the bed and Avery laughed. "This is so weird." She sobered up when she looked at Hunter. "He's in a bad way."

"Briar will fix him," Alex said, confidently. "If she can cure demon burns, she can stop infected wounds."

"They sound like they're from up north somewhere," Avery observed. "Cumbria or Lancashire, maybe."

"In that case, they've travelled a long way to get here. I wonder what they're running from?"

"It's not what, it's who," a young, petulant voice said from behind them.

Piper. She stood in the doorway, pouting in her low-slung jeans and t-shirt, her pale brown eyes made up with dark purple makeup that matched her hair.

"Was it some sort of turf war?" Alex asked from where he leaned against the wall, keeping a watchful eye on Hunter.

"Yes. And we lost. Or rather, he did. And now we're stuck here, miles from home." Her voice dripped with resentment and Holly growled at her, and before they could ask Piper anything else, she turned with a flounce and disappeared.

"She's such a delight," Alex said dryly. "I like her more every time I see her."

Avery glanced at Holly, who was now watching Hunter whimper in his sleep, twitching as if he was dreaming.

"I would imagine this has been a nightmarish few days for all of them," Avery observed.

Within minutes Briar returned with Josh, carrying a gently steaming potion. Josh was carrying a bowl of hot water. Briar had barely settled herself by the bed when Hunter shimmered again and changed back to human form. "Oh good. This will make life easier," she said. "Alex, help lift his head, please."

Between them they manoeuvred Hunter into a sitting position and Briar trickled the potion between his lips, whispering a spell as she did so. Within seconds he relaxed and his breathing deepened, and Alex lowered him back on the bed.

"Right, time to clean up this mess," Briar said resolutely. She chose a selection of herbs and dropped them into the water, and then started to clean the wounds with a soft cloth.

"So, what happened?" Avery asked Josh. "Piper said he lost a fight."

"We live in a small hamlet in Cumbria called Chapel Stile. It's right in the centre of the Lake District, and perfect for Shifters. It's remote and there's plenty of space for us. Quite a few Shifter families live in the area, and we generally get along well. Until recently." He fell silent for a moment, and

Avery wondered if that's all he would tell them, but then he rubbed his face and sighed. "The head of one of the other families died recently and his son took over. He's now the pack's Alpha. He's imposing some new rules and we didn't like them. Hunter was pretty vocal about it, and he was attacked."

"If you don't mind me saying, that sounds quite medieval," Avery said, wondering how bad the new rules could be that made someone want to fight.

"It is. Nothing has happened like that for years." He looked Avery in the eye, finally. "We were taken by surprise. Hunter's a good man. He looks after us, and he's been in his fair share of fights—Shifters are always territorial—but this fight was really vicious."

Avery looked at Hunter's wounds. "It looks like he was trying to kill him."

Josh nodded grimly. "I think he was."

"You should have settled the score, Josh." Piper spoke from behind them again. She leaned on the doorframe, her tone accusatory.

"Shut up, Piper," he shot back. "You're talking rubbish, as usual. If I'd fought, then we'd both be in this mess, and you and Holly would be in big trouble. You know what Cooper is like. He's a misogynist bully."

She glared at him, but dropped her eyes to the floor, seemingly in agreement. "I want to go home."

Josh's tone softened. "So do I, but I'm not sure that's possible anymore."

"Have you lost your house?" Avery asked, incredulous.

"No. I just meant it would be dangerous to return. We might have to sell. Can we have your permission to live here, at least for now?"

Avery was speechless, but Alex snorted from across the bed where he was helping Briar. "Mate, you don't need our permission. Stay here as long as you like."

"He's right, we don't own White Haven," Avery agreed, perplexed by his question. "You can live here if that's what you decide."

"Are there other Shifters in the area?"

"Not as far as I know," she answered. "But then again, this place keeps surprising us lately."

"We like the wild places—the moors, the peaks, and the lakes. But you are on the edge of moorland here."

"Yes, and there are weirder things than Shifters around, I can assure you," she said, thinking of the Nephilim. "Are there witches in Cumbria?"

"Oh yes. And they align with Cooper."

"We align with no one except each other," Alex explained. "Is anyone likely to follow you here?"

"I hope not," Josh said, not meeting their eyes.

Avery had a horrible feeling he wasn't sure about that.

***

The following evening, Avery met the other witches at Alex's flat above the pub, and Newton, their friend the Detective Inspector, joined them.

They had ordered in Thai food, and delicious aromas wafted around the room. Reuben, as usual, had filled his plate, and sat on the sofa with it perched on his knee. He and El were a couple, and El spent a lot of her weekends at Greenlane Manor, Reuben's huge estate. They were both tall and blonde, laid back and well suited. Briar was single, and although she and Newton seemed to have something going for a while, since their battle with the Mermaids, it had fizzled. Newton still struggled to reconcile their magic with his job. He also struggled with the Nephilim sticking around, and he wasn't too happy about Shifters arriving in White Haven, either.

"Shifters? Do you mean Shapeshifters?"

"I don't know any other kind of Shifter," Briar said, annoyed.

"How long are they planning to stay?"

She frowned at him. "As long as they need! And Hunter is badly injured, so he'll have to stay until he's better. That could be weeks."

"How was he tonight?" Alex asked her.

"Slightly better. His wounds don't smell anymore. He'll have scars, though."

"Was he still changing without control?" Avery asked.

"No. My sedative sorted that out. He woke this morning and had some food, and then I dosed him up for the day again."

"He was awake? That's good, right?" El asked from where she sat in her favourite corner of the sofa. "I'd like to meet them."

"And you will, but they're keeping a low profile for now, until Hunter's better," Briar explained.

"Well, I think I should meet him," Newton said, decisively. "We don't want trouble here."

Briar glared at him again. She had very little patience with Newton lately. "They won't bring trouble! Stop being so patriarchal."

"I'm a detective. It's my job."

"It's your job to solve murders. They haven't murdered anyone!"

An awkward silence fell, and Reuben leapt in. "Well, I heard from Gabreel the other day, or Gabe, as he prefers to be called."

"The Nephilim?" Alex asked.

"Well, I don't know another Gabreel," Reuben said with a smirk.

"What did he want?"

"A job for Asher, one of his winged buddies." Reuben owned Greenlane Nurseries, and although it was the winter months, they still had a couple of large greenhouses that they kept stocked, ready for the spring and summer months. They also sold lots of shrubs that kept the place ticking over all year.

"A Nephilim who likes gardening. Nice," Avery said. "Did you offer him a job?"

"I did. A couple of the teens we employed left for University a few weeks ago, so he can fill in for them. He'll start next week. Fully legit, too. They have paperwork and everything."

Newton looked suspicious. "How have they got that?"

"I don't know and I don't care," Reuben said, forking up another mouthful of noodles.

"Strange you should say that," Alex said. "Gabreel came looking for a job with me, too. Well, for Amaziah, actually. Zee for short. So, he starts behind the bar next week."

"Which one is he?" El asked, frowning. "I'm trying to put faces to names."

"Hawk-nose, black hair, dark-skinned—if that helps?"

"Vaguely. The last time I saw them was in a storm, and to be honest, I can't remember them clearly."

"Well, it sounds like we'll be seeing a lot more of some of them," Alex said, helping himself to more food.

Briar looked thoughtful. "I could offer one of them some part-time work. Cassie can only help out a couple of days now that term has started again."

Cassie was one of the ghost-hunters they'd met in the summer; she'd started working with Briar to learn about magic, and to learn a few simple spells to help with their paranormal investigations. She studied Parapsychology at Penryn University with Ben. Dylan, the third member, studied English Folklore.

Newton frowned and looked as if he might complain again, but Briar gave him a challenging stare and he wisely chose not to comment. Avery tried not to smirk. However, Alex simply nodded. "Great, I'll let Gabreel know. I think he's trying to set up a security business as a long-term plan, which sort of makes sense. I think some of the others have managed to get bartending jobs across town."

El placed her empty plate on the coffee table. "So, what are we doing about Samhain this year? I presume we're going to celebrate together?"

Samhain, or All Hallows' Eve, was one of the important dates in the calendar for witches, one of the eight Sabbats, and they'd taken to celebrating them together. The celebrations consisted of feasting, celebrating the turn of the seasons, and cementing their relationships with each other. It was also a time to remember the dead and their ancestors. The energy of such gatherings would be significant, but generally no magic was performed.

Avery groaned. "Genevieve wants us to celebrate with the other covens. It came up at the last meeting. I've been meaning to tell you."

Genevieve Byrne was the leader of the Witches Council, which governed the thirteen covens of Cornwall, and Avery was White Haven's representative. The meetings took place every couple of months, and the latest had been only a few days ago. Avery had refused the invitation to join the celebrations for Lughnasadh after Genevieve declined to help defend White Haven against the Mermaids. She still felt a guilty pleasure over telling Genevieve where to stick the invite.

"Really?" Briar asked, excited. "I'd love to meet everyone!"

"Me, too!" El agreed. "Don't you?"

"I guess so," Avery said, shrugging. "I like it when we do our own thing, but it will be a good chance to meet all the other covens."

"I'm game," Reuben said, having finally finished eating. "One giant party. Sounds great!"

Alex smiled and winked at Avery. "Sounds like that's a yes from us. Where will we all meet?"

"Rasmus's house. He has large grounds on the edge of New Quay, surrounded by a wood. It's very private, apparently. It's where the covens celebrate all the Sabbats. I'll get in touch with Genevieve and give her the good news."

3

The next day was Saturday, the rain had eased, and cheered on by the bright autumnal sunshine, Sally had started to decorate the shop for Halloween.

"Don't you think there are a few too many decorations?" Avery observed from the counter. Sally was stringing up toy skeletons, witches, and ghouls in the windows and around the shelves. On the counter were strings of fairy lights, and in the room at the back of the shop was a mountain of fake pumpkins, ready to fill any gaps.

"No. The more the merrier. It's Halloween, Avery, in under two weeks! The most important date in White Haven!" She grinned, her face flushed, hair tied up on her head, and her sleeves rolled up. "I've got plans for the corner in the next room. You're going to set it up as a reading corner, and we're going to do evening readings of scary stories for kids. I've arranged it with the local school."

"You have?" Avery's heart sank. Lots of kids in her shop. They'd cause havoc! She looked around at her neat displays and tried to dispel the vision from her head.

Sally sighed. "Avery, trust me. It will bring in lots of customers, and parents will be here to supervise them."

"Who's going to read to them?" she asked. Please don't let it be me.

"Me, of course." Dan said, joining them from across the room where he'd been chatting to some customers. Dan was Avery's assistant who was also doing post-grad English studies. He'd also almost met his doom at the hands of Nixie, one of the Mermaids. "It'll be fun."

"Great," Avery said, slightly relieved. "I presume I'll still have to do something?"

"Yes. You, like us, will be dressed up and helping customers stock up on books and their occult needs."

Avery narrowed her eyes. "What do you mean, dressed up?"

Both Sally and Dan looked very pleased with themselves, and Avery had a sinking feeling.

"Well," Dan said, "I'm going to be Dracula. I have a very long, sweeping cloak that I can wrap myself in. I can't wait."

Avery raised an eyebrow. "Really? I didn't take you for a fancy dress type of guy."

"There's a lot you don't know about me, Avery," he said with a certain aloofness. "Sally will be dressed as a zombie. And guess what you'll be?"

"Please don't say a witch."

"Of course you'll be a witch."

She lowered her voice. "Isn't that a bit obvious, all things considered?"

"No. It's perfect. Very meta."

Sally agreed. "I've already bought you a big witch's hat."

"You're kidding me! We haven't done this any other year!"

"Change is good," Sally insisted. "Besides, the Town Council want to make this a really good festival, seeing as Lughnasadh ended earlier than planned."

That was their fault, Avery reflected, since they'd had to get Eve, a weather witch from St Ives, to make a huge storm to cover up their fight with the Mermaids on the beach. It had worked, but consequently the crowds had fled the beach earlier than usual.

Sally continued, "And Stan, our Councillor slash Druid is coming to inspect all the shops."

"I give up," Avery declared. "All right. I suppose it will be fine."

"It will be great, trust us," Dan said, smirking. "I can't wait to see you in costume."

"Be careful," Avery said, "Or I might just hex you."

They were interrupted by the arrival of Ben, one of the ghost-hunters. Avery turned to him with relief. "Hey, Ben. Keeping busy?"

Ben was average height with a stocky build and short, dark hair. He was wearing jeans, a university hoodie, and a jacket shrugged over the top. He greeted the others and then said, "Too busy. Spirit sightings are going up, particularly around Old Haven Church."

"Really? I thought things were slowing down."

"So did I, but not anymore."

"Halloween magic?" Dan asked, wide-eyed.

"Oh please," Avery said. "You missing all the action from the summer?"

"Not really. I'll leave you to it," he said sheepishly, and he and Sally went back to decorating the shop.

Ben fished in his pocket and pulled out his phone. "I'm wondering if these might have anything to do with it. I took pictures of a couple of things we found hanging on the trees around the cemetery."

He showed Avery a photo of a bundle of twigs in the shape of a pentagram strung up high on the branch of a tree.

Avery frowned. "That's weird. I wonder how long it's been there."

"Not long at all. We normally scope out the area every time we go up there, which is reasonably frequently. We have a few night vision cameras set up, courtesy of the vicar."

"The vicar? James?"

"Yep, the same one who looks after the Church of All Souls. He kept in touch after the events there," he said meaningfully, referring to the appearance of the Nephilim and the death of Harry, the verger. Avery was astonished. She had no idea he'd kept in touch with Ben and the others.

"Why didn't you say so?"

"I didn't think of it. Anyway, this is a proven hot spot, so we like to keep tabs on it. This," he said, indicating the photo, "appeared in the last week."

Avery was perplexed. Who could be placing those around the church grounds? Was there another witch in the area they didn't know about? And what were they hoping to achieve? She made a decision. "Show me."

***

Old Haven Church looked beautiful in the weak sunshine. The large, grey blocks of local stone it was made from looked golden in the light, and long shadows were already streaking across the old, lichen-covered gravestones.

Avery looked across to the Jacksons' Mausoleum where Gil, Reuben's brother, had been laid to rest only months before, at the beginning of the summer. Beneath it was a hidden room where previous generations of the witches had gathered to celebrate magical rites. She shivered. It was a creepy place, and she hoped she never had to go back there. Ben had no idea about the hidden room, but he knew all about Reuben's brother and how he died.

The church was locked and the grounds were deserted, and Ben led the way down winding paths between the graves to an older part of the cemetery at the rear. Old Haven Church was out of town, high on the hill above the coast, and very few services or burials were held there anymore. Gil's had been an exception because of the family mausoleum.

At the edge of the oldest graves at the rear of the cemetery was a small wood. The trees were a mixture of mainly oak and beech with some shrubby undergrowth, and at this time of year their branches were bare except for a few hardy leaves clinging on. The rest were thick underfoot.

"This is where we've set up the cameras," Ben explained, as he pointed to a couple of devices situated in a sheltered spot on the edge of the wood, protected from the elements by a wooden box. "We've found that this place is the most likely to have spirit manifestations—probably because it's the oldest part of the grounds. We train the cameras on the graves. But the weird twig-things are further in."

The wood was left to grow wild and unkempt, and he led Avery through the tangle of branches and over fallen, mossy tree limbs and rotting trunks to a small clearing. He pointed to where one item swung from the branch of a huge, gnarled tree in the centre, twigs and feathers bound together in an odd shape. "Does it have a name?"

Avery frowned, puzzled as to who had put them there. "Witch runes, witch twigs, spell-casters. They have lots of names. Their intent is more to offer the warning that a witch is around, to scare others, too. They look spooky to the uninitiated. But why are they here?"

Ben looked as puzzled as she did. "Would Reuben have put them here? Because of his brother?"

"No. This is not Reuben's style. It's pretty old school, to be honest." Avery moved closer and squinted up at it. "I'm not sure I recognise this sign." She pulled her phone out of her bag and snapped a picture of it so she could look it up later.

"Why don't you take it with you?" Ben asked.

"I don't know who's put it there, and I'd rather they don't know that we know it's here. And I can feel the magic around them. I don't suppose you have any footage of whoever put it there?"

"No. They obviously spotted the cameras." He shrugged, "I mean, we haven't tried to hide them. And whoever put these here could have approached from any direction. This wood backs onto fields with only the low church wall between them."

Avery looked around, astonished. "I honestly did not know that the wood was this big, and I certainly didn't know there was a clearing in the middle of it." She turned and explored the surrounding trees, looking carefully to see if there were any more hidden in the tangle of branches, but apart from the couple Ben had told her about, she couldn't see any. And then realisation dawned, and she groaned. "This is a yew tree. That changes everything."

Ben looked confused. "Why?"

"Because yews have huge significance. They're present in churchyards across the whole country. Some have several, many at the gates of the church. They protect against evil, but they are also guardians to the Underworld, death, and the afterlife. Churches were built next to them deliberately," she mused, "not the other way around. Many yews are hundreds, if not thousands, of years old."

"Another case of Christians jumping on pagan traditions?"

"Absolutely. They are a potent force for protection against evil. " Avery pointed. "Look at it. The trunk isn't like a normal tree. It has several trunks forming one tree, and the older it gets, the more the trunks are hollowed out, forming a space within the tree. It keeps its needles all year round, and every bit of it is poisonous."

Ben stepped into the space. "You can walk right into and through this one. It's huge."

Avery frowned. "I'm going to do a bit more research on yews. As for the witch-signs, there's too few to create a big spell, but maybe whoever's put them there is starting slowly. When are you next due to come here?"

"Another couple of days, why?"

"Keep me informed if any more appear. I think we have another witch in White Haven, and I don't know what he or she wants. I'm worried it's nothing good."

Ben led the way back to the edge of the grove and started to exchange the camera memory cards while they were talking. "I'll check these later. If there's anything interesting, I'll let you know. If there's spirit activity, do you want to come up one night?"

She sighed. "I suppose so. And I'd better tell the others."

4

The next night, Avery was with Briar at the Shifters' house. Hunter was sitting up in bed, wincing as Briar inspected his wounds, and Avery stood to the side watching, Josh and Holly next to her.

"They look better," Briar said, looking pleased. "They're already closing up. How do you feel?"

He watched her deft hands admiringly. *Interesting. It seems Briar has another fan.* "I feel a lot better. What did you do?" His voice was deep and resonant with a Cumbrian accent, yet surprisingly gentle.

Briar smiled briefly. "I used some healing Earth magic. Combined with your own natural magic, it worked well. They were nasty wounds. You're lucky I got to you before the infection killed you."

"I know. Thank you," he said, his eyes appraising her.

Hunter, when he wasn't as white as a sheet and covered in sweat, was handsome in a reliable, easy on the eyes kind of way. His dark hair was tousled, and his muscled physique was fit and athletic, although covered in scars. A lot of him was on show, despite the sheet draped around him.

"Before you put my dressings back on," he continued, "can I have a shower? I smell like crap."

"Of course," Briar said, stepping away from the bed. "It'll help clean your bites."

He smiled and stood, pulling the sheet around him. Avery turned to Josh and Holly. "How are you two feeling?"

"Happier now that he's well," Holly said, watching her brother leave the room. She met Avery's eyes. "I still don't know what we're going to do, but at least we have some thinking time."

"We have to go back at some point," Josh pointed out. "I don't think we can stay here forever."

"I know, but part of me doesn't want to fight Cooper." Holly sat on the bed and looked at her feet. "If we go back, it means more fighting, and Hunter might not survive."

"He might win," Josh pointed out.

"Perhaps, but how long would it last?" Holly said, glaring at her brother. "Cooper wants us to influence his businesses at the expense of our own. It's a nightmare, but I don't think it's worth losing a life over. And even though Hunter is a good fighter, he's not a killer. We can sell our house and move here!"

Once again, Piper appeared in the doorway like a ghost. "I don't want to move here. This isn't home!"

"You want to fight Cooper? Go ahead!" Holly said, her voice dripping with disdain. "I'd like to see how far you get. Hunter fights better than any of us, and look what happened to him."

"We ran away. You're cowards," Piper spat.

"Take that back!" Holly leapt to her feet, her voice dropping to a snarl.

"Never." Piper squared up to her. "We ran, and I'm ashamed."

"Shut up, Piper," Josh warned, pushing her away. "Holly has a very short temper right now. You want to get a few bites, too?"

Holly's eyes had turned a molten yellow, and her face started to lose its human appearance. Avery stepped back, alarmed, and she noticed Briar did the same. Avery instinctively called the wind to her, and a gust blew around the room and energy sparkled in her hands.

That was enough to snap Holly out it; her shoulders dropped and her eyes returned to their normal pale brown, watching Avery warily.

"Sorry. Instinct," Avery murmured. "How much control do you have over shapeshifting? I mean, I've never met a Shifter before."

"Very good control," Josh said before Holly could respond. "Except when you're as injured as Hunter, or provoked. But Holly knew what she was doing, didn't you?" He was clearly expecting Holly to apologise.

"I'm tired," she explained. "And annoyed at someone's constant whingeing."

Piper just glared.

"Are you all wolves?"

"Yep, runs in the family—like witchcraft, I guess," Josh said, sitting on the edge of the bed.

"And you turn from a young age?"

"Not really until our teens. Some earlier, some later, but that's the average."

Briar had been listening as she prepared more bandages and salve for Hunter's wounds. "I guess you learn to control it as you grow, like we do. I can sense it—it's a different sort of magic."

Avery agreed. "Me, too. I could sense it when you first walked in my shop. It's stronger when you're worried."

Holly laughed. "The Wolf creeps closer to the surface, then. It's a defence thing."

Briar looked up, frowning. "So, where are your parents? Can't they help with this Cooper guy?"

"'Fraid, not," Josh said, his voice tight. "They both died a few years ago. Car accident." He didn't elaborate further.

"Sorry," Briar murmured, and Avery added her condolences.

Piper narrowed her eyes. "You're asking a lot of questions."

"We're curious, that's all. Ask us about being a witch if you want," Avery shot back.

"Don't care," she said simply and flounced out of the room.

"Sorry," Josh said, sighing. "She's not normally so nightmarish. She's just missing home. And she adores Hunter, so she's been more scared than she wants to admit. She'll come round."

"She'd better," Holly said, following her out of the room.

As she left, Hunter strode back in with a towel wrapped around his lower half, his sheet in his hands. "That's better. I'm all yours," he said, smiling at Briar.

His injuries haven't affected his libido, Avery thought.

"Your injuries are horrendous," Avery said, noting them fully now that he was standing. Huge claw marks were raked down his back and side, and also across his chest. One streaked across his neck, almost hitting his cheek. And he was covered in bruises. "They must hurt."

He winced as he sat down close to Briar. "They do, but the potions helped. Thanks for allowing us to stay here, and helping us."

"I'm sure Josh must have explained that's not how it works in White Haven. You don't need our permission to be here."

"But you've given it, right? Allowed us Sanctuary?" He was strangely insistent.

"Yes. If you want permission, you've got it," she said, bewildered.

"And you are witches?" he asked, wincing again as Briar dressed his wounds with a salve.

"Yes. There are five of us in White Haven, and more across Cornwall. But you have witches in the Lakes, I understand," she said, remembering what Josh had told her.

"Yes, and they control what goes on. They wouldn't appreciate unknown paranormal creatures showing up unannounced."

Strange. She had so much to learn about other witches. "Maybe it's because there are a lot of Shifters where you come from. What about this Cooper character? How much control does he have?"

"Not as much as he wants." Hunter scowled, and Avery wasn't sure if it was in pain or from the thought of Cooper. "He caught me by surprise, the bastard. That's why I'm so badly injured. But I'll go back when I'm healed."

Josh almost jumped in surprise. "We will? I wasn't sure you'd want to."

"Of course I want to," Hunter said, glaring at Josh. "Our home is there. You didn't think I was just going to roll over and let him think he'd won, did you?"

"I wasn't sure what you'd want to do, if I'm honest. He almost killed you, and I had to protect our sisters and get out of there."

Hunter's eyes softened momentarily. "And you did the right thing. But I will go back. It's not over."

Briar spoke softly as she unrolled a long bandage. "Well, you'd better prepare yourself for a long wait. These will take weeks to heal. If you fight too soon, they'll open up again. Lift your arm."

He smiled at her and did as instructed, watching her as she leaned in and wrapped the bandage around his chest, turning slightly to help her.

"At least I know if I get injured again you could help," he said, pleased with himself.

"Not if you're in Cumbria I won't. It's a bit far."

"You wouldn't visit?" he teased.

"Nope. I have a business to run." She kept her head down and concentrated on his dressings.

He fell silent and Avery tried not to smirk. "What do you guys do for a living?"

Josh answered, Hunter clearly distracted by Briar. "We have a family business, taking groups of tourists around the Lakes—day trips, walks, kayaking, hiking, camping. We know the place like the back of our hands."

"Does everyone know what you are?"

"No way. It's a Shifter community, but nobody outside the pack knows. That's the beauty of the Lakes. It's wild and areas of it are remote, so we can shift with complete privacy."

"We keep a low profile, too, as much as possible," Avery said. "Will anyone come looking for you here?"

"Let's hope not," Josh said, tiredly running his hands across his face. Avery noticed, however, he refused to meet her eyes. "We don't aim to bring any trouble to you."

"Don't worry. We handle trouble pretty well."

***

"I think you have an admirer," Avery said to Briar as they walked down the hill into White Haven. It was a calm night, cold and clear, and stars sparkled in the sky above them. It would frost later, the chill was already gathering. Avery pulled her jacket together and huddled into her scarf.

"He's a flirt," Briar said, embarrassed. "It means nothing."

Avery adopted a teasing, singsong voice. "Hunter and Briar sitting in a tree, K-I-S-S-I-N-G."

"You have to be kidding me! How old are you?" Briar exclaimed.

"Sorry," Avery said, laughing. "It's nice. He's nice. I can sort of see you together."

"Really? Mr Hunter Shapeshifter, I'm going back to fight the big bad wolf. I don't think so."

"Do you and Newton catch-up anymore?" Avery asked, hoping she wasn't prying too much.

"No. I'm a witch, he's a detective. It doesn't work. And besides, I have work to keep me busy right now."

"Never too busy for love."

"That's because you're all loved up with Alex. It's not a complaint," she added quickly. "I'm pleased for you. Anyway, moving on from my love life, why are we meeting tonight?"

"I think there's a rogue witch in White Haven. Come on, get a move on. Last one in the pub gets the round."

They arrived at The Wayward Son breathless and with flushed cheeks. Briar was surprisingly quick, and Avery followed her through the door wishing she hadn't made the bet. She headed to the bar and ordered two glasses of wine, white for Briar and red for her, but Simon, one of the regular bar staff, gestured up towards the ceiling. "I wouldn't bother. He's got wine upstairs. He said to send you up."

"Fair enough," Avery said, and they wound their way through the crowded tables to the small room at the back of the pub, and the stairs that led to Alex's flat.

He answered the door with a flourish. "Welcome, ladies." He leaned in and gave Avery a breath-taking kiss, and Briar sidled past them. "Missed you," he murmured.

"Get a room," Reuben yelled from the sofa in Alex's living room.

Avery laughed and headed into the flat as Alex closed the door behind her. "Thanks, Reuben. As usual, you completely spoil the mood."

El was leaning against the counter that separated the kitchen from the living area, giggling. "That's what he's here for. How're our Shifter friends?"

Briar shrugged her jacket off and put it on the back of a chair. "Hunter's better. But he'll be scarred for life. There's some stuff I can't heal."

"Will they go back?"

Avery nodded. "Oh, yes. He intends to fight this Cooper guy."

"I'd do the same," Reuben said. "Let's face it, we did it here. You protect your own space."

"Well, he's not well enough yet," Briar answered. She took the glass of wine that El passed to her. "By the way, Gabe, the Nephilim, came into my shop today, and he brought Eli with him. I think they're shortening all their names so they blend in a bit more. Eliphaz sounds so Old Testament."

"And?" Avery asked, curious.

"Eli is starting with me on Monday—tomorrow, in fact!" She looked baffled. "I must admit, I didn't think one of them would want to work in my shop. It's not exactly exciting. He's going to be bored stupid."

Alex laughed. "It's money. I'm sure he'll be fine. Which one is he?"

"He's tall—"

"Aren't they all?" Avery interrupted.

"Olive-skinned, green-eyed, brown hair, clean-shaven. And silent. Didn't say a word. This could be really weird. Cassie never stops talking."

Reuben grunted. "Just one more thing for the locals to comment on. Ash started a few days ago, too. He's pretty quiet, but can he carry stuff! He works twice as hard as anybody else."

"I wonder where else we'll see them around town?" Avery asked. "In fact, I've been trying to work out which one was at the Church in Harecombe."

"Maybe it's better we don't know," El said.

Alex started to get food ready in the kitchen. "We're bound to work it out one day. Zee starts his first shift tomorrow, so let's hope he can communicate. It's better in a pub to have chatty bar staff."

As he was talking, Avery's phone rang, and she reached into her bag and saw it was Ben. She inwardly sighed. I know what this is about. "Hey, Ben. Let me guess. More witch-marks."

"Plenty more," he answered. "And things are starting to look really weird at Old Haven."

"They are?" she asked, alarmed. The others all turned at her tone. "How weird?"

"There's some sort of design burnt into the ground. Do you want to see?"

She groaned. "Couldn't you have called in the daytime?"

"I've only just found it! Trust me. You'll want to see this."

"You skulk about at night? In the freezing cold?"

"It's the job! Get your ass over here."

He rang off and she looked up at the others. "I had meant to tell you all over dinner, but guess what? Dinner will have to wait. We're heading to Old Haven Church."

***

Old Haven was dark. Very dark. There were no street lights, and no lights along the paths that snaked around the graves. The air was crisp, a low ground mist had started to rise, and an owl hooted in the distance.

"This had better be good," Reuben complained. "I'm freezing my ass off and I'm not in the mood for spirit banishing. If this is Caspian's doing, I'll fry him."

Avery had told them about the witch-signs on the way over, and they had speculated about who could be putting them there.

"This is not Caspian," Avery said firmly. "He's far more direct. And I think he's too busy to be sticking up witch-signs at Old Haven. "

"I agree," Alex said, striding quickly along the path, his torch illuminating the way ahead. "He'd be more sophisticated than this."

It wasn't long before they heard voices and saw lights ahead of them, illuminating the trees' bare branches. The ghost-hunters. They stood huddled together, and turned when they heard the others approach.

"Hey, guys," Dylan greeted them. He was wearing a large puffer jacket that swelled his slim frame. "Glad you could make it."

"I had nothing better to do than drink beer and eat," Reuben said sarcastically.

Dylan grinned. "You'll be glad you came!"

"Will I? I'm not sure about that. So what are we all so excited about?"

"Follow me!"

Dylan led them into the clearing in the centre of the grove and pointed his torch at the ground.

A rune was scorched into the earth.

"What the hell is that?" El exclaimed, dropping to a crouch and reaching out tentatively to touch the scorch marks.

"Well, it's why you're here," Ben said, testily. "We've never seen anything like it before. And there are more of these." He pointed to the yew tree. From its branches hung dozens of witch-signs—twigs of all shapes and sizes, making strange runic shapes.

Avery shivered. The glow from the torch lit the witch-marks up and cast strange shadows on the trees. Coupled with the very large rune burnt into the ground, it was undeniably weird. "Why did you come here at this hour?"

"We came to check the cameras and do some readings with the gear, and I thought I'd check the yew while we were here."

"I can feel the hum of magic here, can you?" she asked the other witches.

"It's faint, but yes, I feel it," Briar said, pointing her torch up into the twisted tree branches.

El lifted her fingers from where she'd touched the scorched mark and sniffed. "Nothing but earth and witch fire. I don't recognise the sign, either." She stood and played her torch over the ground.

"You looking for more marks?" Alex asked.

El nodded. "I can't help but think this is incomplete."

"I agree," he said. "I think this is the start of something bigger. If we compare it to the portal openings, it would have to have more symbols to be effective."

Avery looked across at Alex, startled. She'd been examining the witch-twigs, trying to make out some of the shapes and symbols. "You think it's a portal door?"

"I think it will be, once it's complete."

"Here," El shouted from the edge of the undergrowth. "There's another mark scorched into the ground." She pulled out her phone and started to snap photos as the others joined her.

"What is it?" Briar asked, frowning.

"Looks like a runic letter."

"Could this be the start of a portal to summon demons again?" Reuben asked, alarmed. The last person who'd summoned demons had been Alicia, Gil's widow, who was now also dead, killed by one of her own demons in Reuben's house.

Alex shrugged. He was their own expert in banishing demons, and knew the most about portal signs. "These portals come in all sorts of shapes and sizes, so maybe?" He looked at them apologetically. "Sorry. It's hard to know at this stage."

"Can't you just get rid of the symbol?" Cassie asked.

"I'll try," Briar volunteered. She crouched, and Avery felt her magic rise as she touched the earth. Briar was the most skilled at Earth magic, and it looked as if she was trying to erase the sign by using the earth to swallow it. However, after a few moments of intense concentration, during which the grass surrounding it started to grow, nothing happened to the scorched ground. She shook her head. "No. The earth resists it. Alex, do you want to try?"

He nodded. "Sure." He stood silently for a few moments, and then started to recite a spell, directing his energy to the mark on the floor. Nothing happened, and he sighed. "Damn it."

However, his magic triggered something else. The witch-signs in the trees above their heads started to vibrate, and the magic they felt emanating from them started to grow, pulsing in the air around the group. And then there was a flash of bright white light and a shock wave of magic rolled out, catching all of them unaware. It lifted them off the ground and threw them back several feet. Avery crashed into a tree trunk and crumpled in a heap, where she lay dazed for a few seconds.

Aware they could be attacked again, she struggled to sit up and blinked, trying to clear her vision. She instantly summoned air, meaning to send a whirlwind into the branches above when she hear Alex shout, "No! No one do anything."

She heard the groans of the others around her, and as the flash cleared from her vision, she saw the dark outlines of the others around her, sprawled on the ground, or lying awkwardly against trees. The sizzle of scorched earth filled the air, and she watched the signs on the ground glow with a fiery light before it faded to embers. Otherwise, the feel of magic was diminishing.

"Bollocks!" Reuben exclaimed. "I've hit my bloody head."

"I think I broke my camera," Dylan groaned.

"But is everyone okay?" Alex asked. From the sound of his voice, he was a few feet to Avery's left. Every single light had gone out, shorted by the magic.

There was a grumble of responses, but everyone seemed generally unharmed.

Ben swore. "What the hell was that?"

"Trigger protection response," Alex said. "This is more sophisticated magic than I thought."

Avery sent a couple of witch lights up, hoping that wouldn't trigger anything else. Thankfully it didn't, showing only her friends struggling to rise to their feet.

"Why didn't my magic trigger it?" Briar asked. She stood, brushing leaves and dirt off her skirt and boots.

"I presume my spell was a more direct assault than your Earth magic," Alex guessed. "Sorry guys."

"Not your fault," El said. "We sort of asked you to."

Once they were all standing, and a few more witch lights had been sent up, they inspected the witch-signs and the sigils on the ground. The sigils still glowed from where they had been burnt into the earth again, but the witch-twigs hung from the trees, as seemingly harmless as they had been when they arrived, although a faint glow marked where they had been attached to the branches.

"I don't think we could cut them free even if we wanted to," El noted thoughtfully. "I might be able to fashion a suitable spell into one of my silver daggers that would enable us to sever the magic attaching them to the tree. When we're ready."

Alex nodded. "Sounds good. But we do nothing until we know more about what we're dealing with here."

"What do you think's going on?" Cassie asked, slightly shaken.

"Well, Samhain is coming," Reuben said, "when the veils between worlds arc at their thinnest. I think someone is trying to capitalise on that by creating a breach."

"When you say worlds, which ones are you talking about?" Dylan asked, perplexed.

Reuben's grin was devilish in the dim light. "All worlds—spirits, demons, other realities, and who knows what else. This is an old church with an old cemetery, quiet and secluded, and lots of power is manifesting here. It's going to be a fun Halloween, guys!"

5

The next morning, Happenstance Books glowed with golden light in the weak autumnal sunshine, enhanced by the enormous amount of fairy lights and fake candles glittering in corners and lighting up carved pumpkins.

"Excellent job, Sally!" Stan the Councillor and town Druid said, as he looked around the shop with delight. "I can always trust you to get on board with the town's celebrations."

Avery carefully said nothing, except smiled and raised an ironic eyebrow. She too was amazed by the amount of stuff Sally had managed to pack into the shop. She'd thought it had looked full the other day, but that was nothing compared to how it looked now.

"Thanks, Stan," Sally said, grinning. "I love this time of year, and I love Halloween! We're starting our storytelling evening at the beginning of Halloween week." She pointed to the printed posters that were placed around the shop and in the window.

"Fantastic!" Stan nodded happily as he strolled around the shop, Sally at his side, with Avery trailing after them. "I might be able to bring my grandchildren one night."

He wasn't dressed at all like a Druid today. His long cloak that he'd worn on the beach at Lughnasadh had gone, and instead he was in a regular dark grey suit and white shirt, his one concession to Halloween, an artful skeleton on his tie.

He continued, "I think Halloween is everyone's favourite celebration. Most shops are looking fantastic. And of course, the plans for the bonfire at the White Haven Castle are well underway."

"Will you be officiating again, Stan?" Avery asked.

He turned to her and grinned. "Of course! I wouldn't miss it. Let's hope rain doesn't ruin everything again. What a dreadful storm last time!" His face fell. "Such a shame, and the evening weather prediction had been so good..."

A rush of guilt swept over Avery again. "Oh well, you know what the weather forecasts are like. They're never accurate. I'm sure this time it will be fine."

"And you'll come?" he asked. "It's a week from Saturday, so obviously not Halloween proper, but close enough. We'll combine it with Guy Fawkes too, of course."

The town celebrations for the pagan and Christian festivals always fell on the closest Saturday, and of course five days after Halloween it was Guy Fawkes night, so the celebrations were on the Saturday in between.

Avery grinned. "Of course. I love a good bonfire and firework display. And, of course, your libations to the Gods."

Stan laughed. "Well, you'd know all about that wouldn't you, with all your books on the occult here."

For one horrible second, Avery had wondered if he was about to say something else, but she recovered swiftly. "Of course. I'm fascinated by it."

"We all are! It's the lifeblood of White Haven. The place is steeped in it. My niece is staying with me at the moment, and she loves all of this stuff! Doesn't live here, you understand," he dropped his voice conspiratorially. "Just visiting while her mother goes through a nasty divorce. I must tell her to come and visit here. She'd love it."

"Of course," Sally said, smiling. "It would be lovely to meet her."

"Yes, I'll mention it to her. Anyway," he said abruptly, "I must get on. I have more shops to visit. Keep up the good work, and I'll see you both soon!" And with that, he swept from the shop with a regal wave, and Avery let out a huge sigh. "Bloody Hell, I wondered what he was going to say then."

"You worry too much," Sally said, straightening a display. "So you're going to the bonfire?"

"Yeah, it won't clash with anything we're doing, and it's always fun. Well, hopefully more fun than last time."

"I take it you'll be doing your own celebrations?"

"We have the honour of sharing our celebrations as part of the thirteen covens of Cornwall—on the actual night of Samhain, of course!"

Sally widened her eyes with surprise. "Wow! So you're going? I thought the initial thrill of being part of the Council had worn off?"

Avery groaned. "It has, sort of. But seeing as Genevieve asked again, and I told her to stick it last time, I thought I should show some good will." She shrugged. "Besides, the others should meet the other covens, and it will be good to see Nate, Eve, Oswald, and Ulysses again." She referred to the other witches who lived in Mevagissey and St Ives, and who had helped them defeat the Mermaids.

"Have you told them about your problem up at Old Haven?"

Avery had told Sally about the witch-signs and sigils earlier that day. "No, not yet. Hopefully it's something we won't need help with." She headed to the back room, leaving

Sally to return to the counter. "I'm going to make some coffee, do you want one?"

"Yes, please. And bring biscuits!"

As Avery made coffee, she pondered the witch-signs they had found at Old Haven. Someone was clearly trying to manifest something, but what? She and Alex had talked late into the night, trying to figure out what the sigil was. It looked nothing like the ones they had seen for demon summoning, but then again, it may not be complete yet. Reuben had talked about other worlds, but she presumed he was just spit-balling as usual. But he was right in one sense. Samhain was known for the fact that the veils between worlds became thin and beings could pass between them, especially the world of the dead, when spirits walked abroad. She had a horrible feeling Helena, her ghostly relative, would be more active during Samhain. But old tales also talked about Faeries—the worlds of the Other—when the Fey and other strange beings could cross into their world, or of course the other way around.

There were lots of tales about mythical creatures and Cornwall had many of their own. Cornish Piskies, or Pixies as they were called elsewhere, were small sprites who were mischievous, but mostly harmless, and known to lead travellers astray. There were also Spriggans, little creatures their local beach was named after, who were supposed to be spiteful and vengeful to those who had wronged them. They left Changelings—Faery children—in place of mortal ones. And Cornwall was well known for its tin mines. The remnants of many were strewn across the land and believed to be inhabited by Knockers, who had large heads and wizened faces and who knocked on the walls of a mine just before a cave collapse. Those tales, like those of Mermaids and giants, were children's stories, but Mermaids had proved to be only too real, and Piskies and Spriggans were supposed to be present in the real world, lurking where they couldn't be seen. Faeries, creatures of the Other—they lived *somewhere else.*

Of course, there were the tales of magic about King Arthur and Tintagel Castle on the North Coast of Cornwall. Morgan Le Fay was allegedly King Arthur's half-sister, depending on which stories you read, and she was half-Fey, as her name suggested. She was a witch who moved between the worlds of the Fey and mortals. According to tales from all over Britain and Europe, the Other also contained dragons, dryads, nymphs, and other mythical creatures. It was a place where time passed differently. A day in the Other, could be hundreds of years on Earth. Avery shivered. There were many tales about travellers who had crossed to the Other and returned years later, only to find their loved ones dead. She wasn't sure which was the more unnerving—demons or Faeries with their clever wiles and manipulations.

And of course there was the yew tree. She still needed to read up on that.

Just as she'd poured coffee and made up her mind to distract herself in the shop, someone knocked at the door and pushed it slowly open. James the vicar peered around the edge. He smiled tentatively. "May I come in and talk?"

A sinking feeling flooded through Avery. *He's going to ask about Old Haven.*

She pasted a smile on her face. "Of course. I haven't seen you for while. How are you?"

He threaded through the boxes, looking around curiously as he always did. "I've been better." He looked her straight in the eye. "You know why I'm here, of course."

"I presume you have questions about Old Haven Church."

He nodded. "Why is my church being targeted again, Avery?"

"I didn't know Old Haven was your church."

"Old Haven belongs to the Church of England. It's part of my area, especially because it's used only occasionally. It doesn't need a full-time vicar."

Avery frowned, recalling Gil's funeral. "My friend died in the summer and was buried there, in the Jackson's mausoleum. You weren't there then."

"I had some leave. Someone stood in for me. You haven't answered my question," he said softly.

"I honestly don't know why Old Haven is being targeted." He looked so anxious she knew she couldn't brush him off. "Take a seat. I'll take Sally her drink, and then we'll chat."

She rushed out the door, plonked Sally's drink and a pack of biscuits in front of her, and said, "Give me fifteen minutes. If I'm not out, come and get me."

Sally smirked and nodded, and Avery took a deep breath and headed to the back room.

James was idly flicking through a book on local history, but he put it down as soon as she walked in.

"Do you want a coffee?" she asked, remembering her manners.

"Just a biscuit will do."

She pushed a pack of chocolate digestives over and watched as he took a bite of one. "I'm not sure what's happening at Old Haven, but it's definitely different from what happened at All Souls."

"In what way?"

"Well, someone is trying to manipulate events at Old Haven. Someone is placing witch-signs in the trees, and there's a sign burnt into the earth now. That didn't happen at All Souls. The spirit there arrived all on its own." Avery inwardly winced. *Not exactly true, but she couldn't tell James about the portal under the Church.*

James's lips tightened. "Witchcraft! Someone is performing witchcraft at Old Haven? That's sacred ground. Hallowed. Consecrated to God!" His voice rose with anger.

"Witches are not demons," Avery said, her voice also rising with indignation. "Witches are good. They are not repelled by hallowed earth. Many worship the Goddess, not the Christian God. It doesn't make them evil."

"You speak from experience," James said knowingly, his eyebrows raised.

"Yes," she said, sick of his accusations and stupid ignorance. "I know about witchcraft. There's good and bad to the craft, as there is to anything. But I'm pretty sure this is not about inviting demons into Old Haven." As she said it, a certainty rushed through her, and she was convinced she was right. Her being resonated with it.

He leaned forward. "Then what are the witch-signs for? They are creepy and unholy and I want them gone."

"We cannot move them. Yet."

He narrowed his eyes at her and then sat back. "That's exactly what Ben said. Why? They're just twigs."

"Look, you asked Ben to keep an eye on the place, so he is. There have been increased spirit sightings there. It's an old church, with old graves. Halloween is coming. Maybe somebody wants to stir up ghosts and scare people. Or maybe it's something else. He came to me for advice, and I suggested that we don't move the signs yet. You have to trust me, James. We'll move them when we can."

"Well, that's the trouble Avery, I'm not sure I can trust you."

Avery's heart thudded painfully in her chest. "So, why are you here?"

"I'm assessing my options."

"What's that supposed to mean?" she shot back, annoyed. "We helped you at All Souls, and I'll help you now, but we need time and space to do it."

James rose to his feet, the chair scraping along the floor. "I've wrestled with my conscience ever since the events in the summer. I'm not sure what happened then, but I have to accept I wilfully looked the other way. I will not again. I've decided I'm going to call the police."

Avery stood, too. "And what will they do?"

"I want them to catalogue it and issue a trespass notice. I don't want whoever it is doing this to think they can keep doing this."

"And what about Ben and the filming?"

"I will allow that, but not the witch-signs. I'm going to get them down as soon as possible. And I want the press there."

"The press! Are you nuts? Old Haven will be invaded! I thought you would hate that. In fact, that's exactly what you wanted to avoid at All Souls!"

"I've changed my mind. I will make it clear that this will not be tolerated." And with that, he turned and marched out the door.

***

"I'm worried James is going to get hurt," Avery said to Alex.

"I'm sure he'll be fine. Especially if the press and the police will be there," he answered, trying to reassure her. "What could go wrong?"

"Everything!" she huffed. "I wonder if I should go."

"Don't talk bollocks," he said, incredulous. "You can't use magic, and you being there will look suspicious. Let James go ahead and do what he has to. I guarantee if he can tear those signs down, they'll be back overnight. In fact, he probably can't tear them down. They're reinforced with magic."

"That's what worries me. He could get hurt. And what would be on film?"

"Nothing! Magic will fry the footage."

"Well, from what Ben told me, it's happening tomorrow at midday."

It was a few hours after James had announced his intention to remove the signs, and Avery and Alex sat at the corner table in Penny Lane Bistro, exactly where they had sat months earlier when they were planning to break in and hunt for Helena's grimoire. In fact, Penny Lane Bistro had been Helena's house with her husband, and it was from there that she had been dragged to her trial for being a witch.

"When did he phone?" Alex asked, referring to Ben.

"At about six. I'd been trying to warn him about what James was planning, but he was testing psychic subjects at the university."

Alex smirked. "Were they psychic?"

"It doesn't look like it," she said, laughing. "Anyway, James had already told him. The press couldn't scramble in time for today, so that's why it's happening tomorrow. They were very interested, apparently."

"Of course they were. It's the perfect Halloween story. Especially after the deaths in the churches over the summer."

"I guess there isn't much we can do. I've told Ben to stand as far back as possible." Avery sighed. "I thought we'd ended things with James quite well, and now I find he's been fuming for months. It sucks."

Alex leaned forward and held her hand, stroking her palm. "I know. But we're witches and he's a vicar. And we did act very suspiciously. Anyway, I'm starving. Let's order food first and then we can talk."

"Does your stomach always come first?" Avery asked petulantly.

"Not always." He turned to the menu. "I'm having steak. What about you?"

"You always have steak."

"I'm a red-blooded male and I've been on my feet all day. You?"

"Venison," Avery said decisively. She sipped her red wine and decided he was right. There was nothing she could do about James. Ben and the others would be there—they were going to be interviewed about ghosts. They could keep an eye on James. "So, how's Zee working out?" she asked after they placed their order.

"Brilliant."

"Really?"

"Yep. He's tall and striking, he works hard, and the ladies love him. Including half the bar staff," he added with a frown.

Avery laughed. "Oh! A ladies' man?"

"I'm not sure I'd say that. He's just charming—and huge. And mysterious. I think that helps."

"Mysterious how?"

Alex sipped his pint as he thought. "He doesn't talk about himself much—understandably. No one knows where he comes from or what he does outside of work. And let's face it—we don't know much more, either. I just know they live in that big house on the edge of the moor that's available for long-term rentals. I have no idea how they arranged it, or who sorted their paperwork, and I don't want to know."

"How's Newton with him?" Newton often drank in The Wayward Son, but he was very suspicious of the Nephilim.

Alex raised his eyebrows and exhaled heavily. "Polite but brusque. He'll come around. I don't think it helps that the very handsome Eli is working with Briar."

"Really! Jealous? Well, he should have made a move when he had the chance." She took a satisfying sip of wine. "I'm a bit disappointed. They would have made such a nice couple. But, it's his own fault. "

"You're a hard woman, Avery Hamilton," Alex said, holding her hand and gazing at her in the way that was guaranteed to send her stomach somersaulting. "Remind me to never get on your bad side."

She met his dark chocolate eyes and felt her heart skip a beat. "Keep treating me like this and I don't think you ever will."

"Ever? I like that," he said, rubbing her palm again, and Avery allowed herself a twinge of excitement at the thought that this may last longer than any relationship she'd ever had before.

She wasn't sure if she was pleased or bitterly resentful when the waiter brought their food and their conversation turned more mundane, but just after nine they were interrupted by Alex's phone.

"Hey Reuben," Alex started, but then he fell silent and looked alarmed. Really alarmed. Avery's stomach tightened with worry. "Reuben, I need you to stay calm until we get there. Give us five." He looked at Avery. "Something's wrong with El. We need to go."

6

El was lying on the floor in the middle of her lounge, unconscious.

Her long, blonde hair was spread around her, looking bright against the dark red of the rug beneath her. Her face was pale, and her limbs were spread wide. She was wearing skinny jeans and a t-shirt, and her feet were bare.

The door to her flat had been open and they found Reuben at her side, kneeling as he shook her gently. "She won't rouse at all!" He looked at them, panic filling his eyes.

Avery felt for her pulse. "How long has she been like this?"

"About fifteen minutes. It happened just before I called you." Reuben was almost breathless with worry.

"What were you doing?" Alex asked calmly.

"We'd just had dinner. I'd cooked and was tidying the kitchen, and she walked from the table to join me and just fell!"

"No headaches, dizziness, anything weird? Any sign of fainting?" Alex asked.

"No! It was a normal night and she just collapsed. Should I call an ambulance? I wasn't sure if it was magic."

Interesting suggestion.

"Have you called Briar?" Avery asked.

"I couldn't get through," he explained.

"I'll try." Alex rose to his feet and started to pace as he pulled his phone out of his pocket.

El's pulse was fluttering wildly under Avery's fingers and her eyes seemed to be moving rapidly beneath her closed lids.

Avery looked around the room, perplexed, and asked a question, not really expecting Reuben to answer. "I wonder if she's possessed or something?"

He frowned. "Why do you ask that?"

"Well, you wondered if it was magic. She's young and healthy. Why would she collapse?"

The more she thought about it, the more likely this seemed and she stood, too, looking around the room, eyes narrowed.

"Let's think. We know there's another witch in White Haven. There are witch-signs at Old Haven, and strange sigils on the ground. Someone is trying to conjure something. They must know we're witches—or at least that there are witches in White Haven. Josh could recognise magic and he's a Shifter, so another witch would know us. Maybe that's even why they're here," she said, thinking out loud.

"Are you suggesting that whoever it is, is targeting us?" Reuben asked, wide-eyed. "Some bastard has hexed El?"

"Maybe." Avery shrugged. "That's the only logical solution—improbable though that seems."

Alex joined them. "I got hold of Briar. She was at the Shifters' house with Hunter. They're coming now."

"Both of them?" Avery asked, confused.

"He wants to help," Alex explained. "Not sure whether it's us though or Briar. But, all help is welcome."

"We need to look for witch-signs, symbols, runes, hex marks—anything," Avery said. "I'm wondering if she's been cursed by our mysterious newcomer."

Alex nodded. "Reuben, you monitor El. Yell loudly if anything changes. We'll search the flat."

"And the foyer," Reuben suggested, reaching for El's hand.

"Good idea. I'll look there now," Avery said, heading for the lift.

El's flat was situated on the top floor of an old converted warehouse, next to White Haven harbour. The foyer was locked, and visitors had to ring to be let in, but that wouldn't bother a witch. It was easy to open locks—electronic or otherwise.

The trouble was, Avery thought as she examined the lobby, which contained a large plant, a small table, the entrance doors to the two ground floor flats and not much else, *a hex bag or something in the lobby would surely affect the whole building.*

Outside the locked area of the foyer was the entrance with a row of locked post boxes. There were only five other flats here—two on each floor, including the ground floor. Avery looked in El's post box, but it was empty other than a couple of advertising flyers.

She headed out of the building and around the perimeter, not knowing what she was looking for, but hoping to see something unusual.

Once outside she inhaled deeply, enjoying the fresh sea air and sharp bite of brine and seaweed. The tide was in, and the fishing boats and small sailing ships bobbed on the gently moving water. The harsh glare from the street lamps showed that the road next to the harbour was mostly deserted, other than a few people wandering past on their way to and from pubs and restaurants. The fish and chip shop had steamy windows, and the faint smell of chips and vinegar drifted towards her. Avery shivered. It was cold and she could feel rain in the air.

Avery set off around the side of the building. There was only a short distance separating it from the sea, and as she progressed further around the back of the warehouse, the sounds of the town fell away and she heard the glug and lap of the water.

She felt a prickle run down her spine.

Someone was watching her.

Avery froze, slowed her breathing, and sent out her magic, gently. She didn't want to alarm whoever was watching her.

She turned slowly, scanning the area. To the right all she could see was the road snaking around the edges of the town, past the arcade with Viking Ink above it, heading towards Spriggan Beach.

No. Nothing from that direction.

Avery examined the walls and ground, looking for witch-marks or sigils, all the while feeling the prickle between her shoulder blades, but the building looked and felt normal. This attack was definitely directed at El, and whoever was watching wanted to see their reaction.

She looked towards the deeply shadowed path under the wall on the far side of the harbour. *Someone was there. Should she engage them now?* She had no idea of how strong they were or what they could do. It could be a trap for all she knew.

Quickly, before she changed her mind, she sent a spell to chill the blood—unpleasant, but not fatal. Within seconds there was a cry, and Avery saw a bright blue light flash across the water towards her. She rolled, threw up her defences, and deflected the energy bolt. A figure sprinted towards the road. Avery saw a coil of rope lying on the quayside and she flicked another spell towards it, seeing it rise with satisfaction and trip up the unknown enemy. Her assailant rolled quickly and sent a well-aimed curse at her. Avery flew backwards, hitting the wall of the building with a crushing *thump*.

She dragged herself off the cold floor and stood ready to fight, but it was too late. Her attacker had gone.

Avery ran back down the quay, hoping to see someone running along the street, but instead met Briar and Hunter as they sprinted from the road. Briar was breathless. "Sorry! I got here as quick as I could. Is she okay?"

"She was, but I've been out here for the last fifteen minutes. Someone, another witch, was lurking over there." Avery pointed to where her attacker had been hiding.

Hunter narrowed his eyes. "Show me. I have a better sense of smell than any of you. I may be able to detect something."

If Hunter was still suffering from his injuries, Avery couldn't tell. He looked fighting fit, and he reeked of confidence and aggression.

Briar agreed. "You carry on. I'll head up to El." Without waiting for their response, she headed inside, and Hunter followed Avery.

"You feeling better, then?" Avery asked as they walked.

"Much," he said, grinning. "Briar's a good healer."

"She is. She's a good witch."

"Single?" Hunter cocked a quizzical eye at her.

Avery smiled, despite her worry about El. "Yes. Single. Don't you live a long way from here?"

"Not at the moment I don't."

Avery appraised him. His hands were thrust into his leather jacket pockets, and his jeans hugged his hips. Leather boots completed the picture, along with his charming, confident grin. He was a darker, cockier version of his younger brother, Josh, and he was very different from Newton. "She's not the love 'em and leave 'em type," she advised him, quickening her step. "You hurt her, I'll boil your balls."

"Yes ma'am," he said with a smirk.

"I mean it." They had reached the far side of the harbour, and the opening between the two walls yawned wide and dark, the waves choppy where the calm water met the open sea. "This is where my attacker was watching me and the building. I can feel a residual tingle of magic."

Hunter dropped to his hands and knees and sniffed the ground. Old lobster pots and rope were coiled on the side; the scent of fish and the sea was strong. Avery was certain he wouldn't be able to smell much, but she was wrong.

"Female, old." He sniffed again, looking puzzled. "*Very* old."

Avery frowned. "But my attacker was agile. They ran and rolled. An old person couldn't do that. You must be detecting something else."

He looked up at her and shook his head. "No. I can smell other stuff, of course—fishermen, fish, seaweed, dogs, cats. But I sense magic, too. Old magic from an old person." He seemed very certain.

"How old is *very* old? And how can you tell from a smell?"

He rose to his feet and sighed. "It's hard to explain, but energy has signatures—you can probably detect that, too?"

"Yes, but this isn't energy, it's age."

"Oh, age has energy, too. For example, you smell of youth and vitality, and—" he inhaled deeply. "Roses and honeysuckle. And red wine. And a musky male." He grinned. "Dinner date? And very strong magic. Your magic," he pressed on before she could respond, "is a mixture of old and new. I sense another presence around you. Something smoky and complex, and a trace of violets." He frowned, perplexed. "Someone even older than your mysterious attacker."

Avery was astonished. "You must be able to scent Helena, my resident ghostly ancestor."

"You keep very interesting company, Avery."

"If Helena feels very old, and our attacker not so old, how old are we talking?"

He shrugged and set off down the wall, following the scent. "Hard to say with any great accuracy. How old is Helena?"

"Nearly five hundred years."

He raised his eyebrows. "So, I would guess maybe two hundred. Or thereabouts."

Avery felt goose bumps caress her skin that had nothing to do with the chill October air. "But how could someone that old still be alive?"

He smirked. "Magic?"

***

Twenty minutes later, Avery and Hunter arrived back in El's flat after unsuccessfully trying to follow the scent into town. Unfortunately, the overwhelming smells of others made it too hard, and they lost all trace in the narrow lanes that ran into the centre.

Alex looked up when they entered, frowning slightly. "I was getting worried. What happened?"

"Something really weird," Avery answered, trying to get her head around Hunter's news. El still lay prone on the floor, her breathing shallow, the others crouched next to her. "How's El?"

"No change. But we have found this." Alex gestured towards a silver necklace on the floor that was hard to see because it was almost under a side table. "It's cursed. Clever."

"How do you know?" Avery asked, puzzled.

"I've been trying to retrace her steps," Reuben explained, "and I remembered that as she came over to join me, she paused by this side table and said something like, 'Oh, there you are!' I thought she was talking to me, but then she picked the necklace up and dropped like a stone. I didn't think the two were related. I feel like such an idiot!"

"Don't," Avery reassured him. "Why would you think of a curse? And are we sure it is?"

"Yes, it's definitely cursed," Briar said emphatically. She held her hands a couple of inches above El and ran them over her in a sweeping motion. "I can feel the energy field around the necklace. Whatever you do, don't touch it. But it's muted, disguised somehow. And I can't feel anything from El. Normally, when I'm healing, I can feel how the body's energies feel wrong, but not now. There's just a void." She glanced up. "It's really weird. I just can't decide how it works."

Avery headed over to the necklace and crouched next to it, careful not to touch. She held her hand above it, feeling with her magic; Briar was right.

Alex asked, "How did this witch get hold of her necklace in the first place?"

"I have no idea!" Reuben said. "Like you said, she wears a lot of jewellery. And she didn't mention a missing necklace."

"Well, whoever is causing this," Avery mused, "was outside the warehouse, on the harbour wall, watching. Maybe they activated it from outside."

Briar shook her head. "No. It was already cursed. I think they were enjoying the repercussions, don't you?"

"Maybe." Avery shrugged, perplexed.

"Any clue as to who it is?" Alex asked.

"Someone very old," Hunter said, joining the conversation. Until then he'd been pacing around the room like a sniffer dog. "I can smell them here, too."

"They've been in this flat?" Avery spun around to look at him. "I can't feel other magic!"

"I can. It's faint, but I'm good. I'd be even better in wolf form. If I could have changed in the street, I would have been able to follow them with ease."

"Wolves in White Haven? I don't think so," Avery said.

He grinned. "Tell people I'm a husky. That would work."

"Can we just cure her now and ponder how it was cursed later?" Reuben asked, a dangerous edge to his voice.

Briar sighed. "It's not that simple, Reuben. We have to work out what type of curse it is to lift it." She pulled her Athame and a small, velvet bag out of her medicines box, and then joined Avery. She placed her Athame under the necklace, lifted it gingerly and examined it again. El's cursed necklace was a long silver chain with an ornate amulet attached, and it looked perfectly normal. Briar dropped it in the bag, tying it securely.

Reuben almost growled in frustration. "How long can this last? I know bugger all about curses!"

"If we can't break it, it could last forever," Briar said, securing the necklace in the box. "And that would kill her." Her words fell into deafening silence. "However, there's some healing magic I need to perform that will buy us some time. Can you carry her to her bed?"

While Briar and Reuben ministered to El, Alex joined Hunter and Avery. "You said this attacker was old? What do you mean?"

"I mean, you have a two hundred-year old—and then some—witch, or something, running around White Haven cursing its resident witches," Hunter answered, a slight preen of arrogance to his tone.

"Well, you can put your famous nose to the test and check out Old Haven Church tomorrow. I want to know if our two problems are caused by the same person."

7

El remained unconscious, but Briar promised to stay with her, as did Hunter and Reuben. Alex and Avery left after making sure the others would call with updates.

"Hunter's pretty cocky," Alex said, as they headed to his flat above The Wayward Son.

"But pretty useful." Avery slipped her small hand into Alex's, savouring his warmth. "That nose of his sensed things I couldn't. Yes, I sensed magic, but not age."

Alex shook his head. "A really old witch must mean some sort of alchemy is involved, and maybe a quest."

"Alchemy? Quest?" Avery looked up at him, confused. "What do you mean?"

"Would you want to live for hundreds of years unless you had something to achieve? Our ancestors were powerful, so were some of the others in the Witches Council. They're all dead. Magic does not normally enhance your lifespan, unless…" He looked at her speculatively.

"Unless you do a deal of some sort, or some really dark magic," Avery finished.

"Because you want to do something."

"How can you expand your lifespan for over two hundred years? Have you ever seen a spell for that?"

Alex shook his head. "No. But I know alchemy promised such things."

"The gift of immortality is a myth, Alex."

"But it might not be immortality. It might be a way of eking out life, bit by bit, until you achieve what you set out to do."

"And that would be to open some kind of portal—if the two are linked?" Avery suggested.

"Maybe."

"So, why target El?"

"Because she said she could make a knife or sword that could cut through the magic securing the witch-signs. Eliminating El means the witch-signs remain. This witch has ears and eyes we don't know about."

"A traitor?"

Alex frowned. "I don't think so. A seer maybe? Scrying? Someone who can do it better than me." He threw back his head and shouted. "Can you see us now? We'll find you, old one." He turned to Avery and grinned.

"Silly bugger."

"But sexy as hell, right?" He pulled her close for a long, lingering kiss.

"Now who's cocky?" Avery said as she got her breath back.

"I'll show you cocky." They had reached his flat, and he opened the back gate of the pub with a wicked glint in his eye.

***

Old Haven Church was draped in mist and drizzle when the group arrived there at nine the next morning.

Briar had phoned Avery at six saying that El was still unconscious and that she was staying with her all day. Neither she nor Reuben had slept much, and Briar had asked Eli to cover her shop. As worried as Alex and Avery were, there was nothing they could do, and they decided to go ahead with their meeting.

Hunter was leaning against the main door of the church, sheltering under the broad porch, Piper next to him. She scowled when she saw them, but he gave a wolfish grin. "Ready for some hunting?"

"Always," Alex said as he led the way to the grove of trees.

Hunter matched Alex's stride. "How's your friend?"

"Not good."

"Sorry. Briar was sure she'd figure out something this morning."

"She was trying to be positive, but I think we all know it's not going to be that simple. The more we can find out now, the more we'll help El."

Hunter nodded, quickening his pace.

"Are you helping, too?" Avery asked Piper, hoping to draw her out of her sulk.

She shrugged. "There's not much else to do."

Avery resisted the urge to roll her eyes and said dryly, "Good for you."

Once they reached the wood, Alex said, "We need to work quickly. The press and the police will be here at twelve, with the vicar."

"It'll take minutes only," Hunter reassured them.

As soon as they reached the clearing, Avery shivered. "The magic has grown stronger. Can you feel it, Alex?"

Alex placed his hand on the yew's knotty trunk. "Yeah, and not just around us. The tree has a…" He paused, thinking for a moment. "A pulse, or a breath—it's like the tree's breathing."

There were now dozens of witch-signs hanging not only from the branches of the yew, but also in the surrounding trees, and Avery watched their strange forms and patterns turning in the damp, autumnal air. "I can feel *them*, too, shimmering with magic. It's so unusual."

"In what way?" Hunter asked, as he lifted his head and sniffed the air.

"It feels deeper, older almost—"

"Wilder," Alex said, before she could continue. "Like wild magic just coming to life."

Avery smiled softly at Alex. "That's *exactly* what it feels like!"

Hunter looked thoughtfully between the two of them, nodding, and then stripped his clothes off without a second thought and shifted into a beautiful black wolf with a grey muzzle.

Although Avery was expecting it, it was still a shock. For a few moments his body shimmered and then dissolved, and a wolf was standing there instead. However, Hunter was bigger than a normal, non-shifting wolf—or so Avery thought. *Like I spend a lot of time with wolves.* He stood at least level with her waist, and his paws were enormous. Even in wolf form, she could still see the scars from his fight, where his thick coat was ragged and patchy.

Hunter immediately started sniffing the ground, and they watched him search among the tree roots and narrow animal tracks.

Avery watched him start searching and turned back to Alex. "What does this mean? Wild magic?"

"Isn't all magic wild?" Piper asked, looking mildly bored.

"Yes and no," Avery said, struggling to explain. "The magic we use is disciplined, taught and practiced for generations, guided and shaped by spells and the elements. This feels like it has no borders, no restraints. Plenty for us to think about."

Piper shrugged and fell silent again.

While Hunter searched, Avery thought about the cameras at the edge of the wood. "I wonder if Dylan had any luck with the footage."

"He hasn't called you?" Alex asked.

"No. I bet that jolt of magic fried everything the other night."

Alex stepped into the yew's hollow trunk and rubbed his hand across the gnarled surface. "I wonder how old this is. It must pre-date the church."

"I agree," Avery said. "I managed to catch up on some lore about them. I know they were sacred to Druids. They believed they linked to one's ancestors and guarded a person's path into the Otherworld. It's also sacred to Hecate and the Crone."

"Hecate and the Crone?" Piper asked, curiosity overcoming her sullenness. She leaned against a beech tree, half watching them, half watching her brother.

"Hecate is the Greek Goddess of magic and witchcraft, the moon and ghosts, and one of the many Gods and Goddesses who are sacred to the night and the Underworld," Avery explained. "She is closely linked to the Celtic Goddess, of which there are three aspects—the Maiden, the Mother, and the Crone. The Crone is the old lady we will all become. She relates to death and as such also guards the Underworld." She smiled. "You, as I am still, are in our maiden phase."

"It sounds stupid." Piper eyes flashed a challenge.

"So does the idea of people turning into wolves, and yet you do," Avery pointed out.

"There's a lot of talk about Underworld and Otherworlds in all of this," Alex said, ignoring Piper.

Avery nodded. "In all the reading I've done, the thing that's mentioned most frequently is the yew's links to the Otherworld. And that sigil burnt into the ground in front of the trunk must have something to do with that—I think so, anyway."

Alex sighed. "And we still haven't identified what that sigil is yet."

Hunter paced around their feet. In seconds he shifted back to human form, completely naked, and Avery tried to avert her eyes. *Shifter's aren't shy.* Alex caught her glance, his eyes filled with laughter.

"Well, it's the same smell I found before," Hunter said, a trace of humour in his eyes as if he knew Avery was uncomfortable.

Smug git.

He continued, "An old woman, and old magic. Very different from you guys." He shivered, and headed for his clothes, pulling his jeans on. "And powerful."

"No other scents that suggest she's working with someone?" Alex asked.

"No. Plenty of other human scents, but nothing remotely witchy. In fact," he lifted his head and inhaled. "Some of them are coming now."

As he spoke, Avery heard voices and turned to see Dylan and Ben arrive. "Hey guys," Ben said cheerily. "Didn't think you were coming today."

"We're leaving soon," Avery reassured him, and introduced them to Piper and Hunter. "You're early."

"I was about to check the footage," Dylan said, "but we heard your voices and thought we'd say hi." He looked around, noticing the newly arrived witch-signs. "Wow. Someone's been busy!"

"Yeah, too busy," Alex said, despondently. "You think you'll have any film at all?"

He grimaced. "Unfortunately, I think there's too much magic around for anything to record now. The footage just buzzes." He caught Piper looking at him and grinned, his teeth glinting white against his dark skin.

Piper's interest shot up and for the first time, Avery saw her actually smile. "Cool. Can you show me?"

"Sure. Follow me."

Hunter watched her follow Dylan back through the trees and sighed. "She's bloody hard work sometimes."

"Maybe she just needs a distraction," Avery said. "Looks like she's found one."

Ben had been gazing around the clearing. "This place is seriously creepy. You guys need to get out of here. The police are coming soon, and the press will set up early. James is on his way, too."

"All right," Avery said. "Please try to stop James from touching the witch-signs. I don't think they're safe, and I think he could get a nasty shock."

"I'll try, but I think we'll fail," Ben said. "He's getting angrier about this by the minute."

"Well, so is the witch doing this. She cursed El last night, using one of her own necklaces." She told him what they'd discovered the night before.

Ben looked worried. "This is getting dangerous."

"Doesn't it always?"

"If there's anything we can do to help El, let me know."

"Will do. And if there's anything you can find out about this site, let us know. I'm going to do some research." Avery looked around at the grove. "This has to have relevance to what the witch wants to do."

"Come on, we better go," Alex said, and followed Hunter as he walked back to the cemetery.

Avery nodded. "Call me later, Ben?"

"If we're all still alive," Ben answered.

Avery was pretty sure he wasn't joking.

***

Before Alex and Avery returned home, they headed to El's flat, hoping to see her awake and well, but they were disappointed. She lay under her quilt, unnaturally still.

Briar leaned against the doorframe. "This curse is strong. I can't shift it."

"Even though she isn't touching the necklace?" Avery asked.

"Yep." Briar headed back to the lounge and pointed to where it lay on a side table under a glass cover that looked like one of El's shop displays. "The necklace is still cursed, too. I haven't dared touch it. I have attempted a few spells to try to discover the type of curse, but it's well-disguised."

Reuben was in the kitchen, trying to keep busy. He looked terrible. His eyes were dark with lack of sleep, and thick stubble was already covering his chin and cheeks. "And while the curse remains, El remains under its enchantment."

Briar explained, "Many of my spells are for healing Earth magic. Not many talk about breaking curses. Have you got any suitable spells?"

"I can't think of any off the top of my head, but I can certainly look," Avery said. "I'm heading back to the flat now, so all being well, I'll get straight on it."

"Me, too," Alex agreed. "In fact, I'm not working until later today, so I can stay if you need to head to your shop, Briar? I can grab my grimoires, bring them back here, and keep an eye on El."

She smiled at him gratefully. "Yes, please. There are a few things I need to check on and some herbs I want to collect. I'll come back this afternoon."

"Same goes, Reuben. You should go home and get some sleep."

"Absolutely not. The business is fine, and El is more important."

"Well okay, but you have to try to sleep here. Briar can give you something. You look like shit."

"Cheers, mate." Reuben's normal buoyant humour had deserted him. "That's because I feel like it. I can't believe someone would do this to El!"

"It could have been anyone of us. In fact," Alex said, looking at all of them, "it still could be. Be suspicious of anyone. We need to try and find how she got to El's necklace—whether it was from the shop or here—and we need to increase our protection spells. One of us could be next."

8

Avery walked up the winding streets of White Haven, having declined a lift back. She needed the fresh air to clear her brain, and her shop was only ten minutes from the harbour.

Despite the grim circumstances and her preoccupation with the curse and the strange events at Old Haven Church, her surroundings made her smile. The murk of the day was lifted by the decorations in the shops and cafes. The windows were filled with pumpkins, witches riding on brooms, skeletons, vampires, ghosts and ghouls, and strings of lights. In another week or so, all of these items would be replaced by Christmas decorations, and they would all gear up for another round of celebrations. The Town Council had already decorated the streets with festive lights, but for now, the focus was clearly on All Hallows' Eve.

The numbers of shoppers were lower, now that the summer holidays were over, and on the way Avery nodded to, or stopped and spoke to the locals as they went about their business. This weekend, however, the streets would once again fill with visitors as people came for the fun of Halloween.

Realising she was close to El's shop, Avery ducked down a side street to speak to Zoey, a practicing Wicca Witch.

As usual, Zoey stood behind the counter looking immaculate. Her hair was cut into a blunt bob, but this time the tips were died neon blue, and her makeup was perfect. She didn't often smile, but as soon as Avery entered, her eyes lightened. "How's El? Better?"

"Sorry, no," Avery said, heading over and leaning on the counter. "I've come to see if you remember anything weird happening here over the last day or two?"

Zoey's face fell in disappointment. "I've been thinking of nothing else, ever since Reuben told me. Nothing unusual has happened. We've had some regular customers and some new ones, but no one has struck me as odd."

"No sign of a break-in, I presume?"

"No, why?"

"Someone has been in El's flat. We think it's a woman, an old woman who potentially appears as someone much younger. I just wondered if you'd seen anything."

"Everything has been completely normal," she explained, perplexed. "I've been trying to think of anything that could help, but I just can't!"

"It's okay," Avery said, smiling softly. "We'll get her back, somehow. In the meantime, do you need help with her shop?"

"No. I can manage. I pretty much run the place anyway."

"Okay. If anything occurs to you, no matter how small, let us know."

Frustrated that there was nothing more to learn, Avery continued on to her favourite coffee shop, bought three coffees and a selection of pastries, and headed back to Happenstance Books.

"Anything going on here?" she asked, placing everything on the counter.

"Nope," Dan said, reaching immediately for a pastry, and nodding to the stacks behind her. "Other than that you've got a visitor."

"I have? Who?"

A familiar drawl made her skin prickle. "Me. I have a few questions." She turned to see Caspian emerge from one of the deep armchairs placed around the shop. He was dressed in a dark grey suit, with a pale grey, linen shirt open at the neck. The scent of expensive aftershave drifted over to her, and she noted his well-groomed hair and expensive leather shoes, all topped with a heavy, knee-length wool coat.

"Oh, goodie. I've so missed you," Avery said dryly.

He allowed the faintest of smiles to crease his face, and then it was gone. "Of course you have. I'm a delight. After you," he said, gesturing to the back of the shop.

She grimaced, considered refusing, and then decided she may as well get it over with—as soon as he asked nicely. She folded her arms across her chest. "Say please!"

"Do we have to do this?"

"Yes. They're called manners. It's about time you learned some."

She could hear Dan sniggering into his pastry and tried to ignore it.

Caspian narrowed his eyes, sighed, and then said with exaggerated politeness, "May I please speak to you privately, Ms Hamilton?"

"Why, certainly, Mr Faversham," she replied as she grabbed a coffee and pastry and carried them to the back room.

"Not one for me?" he asked, leaning forward to open the door for her.

"Had I been expecting you, of course I would have bought one." *Liar!* "Instead," she said, resolutely refusing to share her own and reaching for a pack of biscuits, "Would you like a Hob Nob?"

"Splendid, my favourite," he said, sinking into a chair at the table. He crunched into one with great satisfaction, and Avery's lips twitched with amusement. *Who'd have thought Caspian would like a Hob Nob?*

She sat opposite him and reflected on the strange conversations she often had at this table. As she took a bite of her custard-filled croissant, she hoped the sugar would be enough to sustain her. "I gather this is not a social call?"

"No. I'm wondering what on Earth possessed you to let the vicar summon the press up to Old Haven to film him removing witch-signs."

"Well, short of me glamouring the vicar, there was actually no way of stopping him. And besides, how do you know?" Once again, she felt annoyed. His ability to piss her off in seconds was uncanny.

He smirked as he reached for another biscuit. "I have my methods."

"A sneak in the press, you mean?"

"We all have ways of staying in touch with the local news. So, what *is* going on at Old Haven?"

Avery debated how much to tell him, and they watched each other silently across the table for a few seconds. Despite the very rocky start to their relationship, and the fact that Caspian had been responsible for Gil's death, they seemed to have reached an unspoken truce. She chewed on her croissant, savouring it for a moment before coming to a decision.

"There's an unknown witch in White Haven. She has cursed El, and seems to be powering up a spell in Old Haven Church, centred on the old yew tree in the grove behind the churchyard. I presume she thought the place was so quiet that no one would notice what she was up to. Fortunately, Ben and the others head up there quite regularly, and they spotted them. Initially there were just a couple of witch-signs hanging from the branches, but now there are more of them, and two sigils burnt into the ground. The power there is palpable and growing."

Caspian leaned forward. "El is cursed?"

Avery was shocked. That wasn't what she thought he'd lead with. "Yes. Her necklace. We found it on the floor of her flat. Reuben remembered that she picked it up and then collapsed. But we can't work out what sort of curse it is. And she's unconscious. A very weird, unnatural stillness." Avery hesitated for a second, worry bubbling up inside her. "We can't break it, yet. Briar has tried—she's better at that sort of thing—but I'm about to start searching for spells, too."

"Curse spells are notoriously difficult to break," Caspian said. "They have a tendency to rebound on those attempting to break them. Unless you're the one that cast it, of course."

"I know. That's why we're being careful." She tried unsuccessfully to temper her sarcasm.

"A necklace, you say? Silver?"

"Yes."

"Silver holds magic very well, it will be tricky." He broke off and looked into the distance. "I'll give it some thought."

Really? "Thanks, Caspian. We'd appreciate it."

The surprise must have showed on her face, because he grimaced. "I am not without sympathy, and my family grimoires contain many curses."

No surprise there.

He continued, "In the meantime, what will you do to counteract the press at Old Haven?"

Avery snorted. "It's Halloween. Hopefully people will put it down to some prank or hoax. And it's very likely their cameras won't work. Dylan's don't anymore."

"What was he filming?"

"Ghost activity. That place can be volatile."

He leaned back thoughtfully. "Interesting. But that's good—the cameras, I mean. And any leads on this witch?"

"None. But she's old. Very old, according to—" Avery caught herself in time. She wasn't sure she wanted Caspian to know about the Shifters. "From what we can tell, anyway."

"A time-walker?"

Avery almost choked on her coffee. "A *what*?"

He smiled. "Some witches have learnt to defy time. If she's the one who cast your spell, you'll struggle. They're very powerful."

"I've never heard of a time-walker!"

"So, there are some things I can teach you, after all!" he smirked.

"Go on," she said, wanting to throw the remains of her pastry at him.

He shrugged. "They have learnt the secret of defying aging. Immortal creatures, maybe, but essentially time stretches for them. But it takes energy. A lot of it. She'll be staying somewhere close to natural resources she can draw on to replenish her energy. Somewhere isolated."

"Surely the sea is a great natural resource?"

"Yes, but huge and unwieldy. Running water, such as a spring or river, is better. Of course, your abundance of magic over the town will help."

"No one's drawing on that as far as I can tell."

"*Yet,*" he said, reaching for another biscuit. "And now for my next item of business. There are Shifters in White Haven."

"Wow. You really run a spy network, don't you?" Avery said, annoyed.

"I have been approached by the Device witches from Cumbria."

The name sounded vaguely familiar to Avery, but she couldn't quite place it. "Who?"

"You really are an ingénue, aren't you?"

"Don't push me, Caspian."

"Have you heard of the Pendle witches?"

"Of course I have. I'm not an idiot."

He spread his hands wide, smirking.

She groaned. *Of course!*

The Device witches were an old family that went back at least to the sixteenth century, and probably further. They had gained notoriety when they feuded with another family of witches, headed by Anne Whittle, and then both were brought to the attention of the authorities and tried for witchcraft. The families were commonly referred to as the Demdike family, after "Old Demdike," head of the Devices, and the Chattoxes after "Mother Chattox," head of the Whittles. Together they were called the Pendle witches after the area in Lancashire they lived in. The story was notorious because they were accused of ten murders by the use of witchcraft. Of the twelve alleged witches who were brought to trial, ten were found guilty and hanged, one was found not guilty, and the other died in prison.

Caspian continued, "Their descendants, like ours, survived, and they remain two of the most powerful witch families in the north of England. The Devices are now in Cumbria and have been for many years, after moving on from Pendle. They rule with an iron fist. You know there are many Shifters there?"

Avery felt a deep, sinking sensation in the pit of her stomach. "Yes. Some fled after one of them was attacked. He was near death when they came to me."

"That's not the story I heard," he said softly. "They attacked first, and the family they attacked wants revenge—a rematch. Demdike, also known as Alice Device, will see it happens."

Avery fell silent for a moment, her thoughts whirring. "But they fled here after saying they were attacked by some guy called Cooper. They sought Sanctuary here. They claim victim."

Caspian frowned. "Well, I imagine somewhere between the two tales lies the truth. Either way, Alice—the leader of their family—will ensure that the Shifters return. They will arrive here tomorrow. Expect a visit."

Avery frowned, still confused. "Why did they call you and not me?"

"Over the years our families have done business together, but not for a long time. However, in cases such as these, it was natural they should speak to me, as I know you."

"But why are they coming to see *me*?"

Caspian shook his head slowly. "Avery, you have much to learn. It is because you allowed them Sanctuary."

That word again.

She looked at him, astonished. "What year is this, Caspian? We don't grant Sanctuary like some feudal system. People come and go, and are free to live here!"

"That may be so for normal people, but for those like us, who live on the peripheries of the normal world, some old school polices still apply. Especially as viewed by the Devices. Some old families quite like their feudal systems."

"Like yours, you mean? Your unwillingness to let us gain our grimoires."

He shuffled uncomfortably in his chair. "My father's wishes could not be ignored. Do you want my advice or not?"

"Well, you don't offer it often, so go on."

He met her gaze steadily across the table. "Shifters like that system, too. They are wolves—pack animals, despite their human form. Cumbria is wild country, that's why they live there. It is remote, wolves can disappear there. You do not want a Shifter war here. Did the Shifters *ask* for Sanctuary?"

"Yes. And I laughed, but said of course they could stay here."

"Well, there you are then. I suggest you get your boy repaired and send him on his way." He smiled. "He helped you detect the old witch, didn't he?"

"Yes."

"Don't owe him too many favours. It might come back to bite you."

"We saved his life. He better be bloody grateful, or it will come back to bite *him*."

Caspian smiled, and it almost made him look charming. "That's why I like you, Avery. You have fire, and undeniable magic. If you ever get tired of Alex, give me a call."

And with that, he left, leaving Avery staring after him.

9

Avery was seething. Did Caspian just make a pass at her? Cheeky bastard. As if she would ever think about having an affair with him!

Sally laughed when she told her about their conversation. "He's just trying to get a rise out of you, Avery. Ignore him. He will say anything to inflame you."

Dan agreed, although he qualified it with, "But he is single. Why? He's rich, good looking. A wanker, yes, but still… He might mean it."

"I don't care if he means it. How dare he!"

"He's a guy. You can't blame him for trying, Avery," Dan said, frowning. "You have no idea what it's like to be a man and expected to make the first move. It doesn't matter how confident you are, it's still awkward. Give him a break."

"I have a boyfriend. Aren't there mates' rules or something?"

"Yeah, but he and Alex are not mates," he pointed out.

Avery huffed. "Traitor. That's the last time I save you from a Mermaid."

"Ouch. It's a good thing I've sworn off women, then." He grinned and reached for another pastry. "At least I have food to console me."

"So, what else did Caspian want? You were talking a while," Sally said.

They were all standing around the counter. The shop was empty, and outside the rain had returned in such a downpour that the other side of the street was a blur. Happenstance Books seemed isolated from the outside world. Incense smoke drifted around the room, B.B. King was playing, and a tingle of magic hung on the air. Avery loved afternoons like this.

"He came to warn me about the Shifters and the imminent arrival of the ex-Pendle witches," Avery said, and went on to explain their conversation.

Sally looked worried. "Do you think the Shifters are playing you?"

"Lying, you mean? About what really happened?"

"Maybe. You don't know anything about them. They turn up here, one of them nearly dead, and ask for help. They've told you their side of the story. You have no idea what else went on."

Avery fell silent for a moment. Sally was right. She needed to ask some more questions.

Damn it.

***

The old Volvo that was normally parked in front of the house was missing.

Avery paused for a moment on the doorstep before she knocked, and cast her witchy senses wide. She sensed their Shifter magic, but nothing else. Summoning her courage, she knocked resolutely, and for a while, nothing happened.

She was about to knock again when Holly answered the door, looking surprised. "Oh, it's you. I thought Briar had arrived early."

"No. Briar is a little tied up with our friend, El. Can I come in?"

Holly looked wary, but then said, "Sure, but Hunter's out."

"That's fine. I have a few questions, and I hope you can help." *Softly, softly*. She didn't want the door slammed in her face. Blasting the door back open with her witch powers wasn't on her to-do list for the day.

Holly shrugged. "I can try." She turned and led the way to the kitchen at the back of the house. The rain had slowed to a drizzle, and mist swirled around the back garden. Holly turned the kettle on. "Want a drink?"

"Tea sounds lovely." Thank the Goddess for tea. It seemed to pave the way for any conversation.

Avery had debated with herself on how best to start this conversation, and she realised there was no easy way. She could hedge around the fight and what really happened, but ultimately decided honesty was the best way.

"Alice Device is coming to see me tomorrow."

Holly dropped the cup she was holding and looked at Avery in shock. The noise of the shattering cup was ignored as each met the other's eyes. Holly was frozen in place.

Avery spoke softly. "Would you like to sit down?"

Holly nodded and fumbled for a chair, sinking into it absently. She was still mute, and she looked at the table.

"Why is Old Demdike coming to see me?"

"I didn't think they would follow us here." Holly's hands started to shake, and she placed them on her lap, out of Avery's sight.

"What happened in Cumbria?"

Holly swallowed nervously. "I'm not sure Hunter would want me sharing this."

"I don't give a crap what Hunter wants. What happened?"

Holly looked at her, her eyes silently pleading.

"I can't face the Devices without knowing what really happened. Weakness is not an option."

Holly exhaled heavily. "Cooper is the pack leader and Hunter challenged him. He lost, and we fled."

"Oh! So Hunter wasn't attacked in some stealth manoeuvre, he actually challenged Cooper. He started the fight."

"Yes."

"Why lie? And what's the big deal? Cooper is still the pack leader. Why are they coming here?"

"He needs to swear loyalty and renounce his claim to the leadership. He fled—*we* fled—before he could do this. Hunter wants to challenge again. He's buying himself time."

"Time to heal."

Holly nodded. "Yes. If he loses after a challenge, we lose everything. We move to the bottom of the pack. Loss of privileges. And I'm still expected to marry Cooper."

Avery felt the air start to rise and her hair lifted as a gust of wind rattled around the kitchen. Holly looked around, alarmed and confused. "You are to do what?"

"Marry Cooper. We are the oldest families. It's expected. I don't like him. I never have. Hunter was trying to protect me."

Avery was incensed. "You're not a piece of meat! What the hell system do you live in? It's the twenty-first century, Holly!"

"Are you causing that wind?"

"Yes! I can make a frigging hurricane if I want! Are you serious?"

"Yes. Shifters are pack animals. It's patriarchal. And the pack leader is strongly allied to the Devices—Old Demdike. They carry their history with them."

"I have history! We all have." Avery shot up from the table and started pacing the room, energy balling in her hands. She was pretty sure Holly was being honest with her. Avery could usually sense lies—witches were good at that—but their Shifter magic was clouding her judgement. "Are you telling me the truth? Because if I defend you tomorrow, I want to make sure I know absolutely everything. I can make your life just as miserable as them." *Not entirely true, but they didn't have to know that.*

"Yes! Hunter would hate you to know this—he hates to fail. He thought he could take Cooper on. It's knocked his confidence and almost killed him—because of me. I begged him to do it!" Holly started to cry. "I should just suck it up. Marriage to the pack leader is something many other Shifters would want."

"Only if they're stupid," Piper said. Once again she'd sidled to the door, and she stood watching them.

"But you want to go home," Holly said, annoyed. "At my expense."

"Not true." Piper joined them at the table, her shoulders bowed. "I want to go home, yes, but not with those consequences."

"And what does Josh think?" Avery asked.

"Like us, he thinks it's time for change. It would be good for the whole pack," Holly said.

"And what about the other members?"

"Some agree, others don't. There are a lot of us."

"The younger ones definitely want change," Piper said, "I know they do. I think they'll be gutted that Hunter lost."

"They would know?" Avery was struggling to understand the pack rules and what exactly a challenge consisted of.

"Oh, yes. The pack was there, watching the outcome."

"How exactly did you get Hunter away, if it was an arranged fight and everyone was watching?"

"Josh picked another fight, and we sneaked him out in the chaos. We have broken every rule there is," Piper explained, slightly triumphant, and it brought a brief smile to Avery's face.

"I like your style!" Avery fell silent for a second, thinking. "Do the witches interfere with fights?"

"I'm pretty sure not," Holly said, but doubt lurked behind her eyes.

"So, just to be clear, Hunter wasn't ambushed. He picked the fight and lost?"

Holly nodded. "Yes. And we have to return to finish it. We either submit, Hunter dies, or we are exiled."

Avery felt her annoyance settle into cold, hard steel and she sat down. "Why are you in White Haven? Why not somewhere else?"

"We wanted to put a lot of distance between us and them, and this is a long way south. And then we sensed the magic here. It's strong. You're strong. We needed your help, and we needed someone who could stand up to the Devices, if they came looking. We honestly didn't think they would—at least, not so soon. They're mean, Avery. They'll drag us back before we're ready to go.""No, they won't. I'll make sure of that."

***

Avery marched into The Wayward Son with fire burning in her soul. Alex was behind the bar serving a customer, and for a second, he didn't see her. The sight of him calmed her down, fractionally.

His lean, muscled frame looked good in his jeans and black t-shirt. As usual, stubble covered his cheeks and chin, and his hair fell loosely to his shoulders. Her stomach somersaulted. *He was so hot.* And the absolute opposite of Caspian in every way. He looked up and grinned when he saw her, and her stomach flipped once more. Even now, months after they had got together, he still gave her goose bumps.

"Hi, gorgeous," he said, leaning over the bar to kiss her. "I didn't think I'd be seeing you 'til later."

She cupped his face between her hands and kissed him back, enjoying his heat and scent, before she broke away. "Hi, handsome. I've missed you."

"Good," he said, a gentle smile playing across his lips. "But why do I sense there's another reason for your early visit?"

"There have been a few developments with our new friends. Can you get away from the bar for a while? I'm going to call the others, too."

"Sure, give me half an hour. But there's no El, remember, or Reuben. He'll be with her."

"Shit." She rubbed her face. "Have you heard how she is?"

"No change. I called Reuben earlier." He gestured to a stool at the end of the bar, well away from prying ears. "Grab a seat and I'll get you a drink. Want some food?"

At the mention of food, her stomach grumbled and she checked her watch. It was nearly three. No wonder she was hungry. "Yeah, a bowl of fries, please." And then another thought struck her. "What happened at the church?"

"I haven't heard." He placed a glass of red wine in front of her.

Avery reached for her phone. "Crap, let's hope no news is good news. I'll call Ben."

Before she could make the call, a blast of cold, damp air gusted into the bar, and Avery looked up to see a grim-faced Newton approaching. "Newton! Didn't expect to see you here at this time."

Newton did not waste time on niceties. "What the bloody hell is going on at Old Haven Church?"

"Were you there today?"

"Yes, I was there, and it would have been nice if you'd have given me some warning!" His face was thunderous.

"But you deal with murders, why were you there?"

"Because with all the weird shit I've been dealing with lately, my boss has decided that I'm now the new go-to guy for paranormal crap."

"And that's bad?" Avery asked tentatively, before taking a large gulp of wine. It was going to be one of those days.

"Yes! I don't want to be the poster boy for paranormal Cornwall!"

Alex slid a pint of the local Doom lager in front of him. "On the house, mate. You look like you need it."

Newton looked like he was about to protest, and then slid on to a stool next to Avery and drank some anyway. "Cheers."

"So, what happened with the vicar?"

"He ended up being blasted off his ladder. The camera exploded, the cameraman received third-degree burns, and the interviewer, some perky blonde called Sarah, passed out with fright."

Avery put her glass down in shock, glanced at an equally shocked Alex, and asked, "Is James okay?"

"No. He's in hospital, unconscious, with a broken arm."

Avery's hand flew to her mouth. "Oh, no. And Ben and the others?"

"Fine, if not shocked. They were watching from the edge of the clearing."

"And you're okay?" she asked, faltering as he fixed his glare on her.

"No! I'm bloody furious! You said nothing about this! Neither of you!" He turned his glare on Alex.

"Clearly a mistake," Alex said, glancing nervously at Avery, "and could you lower your voice?"

Avery glanced around to see a few heads looking their way.

Newton grimaced, and continued in a low menacing tone. "Why didn't you tell me?"

"I honestly forgot, and didn't really think anything would come of it," Avery said. "I'm so sorry, Newton. We've got a lot on with the Shifters, and with El being cursed."

"Cursed?" His eyes widened with surprise.

"Sorry, didn't we tell you about that, either?"

"Why don't you two head up to my flat?" Alex suggested, seeing that Newton was about to go apoplectic, "and you can get Newton up to date. I'll join you as soon as I can."

With that, Avery headed upstairs, wishing she had some moral support.

Newton paced Alex's flat as Avery gave him all the latest news, everything except about the Cumbrian witches, which could wait until Alex arrived.

"Will they still run the news story?" Avery asked.

"Of course they will. It may even make national coverage."

"But there's no footage of the actual incident?"

"No. But they sent another crew and they have interviewed Ben and me, well away from the grove. The magic there is interfering with their equipment—not that they know it's magic, of course. I suggested that this is a hoax for

Halloween—a very good one. One that went wrong," he said, glaring again.

Avery sat on the floor cushion in front of the fire and warmed her hands, finding comfort in the bright flames. The day was already darkening outside, and Alex's flat was gloomy, lit only by the fire and one lamp in the corner. She liked it like this, it matched her mood, and the quiet, broken only by the crackle of the flames, allowed her to think.

She looked up at Newton. "Please come and sit down."

He frowned but acquiesced, sitting in the large, leather armchair." It's starting again, isn't it?"

"Yes, and we have no idea what this witch is seeking to do at Old Haven, other than maybe open some kind of gateway. It's well protected, and the magic there is growing stronger every day."

The door swung open just then and Alex came in, carrying two bowls of fries, and he sat on the sofa, placing both on the coffee table next to Avery. "Here you go. For you, too if you want some, Newton."

Newton nodded and took a chip absently.

"You filled him in?" Alex asked.

"Yes, and now I have more news for both of you," she said as she pulled a bowl of fries closer.

Between munching on chips, she let them know about Caspian's visit and her chat with the Shifters.

Alex groaned and leaned back, rubbing his face. "Great, just great. Have you heard from them yet?"

"No, but it's just a matter of time."

"Okay," Alex said, coming to a decision. "Let's head to El's flat, meet Briar and Reuben there, and work out what we do next. Want to join us, Newton?"

"Of course I bloody do."

10

By the time they reached El's flat, the rain was pouring again, streaming down El's windows and blurring the view. Her flat, however, was a warm cocoon of light and colour, and Avery, Alex, and Newton shook off their jackets and joined Reuben and Briar in the lounge.

"Any improvement with El?" Avery asked, sure she'd be disappointed with the answer.

"A very tiny amount." Briar looked hopeful, which dispelled some of the shadows beneath her eyes. Reuben looked even worse than he had before.

"Really? How?" Alex asked, placing a bag full of books on the table.

"I've found a couple of spells that talk about lifting curses, so I've been experimenting with them. She's not conscious, but her eyes are flickering a little. I hope that means something's happening. Sorry—that's vague, but I feel like I'm swimming in the dark here."

Briar led the way to El's bedroom, where she lay covered only in a sheet. The room was warm and the blinds were half-closed, keeping the space dim and shadowy. Candles had been placed around the bed, and the air was rich with the scent of incense. A symbol had been drawn on El's forehead, and a line of runes scrawled on her hands and feet. An amethyst was placed over the symbol on her head.

Briar watched her with troubled eyes. "I've been trying to draw the curse out, but without knowing what it is, it's hard. I've examined the necklace as much as possible, but haven't had much success. I'm scared to touch it without protection."

Avery sighed with annoyance at her forgetfulness. "That reminds me. Caspian has offered to help break El's curse."

Reuben had followed them into the room, and he leaned against the doorframe, frowning. "I don't want him anywhere near her! How does that wanker even know about this?"

"Because I was blessed by a visit from him," Avery said, feeling anything but lucky. "He came to give me some information about the Shifters, but as soon as he knew El was cursed, he offered his help. It's unlikely, I know, but it seemed genuine. He says his grimoires have lots of spells on curses and breaking them."

Newton snorted. "Of course they have."

"That's what I said, but I think we should seriously consider his offer." She looked at Alex. "What do you think?"

He shrugged. "Part of me agrees with Reuben, but if you can't make any headway, Briar…"

Briar nodded thoughtfully. "Let me think on it while you bring us up to speed with our Shifter friends." She led them back to the living area.

"You're not seriously thinking of accepting Caspian's help?" Reuben asked, looking aghast.

"I am. The longer she's cursed, the worse she'll get. She'll be dehydrated and starving, and who knows what else."

Reuben sighed with resignation and went to get drinks while Avery told them all about the Devices and their relationship with the Shifters, and about the possibility of their mysterious witch being a time-walker.

"Wow. A lot's been happening while I've been here," Briar said thoughtfully. "Hunter didn't mention this when I checked his wounds early this morning." Then she frowned. "Did he shift again?"

"Er, yes. Is that bad?"

Briar looked exasperated. "Yes! He's a terrible patient. Every time he shifts it disturbs his wounds."

"They did look pretty red," Avery confessed.

"So, you're saying he picked this fight? He confessed!"

"Yes and no," Avery said. "I only know what happened because I went to their house after Caspian visited me and found Holly and Piper at home alone. They told me all about the real circumstances of the fight, and it rings true."

"Well, we always suspected they were holding something back," Alex said. "This puts things in a whole different light."

"They lied to us," Reuben argued. "And brought trouble to White Haven."

"It's something we can deal with," Avery said, trying to reassure him. "And you don't need to get involved. You have El to worry about."

"I'm feeling pretty useless at the moment," he said, running his fingers through his hair. "I've read the grimoires back to front for solutions to curses, and the stuff I've found hasn't been much help with El. I could do with something else to try."

Avery sighed. "We're not looking for a fight. We are buying time for the Shifters. I don't know much about how they live, but it sounds a patriarchal nightmare." She shrugged. "And until I meet with the Devices, we don't even know what they want."

Newton looked impatient. "I'm more concerned about the events right on our doorstep—Old Haven Church, to be precise. What are we doing about that?"

Briar glared at him. "El is my concern right now, Newton."

He looked momentarily chastened. "Well, yes, of course, but the vicar has just been blasted by magic in front of a news crew. We need to stop this from escalating."

"Bloody hell," Alex said, leaning against the back of the sofa and rubbing his eyes. "Once this gets out, paranormal obsessives are going to flock to Old Haven. What a bloody nightmare."

"Yes they will, which puts them in danger," Newton said, thinking through the implications. He rounded on them angrily. "I can't believe you didn't tell me about this!"

"Oh, get over it," Briar said abruptly. "We've had other things to worry about."

Avery inwardly flinched. Briar could be so scathing to Newton now. However, he didn't care. "It's my job, Briar. *You* get over it."

They glared at each other for a few seconds before Reuben hurriedly intervened with a few bottles of beer from the fridge. "So, what's the plan?"

Alex leaned forward decisively. "Old Haven Church is old, but the site it's on is even older. The yew tree has been there for hundreds of years, probably pre-dating the church, which was built somewhere in the thirteenth century. Yews have huge significance. They symbolise death and rebirth, which is partly why churches were built next to them. At Old Haven, it's in the centre of a grove of trees. We need to know more about that site. Why has the witch picked there?"

"You're looking at me with that fevered gleam in your eye," Reuben noted. "What do want me to do?'

"We've brought lots of books with us," Alex started.

"Yes, books on local history, tree lore, old rites… And we thought while you're looking over El…" Avery continued.

"Sure, I could do research." Reuben nodded. "It will help keep me busy. I'm starting to go a bit screwy here."

Avery smiled, "Thanks."

"And what are you going to do?" he asked.

"As I mentioned, Caspian suggested that the witch is a time walker. She has managed to manipulate time to live longer. He says that takes a lot of energy, and we should look at sources of elemental energy to help her renew, particularly water—fresh water."

"A time-walker? It's a term I've heard of, but I don't know much else," Briar confessed.

"Neither do we," Alex said. "But I have an idea for where to find her. We're going to spirit walk."

Reuben frowned. "That could be dangerous if she can do that, too."

"But I can cover a lot of area that way, and I might be able to pick up her energy signature."

Avery added, "He won't be alone. We'll go together."

"Where will you look?"

"Natural springs, waterfalls—I need to start checking uncle Google," Alex said.

"And what about protecting Old Haven Church from paranormal obsessives?" Newton asked, still bristling with annoyance. "The police can't do this."

Alex smiled. "Our friend, Gabe, is looking for some security work."

Newton looked stunned. "The Nephilim guy?"

"It's a great fit, surely! Nephilim protecting the Church. Perfect," Alex said, grinning. "In fact, I'll call him now."

"No, wait," Avery said, stilling his hand. "Let me check with James first. Is he at home, Newton?"

"Maybe. It depends if he's conscious, or has concussion."

Avery sat silently thinking for a moment. She really didn't want to talk to James after their conversation, but she knew she had to. He was injured because she hadn't intervened more forcefully, and the church grounds would be swamped with paranormal enthusiasts unless they acted quickly. And she liked him, despite their differences. He was a good man, and she wanted to help him. "I'll call him now. And Briar, what do you want to do about Caspian's offer of help?"

"Call him. We need all the help we can get."

Avery promptly called Caspian before James. He answered with a slow drawl. "Avery. What a pleasure."

She cut to the chase. "Did you mean what you offered earlier? About El?"

"Of course."

"Then could you come to El's flat? Briar has made virtually no progress, and we need help now."

Avery could sense him bristling with smugness at being asked, and she fought to subdue her annoyance. "It will be my pleasure. I'll be there within the hour."

"Do you need the address?"

"Of course not. I know where she lives." And with that he hung up, leaving her infuriated.

She then called James, but it went straight to voicemail. She looked up at Alex. "I'm going to his house. Want to come?"

"Sure. Newton, we'll call you with news about the Nephilim and the church. Until then, see if you can post a couple of police up there for a short time. We don't need anyone else to get injured."

"And what about these other Device witches?" Newton asked, concerned.

"We'll deal with those when they arrive."

***

"I'm not sure how pleased he will be to see us," Avery said to Alex as they stood poised on James's doorstep, ready to knock.

Alex smiled that slow, sexy smile that always turned her knees to water. "You're adorable, you know that?"

She flushed with pleasure. "Well, thanks, but that doesn't help me right now."

"I'm telling you that you're adorable, and that doesn't help?"

She laughed. "It's awesome, and you're adorable, too. But I don't think James thinks I am."

"Clearly he's an idiot," he said softly as he leaned in for a kiss that left her breathless, and she pushed him away playfully.

"We're snogging on the vicar's doorstep. Behave!"

He laughed as she knocked on the door, and they heard footsteps approach from the other side. The woman who answered looked to be in her late thirties, with shoulder-length brown hair and tired eyes. She was petite in build, shorter than Avery, and she looked up, frowning uncertainly. "Can I help you?"

"Hi, I'm Avery, and this is Alex. Any chance we can chat to James for a moment?"

As soon as Avery mentioned their names her face fell, a trace of fear flashed through her eyes, and she stepped back. Avery's stomach turned. *Was this woman afraid of her?*

"What do you want?"

"Just to talk. I heard he was hurt earlier today."

"Yes, thanks to *you.* His arm's broken and he banged his head."

"And that's why we're here. I did ask him not to go there today," Avery said gently. "Are you his wife? You must be worried. We want to help."

For one horrible moment, Avery thought she was going to slam the door in her face and wondered if they would have to glamour her, which she didn't really want to do. But then his wife stepped back again, opening the door wider. "Come in. I'll take you to him."

They stepped inside and Avery held her hand out, "And your name is?"

She hesitated for a second, and then shook her offered hand. "Elise."

Alex did the same, and gave her his most gleaming smile. "Thanks, Elise. We appreciate this."

She turned her back and led them down a wide entrance hall, and Avery and Alex exchanged a furtive glance. *This was going to be hard.*

The house was warm from the central heating, the entrance hall and corridor were panelled with wood, and the floor covered with rugs. Stray toys were strewn along the way, and as they walked, Elise picked them up wearily. They entered a living room, filled with the chaos of family life, and passing through it, she led them to a door at the back of the house. She knocked tentatively and then pushed the door open. "James, you have visitors."

It was a study, lit with a single lamp, and furnished with a desk overflowing with papers, and several bookcases full of books. James was reclining in a large armchair, the material of the arms and headrest worn thin over the years. A fire was burning low in the hearth, and he sat looking into the flames, vacant. He didn't turn his head.

Elise glanced at them, and then marched over to the fire and threw another log on, prodding it back into life.

Avery moved around the front of the chair very slowly, as if she was approaching a scared child, and dropped to her knees so she was at his eye level. "Hi James, how are you?"

For a second he didn't move, and then he raised his eyes slowly to meet hers, cradling his left arm, which was now encased in plaster. "Not great."

"I'm really sorry you were hurt today, we both are." She nodded to Alex, who now moved into James's line of sight, and he sat cross-legged on the floor, nodding at James in sympathy. Avery continued, "How are you feeling?"

"Pretty confused actually, Avery." He looked across her towards Elise, and Elise straightened and left the room. He waited until her steps retreated. "I'm not exactly sure what happened today, but I'm pretty sure it wasn't a hoax."

"What do you think it was, then?" Avery felt her throat constrict with worry, but she kept her expression calm and relaxed.

James looked away, back into the fire. "I felt a jolt of something flash up my arm and through my body. It felt like every nerve ending was on fire, and it just threw me, right off the ladder and back against a tree. But I saw something…"

Avery looked at Alex, who appeared calm, but she knew he was as worried as she was. She prompted James, "What did you see?"

"A face, a woman's face. Old eyes, so very old. Haunted."

"How did you see her face?"

"In my mind." He turned to her, his eyes equally haunted, and lifted his uninjured hand, pointing to his head. "Right in here. Just for a second. And a voice was shouting something like, 'No, run away, preacher man.' Then I blacked out, but her face is stuck here. Every time I close my eyes, I see her."

Alex frowned and leaned forward. "Did you feel anything? Any emotion?"

"Yes." His eyes moved to Alex. "A raging anger. Who is she?"

"We don't know," Alex confessed. "But we're trying to find out."

"Would you recognise her again?" Avery asked, eagerly.

"Oh, yes. Definitely."

"That may help us, I guess," Avery mused.

James added, "There's power around there. I sensed it. It was eerie. It felt very different from when that spirit was in the church. Those *things* on the tree, you called them witch-signs. Is she a witch? Are *you*?"

Avery felt her breath catch in her throat and she faltered for a second. Before she could respond, James leapt in. "Yes, I see it in your face." He looked at Alex. "Are *you*?"

Alex kept his gaze firmly locked with James's. "There are many definitions of a witch."

James allowed himself a brief smile. "Semantics. What's your definition?"

"What's yours?" Alex countered.

For a few seconds the room was silent, and all Avery could hear were the shifting embers, crackling logs in the fire, and the quiet *tick-tock* of the clock on the wall, which seemed to get louder with every passing moment.

A new hardness entered James's voice. "I've heard of Wicca, of course—witches who celebrate the seasons, who worship the Goddess, who forgo the one true God. But there are also those who sign pacts with the Devil, who wear the Devil's mark, who have familiars who do their bidding, who cast spells and engage with the occult. Which are you?"

Avery sighed and hardened her tone too as she came to a decision. This was not the time for lies, and if this went badly, they could still glamour him. "There are no witches who sign pacts with the Devil, James. That's medieval nonsense.

Innocent men and women were burned for it, including my ancestor, Helena Marchmont. But yes, I am a witch. I perform magic, natural magic." She watched James's face change and his eyes widen with surprise. "*Actual* magic. It has been passed down to me through the centuries, and to Alex, from his family. We have no pacts with anyone, and we are good, our magic used to protect. We protect White Haven, and that includes you."

His eyes narrowed with suspicion and doubt. "What do you mean, 'actual magic?'"

Avery glanced at Alex, and he nodded. Turning to James, she summoned air, and a small breeze drifted around her, lifting her hair. She sent it around the room, ruffling the papers on his desk and lifting them until they floated freely for a few seconds, and then moving on to brush across Alex and James's hair, too. James started, the shock clear on his face. Alex then turned to the fire and made the flames grow higher and higher, creating twisting shapes within them, and then he held his palm out and summoned a flame onto his hands.

James edged back in his chair, a mixture of fear and wonder in his eyes. "Actual magic," he said, exhaling softly.

"Elemental magic," Avery corrected, watching his reaction.

"I think I'm concussed."

Avery smiled. "You might be, but it is real. And it has nothing to do with the Devil."

Alex was watching James carefully, and he leaned forward. "We're trusting you with this information, James. It's a secret—between us."

James nodded in acceptance. "You could have lied."

"Yes, we could have—and still can."

"Are there more than just you two?"

Alex hesitated a second. "Yes, but we won't tell you who they are. It's not important."

James accepted this silently. "And this woman in my head?"

"Another witch, but we have no idea who she is or what she wants," Avery answered. "It's important we keep people away from Old Haven right now."

"And that includes you," Alex added.

"Do those paranormal investigators know about you?"

Avery nodded. "Please believe me when I say that we are safe, James. You have nothing to fear from us, but you also have no idea of the nature of magic and how dangerous it can be. It is powerful and mysterious, and can be used for ill by those who choose to do so."

"Like that witch. She threatened me," he said, starting to get angry.

"Which is why you need to stay out of it," Alex said, insistent.

James stared at him, and it was clear that his moment of wonder was ebbing back towards fear and suspicion. *Had they just made a terrible mistake?* "How do we stop what's happening at Old Haven?"

"We're working on it," Alex said. "But we need time and space."

"As I told you yesterday," Avery said, unable to keep the impatience from her voice.

"You can't just remove those things with your—" he swallowed, "magic?"

"No. But we can protect the area. We have friends who can help; they work in security. Shall I ask them?" Alex asked.

"Who are they?" James looked warily between them. "Other witches?"

"No. But they're strong, and no one can do this better. Their manager," Avery said, inwardly wincing at the lie, "is called Gabe, and you're welcome to meet him."

"All right," he said, resignation and desperation all over his face. "Now, please go and let me try to get my head around this. What do we tell the press?"

Alex smiled. "You don't want them to know now? Because they saw a lot there today."

"No. Not now." He held his hand to his head again, looking appalled. "Can you imagine what they'd say?"

Avery rose to her feet. "They ended up interviewing Newton, the DI, and Ben and the others, so it's already done. Not sure if that will calm anything down, though. We'll be in touch."

11

Once again, Avery and Alex sat within a protective circle on the rug in front of Alex's fire, just as they had done the first time that Avery spirit walked with him.

The room was dimly lit with only candles and firelight, and Avery sat cross-legged and knee-to-knee with Alex. He held the small, silver goblet filled with the potion to help them enter the necessary mind state, and he took a sip before passing it to Avery. She grimaced as she sipped and then passed it back. She had forgotten how bitter it was. "Where are we going first?"

"Up to Old Haven. I thought it would be interesting to see how it appears in our spirit state," he said, reaching forward and squeezing her hands. "And then on from there over the moors. Maybe follow the river up the valley."

Avery nodded. "Do you remember the last time we did this?"

"Of course. It was the first time I kissed you."

Avery reached forward and stroked his cheek, feeling a wave of longing rush over her. "Lucky me. I misjudged you then."

"I know, but I forgive you," he said cheekily, and then pulled her in for a kiss again. "Stop being so distracting. We have work to do."

"All right, I'll distract you later." She lay down and held his hand as they had done before, and listened to him say the spell that helped their spirits leave their body.

She felt herself slip from consciousness into some strange dreamstate, and as before, Alex lifted from his body first and floated above her, his body shimmering silver, a cord linking him back to his corporeal self.

He smiled down at her and pulled gently, and she felt the jolt as she floated to join him. His voice resonated in her head. *Do you need to go around the room again first?*

No, I'm fine, she replied. *Let's get on with it.*

He turned and pulled her through the walls of his flat and out above the streets of White Haven. Although it was cold out she felt perfectly warm and comfortable, impervious to the autumn weather, but the elemental energies looked very different tonight. Rain and wind swirled about them, and the sky overhead was heavy with brooding clouds, appearing purple and grey on this plane. Street lights still sparked brightly below them, and Avery could see the auras of the people who were braving the weather. Above the town was the faint pulse of their magic, released on the night when they broke the binding spell, much smaller than it had been. However, Alex didn't hesitate, pulling her quickly over the town and towards Old Haven on the hill.

There were no people up there. The landscape was quiet and dark, and the bulk of the church was solid below them. But behind it, a dark red glow seemed to vibrate in the night. *Can you see it?* Alex asked, his voice in her head as he guided them closer.

Yes. That's a pretty threatening energy signature. A red aura around a person could mean passion, energy, and strength, but when it was cloudy and tinged with black as this was, it meant anger and negativity. *Does that reflect the witch's aura?* Avery asked. Alex understood this better than she did.

Probably. She built this spell, and as we thought, it's very strong.

As they moved closer, staying clear of the energy field, Avery saw silvery sigils glowing around the area. Wards.

She means business, Alex said. *I wonder if these were added today, after James's attempt to remove the witch-signs.*

Maybe the area doesn't need protecting by Gabe. These wards would discourage anyone from getting closer.

The runes were protective, but also defensive, and Avery could feel their power from here. She wondered what sort of a spell it was.

Maybe James's attempt to remove a witch-sign triggered them, and that's why he heard her in his head? Alex suggested.

Avery agreed, but was distracted by something beneath the cloudy red area that seemed to emanate from the yew itself. *Can you see that?* She pointed towards the heart of the tree.

The yew's trunk and branches were flush with a green aura, indicating life and vitality, and all the other trees and bushes vibrated with the same colour. The yew's, however, was darker and richer, Avery thought probably as a sign of its great age. But within its hollow trunk, she saw a faintly iridescent, white glow.

Alex twisted as he tried to get a better view. *That's a different energy signature.*

I agree. But what does it mean?

I think that whatever she's doing is working, and a portal is starting to form.

But to where? The last one we saw was full of fire and darkness.

Hopefully not to demon realms, then. The witch-signs are resonating, too.

He was right. There were lots of them hanging in the yew and the surrounding trees, and they also glowed with rainbow colours, shaking slightly with power.

Come on, he said, sighing. *There's nothing more we can do here. Let's try to find her.*

They ranged onwards, looking for something that might link Old Haven to where the witch was hiding, but there was nothing.

They passed over swollen streams and rushing rivers, heavy with rainfall. Small waterfalls churned their energy and threw up clouds of moisture, but nothing suggested a witch might be close. They even looked for absences of light that might indicate something was blocking them, but saw nothing.

Alex drew her attention to the moors, well away from White Haven and other small communities. He pointed down to racing shapes, streaking across the ground. Four of them in all, and they seemed to be hunting a small, fleeing creature. *The Shifters.*

Avery gasped. *You're right!* As they dropped lower, she saw how huge and fast they were. They were intent on their quarry, which Avery thought was a fox, and she looked away as they moved around it in a pincer movement. *I love foxes! They can't kill it.*

It's what they do…they're wolves. But Avery detected a trace of regret in his tone, too—if you could call it a tone in your head.

Not tonight they don't, she said, annoyed. She hadn't tried to use her powers on this plane since the last time she spirit walked, but she quickly spelled a charm of protection over the fox, blanketing its scent and draping it in shadow. Then she sent its scent down a false path, causing the wolves to veer in the wrong direction. She smiled gleefully at Alex as the fox ran across the moors to freedom, the wolves now far away.

Avery Hamilton, that was very sneaky, Alex said approvingly.

I know, but I don't care. It's not like they'll starve.

Come on. We're not getting anywhere here. Let's go home.

They headed back to White Haven, passing over the roads that branched below them. Alex's eyes narrowed and he pointed towards dark shapes moving on the road that led directly to the town, a dark mass of grey and black around a swiftly moving car, easy to see against the glow of street lights. *I think the Devices are here.*

If their auras are anything to go by, they are not happy, Avery said.

They dropped down until they were much closer to the car and tried to see inside. There were three figures; a driver and two others in the back seat, from whom a wave of power and determination emanated.

Avery realised one of the witches in the back seat was turning to look out of the window, as if they detected their presence, and she pulled Alex away. *The fun's about to begin.*

***

Avery spent the night at Alex's. They initially talked about how to deal with the Devices, but then, the world tuned out by the wind and rain, Avery decided that getting naked with Alex was much more fun. The Devices could wait.

She woke in the middle of the night, wondering what the weird noise she heard was. For a few seconds, she lay dazed, trying to analyse the sound, and then turned to Alex, but the bed was empty.

Alarmed, she woke completely, leapt out of bed, and pulled on a t-shirt before heading into the main room where she found Alex slumped on the floor of the kitchen, talking to himself—or someone in his mind. *Crap.* Avery dropped next to him, debating whether to try and wake him, but that could be dangerous.

The room was dark, other than the leak of light from the street lamps through the blinds. She spelled the lamps on, but the room looked as normal, and she couldn't detect another presence among them.

She rolled him onto his back and lifted his eyelids. His eyes were white, rolled back into his head, and he continued to whisper words she couldn't make out. He felt icy cold, his skin was pale, and his fists were clenched. She ran to the sofa and pulled a cushion and a blanket free, and then placed the cushion under his head and draped the rug over him.

Months ago, Nate, one of the witches from St Ives, had warned Alex that his visions may get stronger, and for a while, they had. Their troubles with the Mermaids and the Nephilim seemed to have opened floodgates of receptiveness that had led to headaches and sudden collapses. They had been tied to the witches' activities in White Haven, and once he'd had a vision of Gabe, the Nephilim, and had been propelled into his head unexpectedly. It had happened a couple of times at work, alarming his staff, and he had passed it off as exhaustion. With Nate's help he had been able to get them under control, and now they happened only intermittently.

Tonight's efforts must have triggered them again. Avery hated it when this happened; she was powerless to stop them, or bring him out of them. She sat, frustrated, hoping it would end quickly, when she felt the tingle of magic as Alex's protective wards around his pub started to vibrate. Someone was trying to break them.

She jumped to her feet, hands raised, and added her own magic to Alex's spells. For a short time it seemed to be working, and then with a hollow *boom*, the charms fell and she saw an inky black mass start to twist in the middle of the living area. Someone was using witch-flight, which Avery had tried but struggled to master. She quickly threw up a protective barrier of shimmering white energy, blocking whatever it was from coming closer; they might be in the flat, but it wasn't over yet. She was tempted to send a blast of fire at it, but she also wanted to know who it was.

The swirl of darkness coalesced into the figure of a tall woman, standing with arms raised, her dark eyes boring into Avery. She was wearing contemporary dress—dark trousers tucked into knee-length leather boots, a shirt, and a long jacket, and she had long, silky auburn hair, framing a pale face. In the instant before she attacked, Avery registered the shock on her face. *She hadn't expected me to be here.* Before Avery could do anything, the witch sent a blast of pure energy at her, which would have swept her off her feet if it hadn't been for her shield that effectively blocked it.

Avery used her shield as a weapon, propelling it forward with a wave of icy air, and sweeping the unknown witch off her feet and sending her crashing against the far wall. Before she could respond, Avery pinned her there, lifting her off the floor so that her legs dangled inches from the ground.

"How dare you enter uninvited!" Avery yelled, both furious and afraid.

"How dare you look for me!" the woman retorted in a husky voice. She managed to lift her hands and sent a wave of power towards Avery with a swiftness that caught Avery unawares, and she flew backwards, hitting the kitchen cabinets painfully. She fell, winded, and only just managed to find her feet and repel another attack, this one a jet of witch-fire that spewed from the woman's hands across the room. Avery could feel the heat from here, and she managed to deflect it onto a houseplant, which burst into flames.

Alex was still immobile on the ground, and Avery's heart was banging painfully in her chest. She had to stop this woman, *now*.

Avery used elemental air to lift the burning plant off the ground and send it spinning across the room back towards the witch, who in turn hurled it against the wall and advanced across the space. Avery advanced too, but rather than strike with magic, she ran full tilt across the room and rugby-tackled the witch. They crashed into the sofa and rolled over it and onto the coffee table, before falling onto the rug on the far side, barely missing the wide stone hearth of the fireplace.

The witch was winded from her unexpected attack, and taking advantage, Avery punched her in the face. The woman's head flew back in shock, striking the floor, and anger filled her dark eyes. In a sudden display of power, she propelled Avery up until she had her pinned to the ceiling in a vice grip of magic. She held her left arm upwards and tightened her hands as if she was squeezing, and Avery felt her ribs contract. She couldn't breathe and she felt her vision start to blacken at the edges.

With her right hand, the witch wiped the blood trickling from her lip. She stared up at Avery. "You'll regret that, bitch."

Avery couldn't move or speak; her grip was immense. *Shit. She's going to kill me.*

And then out of her peripheral vision, Avery saw Alex rise to his feet, and a huge fireball hurtled across the room.

It hit the witch before she even knew what was happening, and she was immediately enveloped in flames. In a split second she disappeared, taking the flames with her, and Avery plummeted onto the floor, half hitting the coffee table before she dropped to the ground.

For a few seconds, she couldn't breathe and she lay winded, trying to see beyond the encroaching blackness. She felt rather than saw Alex come to a skidding halt next to her. "Avery. Thank the Gods, you're alive."

"Barely," she croaked. The blackness started to recede and she saw his anxious face above hers. "I think I've broken some ribs. That really bloody hurts." She gingerly lifted her left hand and felt her side. Even inhaling hurt.

Alex tenderly felt around her head, and then her left side. "How's your breathing?"

"Painful. Help me sit up."

He eased a hand around her back and virtually lifted her into a sitting position.

"Ouch, ouch, ouch," she said with every incremental movement. Once she got her breath back, she squinted at Alex. He looked equally terrible, with dark shadows beneath his eyes. "How are you? I thought you were unconscious."

"I was. I could feel her mind wrapped around mine like a thick cloud. It was impenetrable, until you did *something*. You must have caused her to lose concentration. I lay still for a few seconds before I acted, and just tried to summon my power."

Avery smiled at him and cupped his cheek. "Lucky me. I think she was about to kill me."

"I would have killed her first. No question." He leaned forward and kissed her gently. "Should I call Briar?"

"No. Let her rest. I'll survive 'til morning. What about you?"

"I'll be fine eventually. I'm just pissed off she caught me unawares. And I need to get my protection spells up again." He flopped back on the ground, staring up at the ceiling, clutching his stomach. "I feel sick."

"I'll make you something," Avery said, trying to struggle to her feet before giving up. "In a minute." She looked over at Alex. "She thought you were alone. She was pretty shocked to see me. If I hadn't been here, I'm not sure what she would have done."

Alex was silent for a second. "Do you think she'd have killed me?"

"I'm not sure. Maybe. She certainly wants us out of action. First El, and now you." A horrible thought struck her. "Maybe she's already attacked Briar and Reuben. I need to call them, it can't wait."

Avery stood slowly, wincing with every movement, pulled her phone from her bag where it sat on the kitchen bench, and called Reuben. It rang for a while before he answered. "Avery. It's four in the morning. This better be good."

"We were attacked in Alex's flat. I wanted to make sure you were okay."

"What!" His tone changed as his brain flipped into gear. "Are you both okay?"

"Yes, just. Are you? Is Briar with you?"

"Yeah, she's sleeping on the couch. Well, she was." She could hear him moving about, and he lowered his voice as he said something to Briar. "Yep, nothing happened here."

Relief swept though Avery. "Good. Is Caspian still there?"

"No, he went home hours ago, but he'll be back later."

"Will he?" Avery thought her confusion would never end. "Why?"

"Well, shockingly, he's been pretty useful." Reuben sounded annoyed but also pleased, not surprisingly. He'd pretty much vowed to hate Caspian forever after he killed Gil.

Avery came to a decision. "I'll let you get back to sleep, but we'll head over in a few hours. This witch means business, and we need to decide what to do."

"Sure, laters," Reuben said, yawning before he hung up.

"So, they're okay?" Alex asked from where he still lay stretched out on the rug.

"Yep. Come on. Let's get your wards up again."

He groaned, sat up, looked around at his flat, and frowned. "And maybe clean. You two made quite a mess."

He was right. The sofa cushions were strewn across the floor, soil was scattered *everywhere*, and the remains of the burnt plant were smeared across the wall and now lay smoking on the floor. Candles and other objects were either on the floor or in random places, and pictures were hanging askew on the wall. On top of that, the smell of smoke hung on the air.

"Your lovely flat! Sorry," Avery said, feeling terrible.

He grinned, rose to his feet, and joined her in the kitchen. "All fixable. Well, maybe not the plant. The important thing is that you're okay." He frowned. "Why is there a bruise on your chin?"

"Is there?" Avery touched it gently. "I think I smacked it off her elbow when I rugby-tackled her."

Alex started to laugh. "And there's blood on your knuckles."

"I punched her, too."

"That's my girl," he said. And then he frowned. "Is that your blood? Because if she's got it…"

He didn't need to explain. Hair and blood were great assets to a witch, and you didn't want an enemy getting hold of them. They could be used to make a poppet—a small figure of someone that you could spell and manipulate.

“No. I’m pretty sure it’s hers. I spilt her lip.”

“Good. Let’s use it.” He threw her a tissue. “Wipe it up and keep it safe.”

12

The next morning, Avery creaked out of bed; every muscle ached, and her ribs felt like they were on fire. After she'd phoned Sally and explained she wouldn't be going in to work until later—and asked her to feed her cats—everyone headed to El's flat. By the time Avery and Alex arrived, Caspian was already there.

The mood in El's flat was all business. Spell books, history books, and reference books were spread everywhere. Incense hung in the air, and the central heating was turned up high, dispelling the cold gloom that lurked outside the windows. Caspian and Briar were seated at El's small dining table, deep in discussion, and Reuben was cross-legged on the floor, an open book on his lap, and a cup of coffee steaming at his elbow. Intriguingly, a selection of different shaped Alembic jars stood in a row on the kitchen workbench, each filled with unrecognisable substances. It looked like a chemistry lab.

It was odd seeing Caspian there, dressed in jeans and a t-shirt rather than a suit, and he looked up as they entered, his eyes brushing across Alex before coming to rest on Avery. She met his eyes briefly before she looked at the others, calling, "Hi, guys."

"Hey Ave, Alex," Reuben said, twisting to look at them. "You two recovered?"

"Just about." Alex headed to El's open kitchen and placed fresh pastries down, closely followed by Avery with a tray of coffees. "Well, maybe not Avery. She's a bit sore." He pulled her close and kissed her forehead.

"But I did manage to buy coffees despite feeling battered and bruised," she explained with a grimace.

Briar groaned in appreciation and joined them at the counter. "You stars. Just what I needed. Can I do anything to help you heal, Avery?"

Avery shook her head. "No, El's more important. As is coffee. Two lattes, two flat whites, and a moccachino in case someone wanted a chocolate hit, too," Avery said, pointing them out.

"Mine!" Reuben shouted. He held up his hand expectantly.

Briar turned to him. "You've got a coffee!"

"I can have two!" he protested.

"It's all yours, don't panic." She picked it up and took it over to him.

Caspian walked over to join them, smiling smugly. "One for me, too? I am lucky."

"Well, you're helping, so why not?" Avery said, trying to avoid his stare.

"And you even get a pastry," Alex said, archly. "Must be your lucky day."

Caspian gave him the coolest of smiles. "To be here with all of you fills my heart with joy."

Briar sighed, exasperated. "Stop it, both of you. We're actually making good progress, thanks to Caspian."

Alex adopted a lofty expression. "Good. So is El out of her curse-coma yet?"

"No, but we now know what type of curse it is," Caspian said. He pointed to the table where the cursed necklace lay on folds of velvet, well out of reach of an accidental touch. "I found some spells which work to reveal the nature of the curse, and through a process of elimination—"

"Endless elimination," Reuben added with a groan.

Caspian ignored him. "By testing various potions and herbs in the alembic jars, we have found it is an earth-based curse."

"What does that mean?" Avery asked between sips of coffee.

"Earth elemental magic, bound into the silver, has suffocated El's mind and bound her magic into Earth and darkness."

Avery paused, horrified. "That sounds awful. So, her mind is trapped—as if she's buried alive?"

"Sort of," Briar said. "If there's an excess of Earth magic, then we'll need Air, Fire, and Water to balance it."

"The witch attacked me last night," Alex said, thoughtfully. "And I experienced a similar sensation. She suffocated me, and I thought it was with her mind, but after thinking about it, the weight of it suggested an earthiness. I was almost crushed under it."

"So, our new arrival is an Earth witch," Caspian said thoughtfully.

Avery frowned. "But she travelled using witch-flight. I thought that was something only an Air witch could do?"

He shrugged. "If she's been around as long as we think, she's probably mastered many skills most of us would never achieve in one lifetime."

"But I'm an Earth witch," Briar said, offended. "I don't do things like that!"

Caspian sighed. "We can do as many positive or negative things with our powers as we choose, you know that, Briar. Earth can nurture and create life, or suffocate and bury it.

Fire can warm or burn, air can caress or batter like a hurricane, and water can give life or drown it." He took a sip of coffee and reached for a croissant. "Using Earth magic to curse is also quite inspired at this time of year."

"Of course," Briar said. "Its season is winter, its nature is grounding, and the cave, its natural manifestation of protection, can be a prison."

Alex nodded thoughtfully. "El's predominant strength is Fire. The complete opposite to Earth on the natural cycle."

"But how do we break it?" Reuben asked impatiently. He still sat on the rug, watching them through narrowed eyes.

Caspian suggested, "We free El from its binding using all the elements. It will take all of us, but now that we know what we're fighting, we can target it more effectively."

"And we've almost finalised the spell," Briar added.

Avery felt a flush of relief race through her. "Fantastic. When?"

"Noon." Caspian moved back to his spell book. "Earth magic is strongest at midnight, therefore weakest at midday. Fire is strongest at midday. We need to place her in the centre of a pentagram. We'll draw it on the floor." He pointed to where Reuben sat in the middle of the rug, and then looked back at Avery and Alex. "You injured the witch last night?"

Alex nodded. "A combination of a fireball, a rugby tackle, and a punch to her face."

"You punched her?" Briar asked, wide-eyed.

"Avery did," Alex explained with pride as he pulled her close and kissed her cheek.

"Nice one!"

Avery laughed, but was uncomfortably aware of Caspian's appreciative glance in her direction, and she studiously ignored it.

"Good," Caspian said. "She'll be recovering, and that will make our life easier. A spell, as you know, is always connected to the witch who cast it, and it's no different with curses."

"And is El at all improved today?" Avery asked.

Briar shook her head. "No. She has sunk deeper into the coma again."

Their conversation was interrupted by Avery's phone ringing, and she saw it was Sally. She retreated to the far corner of the room as she answered it. "Hi Sally, everything okay?"

"I'm afraid not, Avery." Sally's voice sounded clipped with annoyance. "You have two visitors here who are refusing to go until they have spoken to you. They are interfering with the smooth running of this shop."

Avery imagined Sally was staring right at them as she spoke. *It must be the Devices.*

"Did they give a name?"

"No, other than that they have travelled a long way to see you."

"Well, tell them I have business to attend to, and will see them when I'm free," she answered. And then she dropped her voice, just in case they could hear her. "And don't offer them coffee."

She looked across to Alex as she hung up. "The Devices are here."

"Great. Right on cue," Alex said.

"Need my help?" Caspian drawled.

"No," Avery said abruptly, and then she softened her tone, remembering he was helping them. "You concentrate on El. Me and Alex will meet them and will be back here before midday. Need us to bring anything?"

"Alex, do whatever you need to do to prepare yourself to connect with El's spirit. Avery, just bring yourself."

***

"What's going on with Caspian?" Alex asked Avery as they walked up the hill towards Happenstance Books. "He seemed *odd* around you. Creepier than normal."

Avery paused for a second, and then decided honesty was the best option. "He told me if I got bored with you to give him a call."

"He did what?" Alex asked, stopping in the middle of the street. "The cheeky bastard!"

She turned to him and laughed. "Very. Clearly I won't, because he's an arse and you're awesome, so you have nothing to worry about, other than maybe me punching him, too."

"I'd pay to see that," he said, and then he frowned. "When did he say that? You didn't tell me."

She rubbed her face, moving out of the way of a local who nodded as he passed. "Yesterday? When he came to ask about Old Haven and the press. So much has happened, I just haven't had a chance to say."

He looked mildly offended. "As long as that's the only reason."

"Of course it is," Avery said, rushing to reassure him. She pulled him into a shop doorway, out of the drizzle, and wrapped her arms around him, inhaling his gorgeous Alex scent. "You know I have zero interest in Caspian."

"Just checking," he murmured, his dark eyes appraising her.

She rose on her tiptoes and kissed him. "Never doubt my feelings for you, or my loathing of Caspian."

He grinned. "Come on then, or the Devices will be steaming."

***

As soon as Avery entered Happenstance Books, she could feel a chill in the atmosphere, and it didn't have anything to do with the heating.

Sally silently glowered at a couple of witches who sat on the sofa under the window, watching everyone with steely eyes. Other customers had retreated to the far reaches of the shop, leaving the main area deserted. Avery met Sally's furious glance with raised eyebrows, and immediately turned to the newcomers, who rose as one to greet her.

There was a man and a woman waiting. Avery estimated the woman was in her sixties, with long, white hair and a fine-boned, aristocratic face, accentuated with high cheekbones and pale brown eyes that were almost amber. She wore a long, sweeping black coat that covered clothes made of velvet and silk. The man was younger, maybe late forties, with salt and pepper hair brushed into a neat side-part. His clothes were also clearly expensive; a sharp, three-piece suit and a fine wool overcoat. Power emanated from them. In fact, Avery was pretty sure they were projecting it to instil fear. Unfortunately, all it did was annoy her.

Avery spoke first. "I believe you're waiting for me? I'm Avery Hamilton, and this is Alex Bonneville."

The woman answered, a trace of Lancashire to her accent. "We did not expect to wait so long, Ms Hamilton."

"I don't know why not. It's not like you made an appointment to see me."

Her expression froze, and she almost hissed. "Mr Faversham advised you I would be coming."

"But he is not my secretary. And your name is?"

Avery could tell the woman was itching to use magic, and she felt Alex bristling beside her. "Alice Device, and my son, Jeremy Device."

"Excellent. Please follow me." She led the way once more to her back room, Alex following at the rear.

Once inside with the door firmly closed, Alex leaned against it watchfully, and Alice rounded on her. "Your impertinence is outrageous."

"So is yours!" Avery said. "This is my shop, you arrive here unannounced and uninvited, and then have the nerve to criticise me. What century are you from?"

"Our apologies," Jeremy said, intervening smoothly. "We have travelled a long way. I think you know. I detected your unique—" he paused, "energy from last night. It was you, wasn't it? Hovering over our car?"

Avery turned to him speculatively. "Yes. We thought you'd noticed us. Impressive."

"One of my gifts." He bowed his head, but didn't drop his eyes.

Avery took a deep breath and gestured to the table and chairs in the centre of the small room. "We're tired, too. Please take a seat."

Alice looked dismissively around the room, which was as usual, filled with boxes of stock. "May we not sit somewhere more comfortable?"

Avery had no intention of taking them up to her flat. "Unfortunately not."

"We'll get to the point," Alice said, still standing. "The Shifters, Hunter Chadwick and his family, have hidden here. They are to return to Cumbria immediately."

"Have you asked them?" Avery knew that they had not, because their old-fashioned views meant they had to ask the witches of the town first.

"Of course not," Alice confirmed. "They are under your protection."

"Yes, they are," Avery said, deciding that although she hadn't understood exactly what she had agreed to initially, they absolutely were now. "Returning to Cumbria at the present time is out of the question."

Alice stared down her nose at Avery. "You clearly have no understanding of what they have done."

"I believe Hunter challenged some guy called Cooper to save his sister, and unfortunately lost the fight. His brother affected a rescue due to the severity of Hunter's injuries. He is still healing."

"That guy is Cooper Dacre, the leader of the pack, and he demands Hunter makes peace or die in a re-challenge. The fight was not completed. It leaves the whole pack in a state of flux. It is unacceptable."

Interesting that a pack suffered from political instability.

"Hunter suspects interference, and fears for his family."

"How dare you suggest we interfered with the fight," Alice said, bright red spots of fury springing up on her pale cheeks.

"I didn't, he did, and actually didn't mention you at all." Avery paused, letting her inference hang on the air. "You may return to Cumbria now and we will tell you when he is fit enough to travel."

"He returns with us today."

"No. They sought Sanctuary, and we granted it. We decide when he is ready to leave."

Alice fell silent, glaring at Avery with seething resentment, and Avery knew there was nothing she could do.

Emboldened by her progress, and feeling Alex's solidarity from behind, she asked, "Did you oversee the fight?"

"We witness all challenges."

Avery decided guile might be best. "I don't understand the rules of Shifters and their society. It's complex to those who don't participate in it. You work hand in hand with the ruling pack? The Dacres?"

"Yes. It has been our way for hundreds of years."

"So, should a challenger win, your allegiance is to them?"

Alice blinked. "Yes, of course."

"Sounds fascinating. I would love to witness a challenge, wouldn't you, Alex?"

"Absolutely," she heard him reply.

Avery continued. "I believe Hunter is planning to challenge again, once he recovers and seeks to leave White Haven. I would like to watch, if that's possible. I have never been to Cumbria, and of course it's an area famous for its rich history of witches, your family included."

"Challenges can be bloody affairs, Miss Hamilton, and are absolutely forbidden to outsiders," Alice said, and a wave of magic reached a snaky tendril out between them, as if probing Avery's defences.

Avery stopped it dead. "Such a shame."

Alice's features suddenly transformed, and her facade of grace disappeared into a snarl as a flare of magic reared up between them. "You mess with things that are beyond your reach, young witch."

At that, Avery had enough, and a swirl of wind rose around her, whipping her hair up and off her face and pushing Alice back a step. "They asked for our help, and they will get it. Don't you dare threaten me! You have no authority in White Haven!"

Alice lifted her chin defiantly. "And you will have none in Cumbria. Step carefully, Ms Hamilton. Jeremy. A card, please."

Jeremy reached into his pocket and extracted a business card that he handed wordlessly to Avery. She received it without breaking eye contact with Alice. "Thank you. I will inform you when he is fit to travel."

Alex opened the door and without another word, Alice swept from the room, Jeremy following, and within seconds they heard the shrill jingle of the door bells as they left the shop.

Avery looked up at Alex. "Holy cow."

"I think we've just made another enemy," he said, kissing her forehead gently.

13

El's flat had been transformed in Avery and Alex's absence. The blinds were shut and there were candles everywhere, brightening the space with a golden glow. The sofa had been pushed back, the rug rolled up, and a pentacle had been drawn on the floor—a circle that encompassed a pentagram.

The scent of natural oils filled the rooms from several oil burners, and Avery detected mint and rosemary, among others. As she breathed deeply, she felt her head clear and new resolve fill her. "An energising spell," she said to no one in particular.

Briar was still putting the finishing touches on the pentagram, but she glanced up at her. "To help with lifting the curse."

"Good thinking." She slipped her shoes off, and placed her coat in the corner, out of the way, as Alex did the same.

"How did the meeting go?" Caspian asked. He too was ready for the spell. He already sat at the pentagram point of Fire, his grimoire in front of him, and he had also removed his shirt, revealing a pale, lightly muscled chest on which a strange rune had been drawn. The design was echoed in many smaller runes that trailed down his arms and hands in one long chain.

"Depends on which way you look at it," Avery explained. "They left without the Shifters, but they weren't happy."

"But guess who's going to Cumbria when the Shifters return?" Alex said, settling himself at the point of the Spirit at the top of the pentagram. He looked at Caspian. "I presume this is where you want me to sit."

Caspian nodded distractedly. "You're going to Cumbria? Is that wise?"

"We have no choice." Avery sat at the point of Air, between Alex and Caspian. "I suspect they will interfere with the fight. Holly pretty much accused them of it."

"Haven't we got enough going on?" Reuben asked, exiting the bathroom wrapped in only a towel and rubbing his hair dry with another.

"Well, we're not going now!" Avery chided him, trying to look only at his face. Reuben's remarkable physique was very disconcerting. "And why are you showering *now*?"

"I went for a surf," he explained. "I needed to clear my head and connect with my magic. I've found it's the best way for me to do it. Back in a tic, and I'll bring El," he said as he bounded out of the room.

When he returned in board shorts and a t-shirt, he carried El in his arms, and he carefully placed her in the centre of the pentagram, her head at the point of Spirit within inches of Alex, and her arms and legs spread to the other elements. She was clothed in loose white cotton trousers and shirt, her skin was pale, almost grey, and her lips were colourless. Avery's heart sank. She looked on the verge of death, and all other concerns fled from her mind. The only important thing now was El.

Reuben sat at the point of Water, completing the pentagram, as Briar sat at Earth. A candle burned in front of each of them, the colours corresponding to the elements.

"What now?" Alex asked, looking to Briar, but Caspian answered.

"El's mind is cursed by the Earth element, and she suffocates beneath the weight of it. She's hanging on by a thread. We need to draw it out, and destroy it. Alex, you must reach for her mind, help her surface, lead her to light and warmth. She will be confused. The rest of us will balance the elements. Briar, as an Earth witch, will be the best placed to bring Earth out of her, and I will nurture with Fire, El's own element."

"Is that your natural element?" Avery asked, realising she hadn't got a clue what Caspian's strengths were.

"No. Like you, my strength is Air, which is why I have witch-flight. No other elemental strength can master that." He looked puzzled for a moment. "Have you mastered it yet?"

"No, it evades me," she confessed.

"I can give you some pointers," he said, his dark eyes holding hers for a second before he turned back to his grimoire. "Anyway, I will fill the place of Fire. I can add my strength to El's emerging power. And then comes the hard part. The curse is like a live thing—it will try to attach itself to something else. I suggested we put it into another animal, like a rabbit. That would be the cleanest option."

"But I said no," Briar interrupted, glaring at Caspian. "I will not allow the death of another creature. And the curse *would* kill a creature that small."

"So, we must trap the curse in something else." He gestured to where a large jar of water sat at his side. "You may be wondering why I am covered in runes. They will help to draw the curse up and out into this where we can trap it. It is decidedly more difficult and not without great risk, but if we don't, El will die."

The risks they were taking suddenly sank in, and Avery turned to him, shocked. "The curse will pass *through* you? But what if you can't control it, or restrain it?"

"As soon as the curse lifts from her body, you must join your strength to mine and help me. All except Alex. Never let go of your connection to her mind. *Never*!"

Alex nodded, and then closed his eyes to compose himself.

"You didn't answer my question," Avery said, staring at Caspian.

"I will be cursed if I fail, so I do not intend to fail." He looked to his left at Briar, and then Reuben next to her. "Repeat the words of the spell after me. This will not be quick—or pretty—so be prepared."

It was now a few minutes to midday and the rain had returned, filling the flat with a muted, steady drumming that drowned out the sounds of the town. Avery stared at her candle, took deep, calming breaths, and then closed her eyes as she waited for Caspian to begin.

He started to intone the spell, line by line, which they repeated after him. He called upon each of the elements, and Avery opened her eyes to watch him. His voice was sure and steady, and as he called upon each element, their respective candles flared brighter. Avery felt Air surge to her, and she channelled it, holding it close. Caspian reached forward to hold El's left foot, and they each reached forward too, grasping the closest limb, which for Avery was El's left hand.

El's skin gave off an unearthly chill, which reinforced Caspian's belief that she was close to death. Avery's resolve strengthened. She could not lose El. *Reuben could not lose El.* Avery looked up at Alex, but his eyes were closed as he held El's head gently between his hands. An empty potion bottle sat next to him on the floor, and she realised he'd taken something to help his spirit reach El.

At Caspian's nod, she released Air through her fingers and into El's, feeling it course through them both, invigorating El's senses. She felt Fire from Caspian and Water from Reuben, and lastly the lightest touch of Earth from Briar, carefully so as not to overwhelm.

And then the battle began. Slowly, as if from the darkest depths of the ocean, a heavy swell of icy cold started to lift, wrapping its weight around all of them. For a second, Avery felt herself panic as its dense fingers started to envelop her, and dread filled her thoughts. *Nothing would work. They would all die. It was pointless, why even try?*

But Air cleansed her thoughts, and the scent of the energising spell reinforced her will. The curse was trying to undermine them, seeking their weaknesses.

Caspian was calling it to him, opening his body to it, but it struggled, resisting his call, clinging on to El like a fungus. All the elements were mingling now, and although Avery's eyes were open, watching El's immovable form, her mind battled beneath the surface of her skin.

Their battle to banish the curse lasted for a long time. They gained and then lost as the curse ebbed and flowed, its strength waxing and waning, until finally the weirdest thing happened. The Earth curse reared up like a cobra, straight out of her body, a dark surging mass of brown and toxic green, streaming out of El's pores as the other elements gained strength. Caspian called it once more and it headed into the rune on his chest. Caspian cried out like a wild animal as the rune blazed with a fiery light.

Caspian still held El's foot tightly, and Avery felt his connection. She raced through El's body, joining her power with his, and felt Reuben and Briar do the same. All of his runes blazed, and she saw the curse swirl around the blazing marks as Caspian herded it down his arm to the water at his side. He plunged his left hand into the jar, his features screwed up with tension and concentration—and pain. He roared again and drew on all of them.

He was right. The curse was like a wild animal, and it kicked and surged and battled beneath Caspian's skin, the runes barely containing it.

Part of Avery's awareness was still with El, and she felt her stir, life creeping back into her limbs. Alex was there, a faint presence, but he was concentrating only on El's mind.

Caspian's hand was fully immersed in the water and he pushed the now thrashing curse out. It clung on desperately, wriggling like a giant eel beneath Caspian's skin. With one final act of will, he cast it out of his body. The water churned like it contained a maelstrom, and Avery lifted its lid with a jet of air, and slapped it on the jar with a resounding *smack*.

Silence fell and Caspian sprawled backwards on the floor, his chest heaving, the runes glowing with a dirty red light.

Reuben and Briar deflated like balloons, falling forward over their knees. Avery could barely breathe. Her ribs ached again, her head thudded, and stars swam before her eyes. The cloying feel of the curse seemed to hang around, but El stirred like a cat after a long nap.

Alex opened his eyes and called softly, "El, can you hear me?"

For a second she said nothing, and his voice became more urgent. "I feel you, El, you're here. Open your eyes."

And then she groaned. "What the hell just happened? And why am I starving?"

Alex laughed with relief. "Welcome back."

Reuben let out a weak cry of delight and shuffled forward to hold her, pulling her into his lap, and Avery reached for Alex's hand. "Well done. Are you all right?"

"Exhausted, but okay. You?"

"Same." She looked over at Caspian and Briar. "Are you both okay?"

"I guess so," Briar said, shuddering. "That was horrible, just horrible. I feel tainted. For a long while there, I felt we were doomed to fail."

"I think that's the effect of the curse," Alex said. "It was designed to crush you, mentally and physically."

Caspian was still silent, and Avery shuffled over to him. "Caspian, speak to me. Are you okay?" The runes had smeared off his skin, but they had scarred his body; she could see red welts starting to blister. She looked at Alex and Briar anxiously. "Guys, I think something's wrong."

But then he opened his eyes and croaked, "I'm okay. Barely. Someone seal that jar before the damn thing gets out again." And then he closed his eyes tightly again.

Briar had already prepared a spell to seal the jar, and she rose wearily to her feet and cast it. The water within was murky, and reminded Avery of the binding spell Helena and the other witches had cast that sealed Caspian's ancestor, Octavia, within it. She presumed he would remember this, too. She looked at him lying on the floor, his chest rising and falling in shallow breaths. He had risked much to help them, more than she had initially realised. More than she had herself, she felt ashamed to admit. She hadn't realised the effects of the curse would be so serious until it was almost too late. *What did this do to their relationship with him?*

As if he sensed her staring, he opened his eyes. "Something on your mind, Avery?"

"Many things. You could have died then. And your runes seem to be baked in."

He held his arms up and laughed dryly. "So it seems. They will fade in time."

"I have a balm that will help," Briar said, her expression serious. "That was incredibly brave, Caspian. I'll be honest, we couldn't have done it without you. I had no idea how to break that curse."

Alex spoke from behind them, his tone suspicious. "Most unlike you, Caspian. What's going on?"

Caspian sat up slowly and looked at them one by one, considering his words. "Time has proven to me that you are not my enemy."

"You're still responsible for my brother's death, and you tried to kill me once," Reuben said, still holding El in his lap, and Caspian's head fell. "But, you've saved El, and while Gil's death can never be forgotten, this is a start. Thank you."

Caspian considered him for a moment in silence, and then nodded. "Good. Then I guess I should go."

"Not yet, you won't," Briar said. "You have injuries I need to heal."

El croaked, "Can you all stop talking and get me some food!"

Briar leapt to her feet and headed to her box of healing balms and potions. "No food for you yet, El. It's too soon. You haven't had food in your stomach for almost 48 hours. I have a healing potion for you to drink first, and then plenty of water."

"Then food?" El lifted her pale face and squinted at them.

"Soup only," Briar chided.

Avery laughed. "Good to have you back, El! Nice to see nothing much has changed." She looked at her watch. "That took ages!"

"I told you it would take time," Caspian explained. "It was a deep curse, well thought out, well executed. Our mysterious witch has impressive powers. We need to decide what to do now."

Avery smiled. He seemed to have involved himself in their fight, which was unexpected.

But let's face it. We need all the help we can get.

Alex must have shared the same thought. "She's attacked three of us, admittedly one by default. Are you sure you want to involve yourself in this?"

"With luck, she won't know about me yet. That gives us an advantage."

Alex stretched and rose to his feet. "We'd better plan our next steps."

***

El still looked pale, but Briar's potions and soup had restored some of her colour. She sat curled up next to Reuben on the sofa, her head on his lap, covered by a blanket.

The blinds were open, but the day was still dark with thick clouds and pouring rain. They had cleared the pentagram and circle, and cleansed the air of negative energies, and now they sat around drinking tea and eating biscuits.

"So," Reuben summarised, "El has been cursed, you were attacked, Alex, in your sleep, your protection spells were shattered, and Avery was battered like a ragdoll. Have I missed anything?"

Avery was affronted. "We did get the better of her, eventually."

"Only because you were there," Caspian pointed out. "Who knows what may have happened to Alex if you weren't."

"Maybe we need safety in numbers," Briar suggested. She was sitting on the floor, leaning back against the armchair, her feet curled under her. "She's seems to be singling us out for attack."

Caspian agreed. "As it gets closer to Samhain, it might get worse. Whatever she's planning must coincide with that night. She does not want you interfering."

"You should all move in with me," Reuben said decisively. "I have plenty of room."

"But what about my shop?" Avery asked.

"I'm not suggesting we don't go out. Everyone still goes to work, but at night we're vulnerable. There are too many people around in the day to attack."

Alex nodded. "You're right. It would be safest, and then we could ward your house with our combined magic."

"Can I bring my cats? I'm not leaving them behind," Avery pleaded.

Reuben smiled at her. "Of course you can."

"All right then. From when? Tonight?"

"Yes. We've saved El. If the witch knows, she could try again." He looked at the others. "Agreed?"

"Agreed," they all murmured.

"Before I go," Caspian said, "may I ask what you've found about Old Haven's site? The grove?"

Reuben shrugged. "Sure. Not much as yet, unfortunately. But, I've been doing a bit of reading around the Druids of ancient Britain. They revered trees and developed a whole system of belief and the Ogham alphabet around them. The oak was the tree they revered the most, but the yew is considered the link to the spiritual world through our ancestors, and are the guardians to the Otherworld. It has particular significance at Samhain, when the gateways between worlds are at their thinnest. And Samhain is also the night of the Crone. That grove behind Old Haven is probably a remnant of one of many old groves revered by the Druids. And we all know that because of the pagan beliefs about the yew, churches were built next to them. Old Haven is no different. The groves are power centres if used in the right way, and this witch is clearly manipulating it."

"To open a gateway to the dead?" Briar asked.

"Or Faerie," Reuben said, looking amused. "It sounds ridiculous, but…"

"When me and Alex were there yesterday morning," Avery said, "I could feel the wild magic there. It felt different, ancient, as if anything could happen."

Alex added, "We spirit walked last night. There was a strange light within the yew tree's hollow trunk, as if a portal or a doorway was already starting to build."

Caspian nodded. "Any sign of the witch?"

"None. She has disguised herself well."

Caspian rose to his feet. "If you find anything else, let me know, and I'll do the same. The repercussions of opening this portal could be big. I mean, is she planning on closing it again, or is it to remain open forever, allowing passage back and forth? That could be disastrous. Such a portal between the worlds of Fey and man hasn't existed for years—if that's what it is." He frowned. "Are you all planning to attend the Samhain celebrations for the Witches Council?"

"I said we would," Avery said. "But this could change everything."

"Genevieve would not be happy if you failed to attend again."

"She'd also be furious if we allowed a doorway to open to another world. Maybe we could come for a short time and try to do both," Avery suggested.

Caspian laughed as he headed out the door. “Good luck with that!”

14

Avery was exhausted. She needed a good sleep, but she still had a few hours' worth of work to finish first. And then she'd have to let Hunter and the other Shifters know about the Devices' visit.

She sighed as she entered Happenstance Books. It was a hive of activity; Sally and Dan were both busy at the till, serving a line of customers.

Avery busied herself helping out the many kids with their parents who were looking for spooky reads. The children's section, like the rest of the shop, was fully decorated for Halloween, and Dan had prepared the reading area for the storytelling that would start the next night, which marked one week until Halloween. Late night Thursday shopping would continue until Christmas, a request disguised as an order by the Town Council.

Avery inwardly sighed, as part of her wished it were already over. This time of the year was so busy, but she couldn't complain. Business meant money. If only she didn't have a rogue witch, the Devices, and Shifters to deal with. As soon as Sally and Dan were free from customers, she updated them on El and everything else.

They looked horrified. "I didn't know about El!" Dan said, perched on the stool behind the counter. "Why didn't you say something?"

"Sorry, the last couple of days have been so busy, I guess I didn't want to worry you. But look, you both need to be vigilant. Anything strange happens, let me know. I'm increasing my protection on the shop, and I'll be sleeping at Reuben's until this is over—all of us will be there. And I'll take the cats."

Sally frowned, and pointed at her chin. "Is that bruise from last night?"

Avery nodded, feeling gently to see if it had swollen. "Unfortunately. This woman frightens me. She has no boundaries."

"And the Devices? That pair were insufferable," Sally complained.

"They've hopefully gone by now, but it's not over. Far from it. But that battle is for another time." She mulled on the fact that once they got through Samhain, there was a whole other problem to deal with in Cumbria, and she had no idea how that would go. "I just wish we weren't staying open so late on Thursday. I don't like the idea of you leaving here at that time of night."

"It's not me I'm worried about," Sally said. "And between all you witches, there are lots of staff to target. She can't be everywhere at once. Besides, it sounds like she's too busy at Old Haven."

Avery nodded, slightly comforted by Sally's logic. "True. Come on. Let's lock up. Tomorrow's going to be a long day, so I think we need a good night's rest."

"Pub for me," Dan said with a grin. "I'll try not to overdo it. Coming for a quick one?"

Sally shook her head. "I better get back for the kids. And I'll bake a cake for us to keep us going tomorrow," she added with a smile.

"Yes!" Dan said, punching the air. "I love your baking, Sally."

She looked at him with a warning in her eye. "And I'll be bringing in cupcakes for the kids. They are not for you! Not one!"

"Spoilsport," Dan grumbled as he shrugged his jacket on.

"And I'm going to pack and reinforce my protection spells on the shop," Avery said.

"Okay," Dan called with a spring in his step as he headed towards the door. "Don't forget, it's dress-up day tomorrow. Halloween week is here! Your costume is in the back."

"Bollocks!" Avery said with feeling.

***

Avery locked up the shop, picked up the box containing her costume from the back room, turned the lights off, and wandered up to her flat.

The cats greeted her by rubbing her legs and yowling for food. She tickled their ears and fed them, locked the cat flap that led to the garden so they couldn't make a bolt for freedom, and then pulled their carry cages out of the cupboard. Then she headed up to her bedroom to pack. In the end she decided to take only a few clothing items for the night and evening, since she could change for work when she arrived back in the morning. She grimaced at the box. *Damn it. She had to dress up.*

She held up the costume to the light. It was a long dress with a bodice, the skirt made of panels of black and green, and there was a thick belt with a silver buckle to wrap around her waist. A full-length, dark green cloak and black witch's hat finished it off, along with lace-up calf-height boots that languished in the box. She had to giggle. It was her own fault; she shouldn't have let Sally go and choose it for her.

Leaving the costume on her bed, she checked her shelves for useful books to pack with her grimoires, and also gathered her own spell casting equipment—her Athame, chalice, and silver bowl. She felt naked without them close by. A prickle at her neck alerted her to Helena's arrival, her ghostly ancestor, and she turned slowly, always unnerved at her appearance.

Helena stood stock-still in the middle of the room, watching Avery. As always, she wore a long black dress, over which was draped a long cloak, and her dark hair fell across her shoulders and down her back. A faint whiff of violets wafted across the room, and her pretty face creased into a frown.

Avery nodded to her, noticing that she was more corporeal than she had appeared for months. *Was this the effect of Samhain?* "You look worried, Helena. Don't be. I'll be back. A rogue witch is making life difficult."

In the blink of an eye, Helena reappeared inches from Avery, and Avery stepped back, startled. "Bloody Hell, Helena, what are you doing?"

Helena leaned forward and lifted her hand, as if to brush Avery's face. Avery's heart was thudding in her chest. Helena hadn't been this close to her in a long time, and it reminded her of when she'd possessed her body and her mind. *What if she wanted to do that now? What if she was stronger now, and could do it without being invited?* She'd wanted to kill her then, and it was for that reason that Avery had warded her bedroom against her. But, she reminded herself, Helena had helped her find the spell to unveil the Mermaids during the summer. *I have nothing to fear.*

Helena opened her mouth and started to speak, but Avery couldn't hear anything. "I can't hear you, I'm sorry."

Helena gestured again towards Avery's bruise and frowned. Avery never ceased to be astonished by Helena's awareness, and it was definitely stronger than usual. "I don't know who she is! She's trying to open a portal at Old Haven Church. We don't know why or for what purpose. But she's strong. I'm not safe here at night."

Helena stepped back and moved towards the town map that Avery still had pinned to her wall, the map that marked the old pentagram over the town based on the houses where all of the witches' ancestors lived. She pointed to Old Haven Church on the map.

"Yes, that's the place," Avery said.

Helena's expression changed to one of alarm, and then she pointed to Avery's bags with a questioning glance.

"I'm going to Greenlane Manor," she said, pointing it out on the map. "The Jacksons' place."

Helena nodded and then disappeared.

Avery looked around the room, perplexed. "Helena?"

Weird. Maybe she'd gone to Old Haven? Avery shook her head. There was no point waiting. Sometimes she didn't see Helena for weeks; she always wondered where she went. To the spirit realm, or other places in White Haven?

Regardless, it was time to go to Reuben's.

***

Alex had decided to take his own car to Greenlane Manor as he was working until last orders, so Avery went on her own, finding only Briar's car waiting in the driveway.

The house was dark, other than lights by the front door and a couple of lights on the first floor. She knocked at the door, and within seconds Reuben flung it open, and the sound of drum and bass thudded after him. He grinned at her. "Come in. I'm cooking, so I hope you're hungry." He reached forward, took her bag, and led the way to the kitchen, and she followed with her cats. "I'll show you your room in a minute. I just need to check the food."

"Honestly, you didn't need to cook, Reuben," she said, quickening her pace to keep up with him. "I presumed we'd order in." She followed him down the long hall, lined with antiques, into the kitchen at the back of the house, which was a vision of high tech modernity. There seemed to be an acre of work surfaces and gleaming stainless steel appliances, and the smell of something spicy tickled her nose. And it was a mess. Bowls, spices, and chopping boards were strewn with the remnants of food. "Wow! You've really taken up the whole kitchen, Reu!"

"I know." He didn't sound the least bit regretful. "I'm a creative cook. But trust me, it will taste great!"

"I believe you," she said, watching him as he turned down the sound system, artfully built into the wall, and then stirred a large pot, turning the heat down. He dipped a spoon in and tasted it. "Perfect. You like curry spicy, right?"

"Of course. What is it?"

"Lamb *Maas*. My specialty. El loves it. This is her treat," he said with a wink. Underneath his forced cheer, Avery could see the worry on his face, and she squeezed his arm.

"Is she okay? Any after-effects of the curse?"

He frowned and ruffled his dark blond hair. "She's sleeping at the moment, but she seemed a bit flat actually, once the relief of being awake had worn off. I think the curse has left her feeling depressed."

"It doesn't surprise me. It was pretty toxic. You must have felt it."

"Yeah, true. I did. I guess I just wanted her to bounce back to normal."

"I'm sure she will, she's resilient, but she was out for almost two days. Any longer and we'd have had to take her to hospital for a drip. How the hell would we have explained that?" Avery rubbed her face. "It was way more serious than I thought. I'm sorry I didn't help you find a solution. I just thought it was something easy that Briar could break."

Reuben shrugged. "You were side-tracked with other things."

"Not an excuse. El's my friend. Nothing's more important than her."

"Avery, you did what you could, and helped when you were needed most. And you're right—she'll be fine. It will just take time." Her cats meowed pitifully, and Reuben looked down at them and laughed. "I think your cats are going stir crazy. Let me show you your room."

He lifted her bag once more and took her up a small set of stairs, almost hidden in the corner of the kitchen, which led onto the first floor landing. He guided her down a series of passageways until he reached a door. He flung it open and announced, "Your room, madam. With Alex, of course—unless you'd rather have your own?"

"No, you twit, of course not." She gasped as she looked at the room properly. "Holy cow, Reuben. This is amazing!"

"I know. This is all Alicia's doing," he said, referring to his brother, Gil's dead wife. "She may have been a devious, two-faced, demon-summoning bitch, but she did have great design skills."

Avery's eyes were wide as she entered the room and admired the highly polished wooden floor covered in expensive Persian rugs, rich colours, gorgeous antique furniture, and fine linen. "Who normally sleeps here?"

"No one. I just make sure Deb, the housekeeper, keeps it ready."

Avery marvelled at the awesome things that money could buy, and pulled the curtains back to peek at the view. The room overlooked the back garden that was partially illuminated with accent lights pointing up into the trees, but it was otherwise dark, a light grey colour marking the sea at the end of the garden.

She turned to him. "Thanks, Reuben. This is fantastic. You know I may never move out now."

"And that would be fine. You have an en suite, too," he said, pointing to a door on the right. "I'll go back to the kitchen, come down when you're ready. I thought we'd eat somewhere between seven and eight," he said vaguely.

"What about the protection spell for the house?"

"We'll do that later." Halfway out of the door, he hesitated. "By the way, Briar's about three doors down the hall, that way," he said pointing to the left. "Laters."

Once she was alone, Avery freed the cats, who scampered off to explore, stretching out as if they had been imprisoned for hours. Then she looked around the room again, unpacked her few belongings, gasped at the beauty of the bathroom, poked around in drawers and cupboards, and then threw herself on the bed and grinned. She loved her flat, but this was amazing. And she'd be sharing it with Alex. As she lay there, propped up on the full pillows, she realised how busy her head was with worries about Shifters, the Devices, strange portals, and Druids' trees. Maybe she'd rest her eyes, just for a short while.

The next thing she knew, there was a light tapping at her door, and Briar called out, "Avery, are you all right?"

Avery peeled an eye open and groaned. "Yes, come in!"

Briar popped her head around the door. "Were you asleep?"

"I didn't mean to be. It sort of snuck up on me." She sat up, blinking the sleep away. "I didn't know I was so tired."

"Not surprising, considering you were attacked last night." Briar headed over carrying two glasses of wine, one white and one red. She handed the glass of red to Avery. "Reuben sent me up with this."

"Wow. He's a great host." She took an appreciative sip. "Perfect. And how are you?"

Briar sat on the end of the bed, legs crossed, sipping her wine. "Okay, but like you, I need a good sleep. Breaking that curse took it out of me. It was slippery." She shuddered. "Yuck. How are your bruises?"

"It's my ribs, really," Avery said, feeling her left side. "I crashed onto Alex's coffee table, and it completely winded me. Now it just aches."

Briar considered her silently. "You were lucky. Things could have been much worse. Come on, let's go and eat, and then we can protect this place—properly. I want a good night's sleep without fear of attack."

Reuben was waiting in the snug next to the kitchen, sitting next to El. It was a small, cosy living area, much less formal than the large lounge at the front of the house. It was filled with an overstuffed corner sofa, squashy armchairs, and a huge TV screen was fixed on the wall. An ornate wood burner was placed in the corner, and a crackling blaze heated the room.

"Hey, El! You're up," Briar said, sitting next to her. "How are you?"

El still looked pale. "I've been better, but I'll survive."

"Good to see you up and about," Avery echoed. "At least you have Reuben to look after you."

El laughed weakly. "He's doing a great job. I can't wait to eat some proper food."

Reuben interrupted, pointing at the screen. "Guess who's on the TV?"

Newton's face was there in close up, talking to the interviewer, and a view of Old Haven Church was in the background.

"Oh no," Avery said, "has something else happened?"

"As predicted, quite a few ghost-hunters have turned up, trying to get access to the grounds, and the police have had to intervene. And look who's there now."

The interview was from earlier in the day. Dark grey skies loomed over the churchyard, and Newton was wearing a heavy coat with the collar turned up. Reuben turned the volume up, and they heard Newton explain how the Church had hired a private firm to protect the grounds. The camera panned back to show the alarmingly tall Gabreel staring intently at the interviewer as she asked, "Do you think this is overkill on the part of the Church to cordon off the grounds of a place of worship?"

Gabreel frowned. "My job is to protect the public from harm, and as there seems to be a hoaxer at this site who has no qualms about injuring innocent people, I think it's the best thing the Church could do right now."

"And how do you plan to protect this area?"

"I have half a dozen staff who will take turns monitoring the grounds, day and night."

"Is that all? This is quite a large site."

"I have a very effective team," he said, with a look that almost dared her to disagree.

"But what will you do?" she pressed, clearly spoiling for an argument.

"Patrol the grounds."

At his tone of finality, she turned back to Newton. "And do the police approve of this plan of action?"

"Absolutely," he said. "The police are not a private security force. Obviously, we support this decision, and are currently working to identify the hoaxer. Several people were injured yesterday as a result of this hoax, and they will be prosecuted when found. The security firm allows us the time to follow up leads."

The camera panned around now to frame the interviewer, who must be the perky blonde that Newton had referred to the day before. "So, for now, the Church grounds are closed, and we advise all ghost-hunters to stay away from the area for their own safety. Sarah Rutherford, Cornwall News."

Reuben muted the TV again. "Do you think we should check the place out again?"

"Now?" Avery asked, horrified.

"No, tomorrow," he said, looking at her like she'd gone mad. "Gabe's up there doing his thing. I'm sure everything will be okay. And besides, the food is ready."

They spent the rest of the evening eating, drinking, and relaxing, and by the time Alex arrived, Avery was already half dozing on the sofa, lulled by the warmth and good company. He joined them on the sofa after grabbing a beer.

"Everybody's talking about Old Haven Church," Alex informed the group.

"Everyone?" Avery asked, doubtful.

"*Everyone*! 'Who's responsible?' 'Is it serious?' 'How badly was the vicar hurt?' 'Is there a demon gateway in the Church grounds?' 'Is Halloween magic making spirits rise from the dead?' 'How bad will it get by the time Halloween arrives?'"

He listed everything off and rolled his eyes. "Everyone has an opinion, and everyone wants this to be the worst thing possible. Most people are really excited, and quite a few are planning a midnight visit."

Reuben laughed. "I'm tempted to go myself, just to see how Gabe handles it. Is Zee going?"

"Yep," Alex answered in between sips of beer. "Not that he told the punters that. It will be a nice surprise for them to see him at his other job."

El yawned and asked, "So, what now?"

Reuben smiled. "Now we ward the house with a kick-ass protection spell, and then we sleep."

15

Avery was woken by the insistent ringing of her phone as it vibrated its way across the bedside table.

She grabbed it and answered before she even registered who was calling. "Yes?" she groaned.

A hysterical female voice answered. "Avery! Alice has taken Hunter and Holly! We need help!"

Avery's brain kicked in and she shot up, aware of Alex waking next to her. Piper. She put the phone on speaker and flicked a lamp on. "What? Are you kidding?"

"No! They barged their way into the house, attacked Josh and me so we couldn't fight, and have taken Hunter and Holly! I thought you said we were protected!" Anger entered Piper's voice as she accused Avery of lying.

"You were! No, you are. I told them that." She was halfway out of bed now. "Where have they taken them?"

"Cumbria, of course! To fight Cooper."

"We'll follow them," Avery said decisively.

"You'll come now?"

Alex intervened, a restraining hand on Avery's arm. "No. There's no point. We are not going to engage them on the road. It's too dangerous for everyone. When will the challenge take place?"

"As soon as they can arrange it, probably midnight tomorrow. Maybe the day after. We have to go now!"

Avery's mind was whirring with possibilities as she looked at Alex's resigned face. "No, Piper, Alex is right. We can achieve nothing right now. But we will go with you, tomorrow morning. We'll all travel together. Now, promise me that you'll wait."

Piper was silent for a moment. "What if they hurt them?"

"Be logical," Alex said, his eyes heavy with sleep. "Hunter needs to fight, and Holly is collateral. We follow tomorrow. Agreed?"

Her voice was quiet. "Yes, okay. You won't change your mind?"

"Absolutely not," Avery said firmly. "I have a score to settle with them. They have violated your Sanctuary. See you tomorrow morning. We'll be at yours at eight."

She rang off and looked at Alex. "That bitch!"

"Caspian warned you about them."

"These are their rules, not mine!"

"Maybe they didn't think you meant it."

"Did I sound like I meant it?"

"Yes. But they're old school and used to getting their own way. Are you sure you want to follow them up there? This will get ugly."

"Yes!" Avery said, incensed. "Don't you?"

He held his hands up in surrender. "Of course! Now come here." He spelled the lights out and lay down, pulling her close. "Try to sleep. We've got a long day tomorrow."

***

The morning had started badly. Alex and Avery had met as agreed at the Shifters' house, only to find that their Volvo had been sabotaged and wouldn't start, and neither Alex nor

Avery could spell it to start again. They ended up going back to Reuben's in Avery's van and borrowing Gil's BMW that was still in the garage. Driving the seven-hour journey to Cumbria wasn't possible with either Piper or Josh unsecured in the back of Avery's van. By the time they left it was closer to nine, and the rush hour traffic was still in full swing. Alex was taking the first stint at the wheel, as he was far more used to the Cornish roads than Josh or Piper.

The one good thing about having to head up to Cumbria, Avery mused as Alex navigated onto the A roads that led to the motorway and the north, was that she could put off having to dress up as a witch in her own shop. When she phoned Sally to tell her she had to take a couple of days off, she accused her of doing it deliberately.

"I did not! This is an emergency," she stressed. "I'm sorry, I really am. And I'll get the others to keep an eye on you. Call either Briar or Reuben if you're worried about anything. Or Newton." She knew he'd help if he could. "Anything suspicious, don't hesitate."

"All right," Sally sighed. "But I was looking forward to today."

"I was looking forward to your cake, and to seeing you two dressed up. But I'll be back, and I'll wear that stupid costume then."

"Stay safe, Avery. I don't like the Devices, and I don't trust them. Be careful."

"I will," she promised.

The other witches hadn't been happy when she saw them at breakfast, either. "We should all go," Reuben said recklessly. Now that El was better, his usual bounce had returned, and Avery could tell he was itching for action.

Alex just looked at him with a measured stare. "El is still recovering from her curse, and we still have a rogue witch down here. You three have to stay and look after White Haven. We'll be okay."

"Take my short sword," El had insisted, referring to the sword she had fashioned that enhanced elemental magic. "You can collect it from my shop. You both wield it well, and it may help you."

That sword was now in the boot of the car, and Avery could feel its magic from where she sat in the back next to Piper, who chewed her lip and fidgeted as she gazed out of the window.

"Tell me about the pack," Avery said, as much to distract her as to learn more about what they were facing. "How many are in it?"

"About ten families, all spread across the small towns and villages in the Lake District. That makes about 30 or 40 Shifters," she estimated.

"Including children?" Alex asked, listening as he drove.

Josh shook his head. "No. They are not full pack members until they hit 16."

"And do regular people have relationships with Shifters?" Avery asked.

"Sure," Piper said, "or else there would be a lot of incest! Consequently, not all children are Shifters. You can usually tell by the early teens. When hormones kick in, that's when shifting starts. Some kids miss a lot of school until they start to control their changes. You really don't want to shift in class!"

"So, I guess, you live under the radar, like we do?"

Josh looked over his shoulder. "Yep. Just as we told you. We have a regular business, but the pack always comes first. You swear fealty to it at 16."

"Does the community know, or even suspect, that Shifters live among them?"

"Maybe, but no one says anything. We're spread across the countryside. It's big, remote, and we take care not to draw attention to ourselves."

Alex twisted in his seat slightly, still watching the road. "So, this challenge. What is it, where does it happen?"

"Castlerigg Stone Circle. Anyone can challenge the leader—the Alpha—but most don't unless something really bad is happening. The Alpha is strong, and brings stability."

Avery frowned. "So how long has Cooper been the Alpha?"

"Just under a year. He succeeded his father."

"Is that normal?"

Josh glanced at Piper nervously. "Not really. Normally, the strongest succeeds. When an old leader grows too weak, others challenge him. But there hasn't been a real challenge for hundreds of years. It was a line of succession."

"Why?" Avery asked, sensing something suspicious.

Piper answered, her tone dry. "The Dacres are a very rich family. They have power and influence and like to maintain leadership. They fight dirty and have the Devices on their side, and to be honest, many other members, too. They take care of us if we take care of them. Unfortunately, laying claim to Holly was one step too far. To take them on is huge. Hunter didn't care about that."

Avery was struggling to understand. "So, Holly marrying Cooper is politically motivated. But why her? If they're so rich, what makes her special?"

"Because we are one of the oldest families, and have a strong line of Shifters. Alphas have come from our family in the past. It's believed that we will create other strong Shifters. Plus, when two Shifters mate, their children are *always* Shifters, too. Cooper wants Shifter kids. He has no brothers or sisters. He needs an heir if his family is to continue to be the Alpha."

"You said other women would like that chance, so why not choose them?"

"Because there aren't many Shifter women, that's why," Josh said. "Shifters are more likely to be male."

Piper smiled softly. "We're rare, and therefore precious."

Avery exhaled heavily, "Wow. That's mad. What a weird life."

"Any weirder than yours?" Piper asked, narrowing her eyes.

"Yes! I don't get married off to some witch just because I'm a female with a strong lineage, for breeding purposes!"

"And," Alex added, "witches are pretty much an even split of male and female, despite the popular image being that witches are women."

Avery thought for a moment. "Are there other Shifter communities across the country?"

"Sure," Josh answered. "Many farther north than us, especially in Scotland. There is some movement between packs, but it's not common. Newcomers bring challenges."

"And new packs?"

"Happen rarely," he said. "Unless you can persuade some members to leave together. They have to be really unhappy to do that. It means moving to a completely new area."

"So Hunter has to win, or what would happen?"

"Everything we said," Piper explained. "Holly will marry Cooper, and essentially Hunter has to swear fealty to him."

"But I don't think he will," Josh added, worried. "He'd rather die first."

"And Cooper would be only too pleased to see that happen," Piper said, and then turned and looked out of the window.

"And Holly?" Avery asked. "She wouldn't refuse Cooper?"

"Like we said. He's powerful. He influences businesses and the locals. One word from him and our business could fold. We'd become virtual outsiders in our own community, and our income would be gone. We'd have to leave and start again. Our whole lives are there—friends, work, our home. Holly knows what the consequences would be."

"So she'd essentially sacrifice herself for all of you," Avery said, not sure whether to admire Holly's decision or not.

"Yep," Josh said, looking uncomfortable.

Alex sounded incredulous as he put in, "You know that life elsewhere would be fine. You'd start again. So what?"

Josh looked at him sharply. "Would you?"

"If it meant saving Avery, or anyone else I loved from that, of course I would."

Avery blinked in shock. *Loved? Was that meant for her? Did he love her?* They'd never had that conversation. *Did she love him?* She looked at him for a moment, meeting his eyes in the rear-view mirror. *Yes, of course she did.*

She dragged her gaze away and turned back to Josh. "Would you challenge?"

"I'm tempted, but I know my limits. I'm not as strong as Hunter or Cooper."

Alex glanced at him. "You must have good friends—other Shifters who would support you."

Josh nodded. "Yes, we do. I phoned them early this morning. We have a couple of families who are really sympathetic to us, and are willing to help us discretely, but no one who would put their life on the line. I've asked them to tell us if they hear anything about a meet. They agree with me. It will happen tonight, but there's no word yet."

"We need to meet them, before the challenge. There must be a way of trying to get them to help you," Alex said, insistent.

Josh rounded on him, annoyed. "How? We can't guarantee we'll win. I keep telling you, and you're not listening. We don't have that kind of support or leverage! *We are completely screwed!*" Josh's eyes had taken on a frightening yellow ring that looked like fire around his pupils, and they could hear a small snarl in the back of his throat. Piper shot upright, out of her relaxed slump on the backseat, and Avery felt a tingle in her palms as she summoned her magic.

"Calm the fuck down, Josh. It's just a question—I'm trying to help!" Alex yelled back.

Piper reached forward a hand and laid it on Josh's arm. "Josh, please."

He took a deep breath and looked away, out of the window, and Avery felt the tension subside.

"Tell me about the Devices," Avery said, hoping to find other avenues to help. "Everything. What are their motivations, weaknesses, roles in the community?"

Piper spoke up first. "Like the Dacres, they're rich. Big house, good community standing, own many local businesses."

Alex snorted. "No wonder they reached out to Caspian. Their families sound similar."

"Why do they care if Cooper loses?" Avery asked.

"They know that other pack members would rather keep our lives more independent, away from the influence of the Devices. They would lose their power over us."

"Does that matter?" Avery asked, incredulous.

"It does to them."

"And does anyone know of their links to the Pendle witches of the sixteenth century?"

"Maybe a few locals make the connection, but no one would believe they're witches," Josh said, turning around. Avery was relieved to see that his eyes had returned to their normal colour. "Same as you and your ancestor, Helena."

Avery looked at him, astonished. "How do you know about that?"

"Briar told us. We were asking about all of you and your history. She explained the mysterious cloud of power above White Haven. That's what drew us to you."

Avery thought for a moment, watching the countryside streak by. They were on the A30, passing through the rugged beauty of Bodmin Moor, looking more brooding than usual under the grey overcast conditions.

She exchanged a worried glance with Alex in the rear-view mirror, and she knew exactly what he was thinking. *How would the Devices interfere, and what could they do to stop them?*

"How many Devices are there?" she asked abruptly.

"Alice, her daughter, Rose, and Rose's two children, who are both younger than me, and Jeremy and his children. I don't think Alice's grandchildren will interfere, just Jeremy and Rose."

Avery realised she had no idea how they'd captured the others the night before, so she asked now, feeling it would help her understand how they fought.

"They knocked on the door like civilised people," Piper said. "It was nine at night. Hunter answered, and they said they wanted to talk, that they understood we were under your Sanctuary, but they needed to discuss terms. He was suspicious, but let them in."

Josh continued. "We were in the lounge, and we came to the door to see what was happening. As they entered, Jeremy did something—released *something* from his hands."

"Yeah, it was like this little cloud of blackness," Piper said, struggling to articulate what it was. "But it rushed across to us like a mini whirlwind, and that's all I remember."

Avery frowned. "You passed out?"

"Yep," Josh said. "When we woke up, it was three in the morning, and we were freezing our asses off on the floor. Hunter and Holly had gone."

"You're sure they'd have headed back home?" Alex asked.

"Yes. They'll have either gone to Cooper's house or their own place."

"So, if they've travelled all night, they'll be there by now," Avery said. It was about seven hours to Cumbria, give or take some time for stops and traffic.

"They won't want to waste any more time," Alex said. "They know you'll follow. Can this fight happen in the day?"

"No." Josh shook his head. "All challenges take place at midnight, in the open, at Castlerigg Stone Circle."

"Are you sure?" Avery asked.

"Always," Piper agreed. "It's sacred ground, our spiritual home."

Piper was looking tired, and the shadows under eyes were darkening. Her normal retreat into snark had gone, and instead she looked defeated as she leaned back against the seat and closed her eyes.

Avery fell silent, trying to come up with a plan, which she decided was virtually impossible without knowing how the night would unfold. She thought of El's sword in the back of the car, and was glad they'd brought it with them. Tonight could get very ugly.

16

Avery took over the driving from Alex just before Birmingham, negotiating the horrible M5/M6 interchange on the way to the north, and the traffic was horrendous, slowing their progress to a crawl in places. They'd finally had a call from Josh's friend mid-morning, who confirmed the challenge was to take place that night, but there was no other news. While Avery drove, Josh and Piper slept in the back of the car; they would all need their strength for the night ahead.

Josh drove the last two hours of the journey, and they finally exited the M6 and followed the A590 and then the A591 to Ambleside. Josh was navigating them to the Devices house, where they hoped to see Hunter and Holly.

"I doubt they'll be there," Alex said. "They'll have hidden them somewhere. They must know we'd look for them. Or at least you would." He grinned suddenly. "They must have hoped that damaging your Volvo would have stopped you. Idiots."

"Agreed," Josh said. "They will hide them before taking them to Castlerigg. They won't risk the challenge being stopped now. Once there, the pack will ensure it happens."

"Will they?" Avery asked. "Why?"

"A challenge leaves uncertainty. No one wants that."

Avery shook her head, perplexed. If some of them wanted change, surely they should support Hunter. Many were obviously scared of Cooper and his supporters. Avery already hated him. He sounded like a bully.

The Devices lived on the outskirts of Ambleside, a popular tourist town in the centre of the Lake District at the head of Lake Windermere, surrounded by rugged hills and tumbling streams. As they passed the lake, it was dusk and they again hit traffic. Avery checked her watch, worried. It was nearly six. Traffic, road works, and a couple of stops had delayed them all along the way, and who knows what might delay them further here.

They wound down narrow lanes, but because of the encroaching night, Avery caught only a glimpse of the wild beauty of the landscape, though she couldn't help but get lost in the view. It was wilder than Cornwall and the perfect place for wolves to roam free, unseen and unheard. By the time they got to Ambleside, their surroundings were lost in darkness, but the town looked quaint with its winding streets of grey stone buildings, and the bright yellow of street lights illuminating shops and pubs. Any other time Avery would have loved to wonder the streets and explore, but there was no time for that now.

The Devices' house was a large stone building, set at the bottom of a hill. It had a long drive, which offered only a peek at the house, and for added privacy, it was surrounded by a large, walled garden offering glimpses of mature trees and shrubs.

Josh parked at the side of the road and turned to the others. "At least the darkness will offer us some cover. Once we slip into the grounds, me and Piper will change and head to the house as wolves. Maybe you should wait here until we give you the all clear?"

Alex looked incredulous. "No way. They're witches and are obviously quite happy to use their power against you. We're coming."

"Agreed," Avery said, reaching for the door handle. "We should check for magical traps and protection spells."

They exited the car and Avery shivered as she pulled her jacket on, thankful she'd borrowed El's heavy parka. It was cold, almost icy, with the wind bringing a chill from the mountains. She reached into the boot for El's sword. "Do you want it, Alex?"

He shook his head. "No, you use it better than me. But stay close."

The lane they were on was deserted, and Alex and Avery stood at the bottom of the drive, feeling for magic. "Nothing yet," Alex declared.

"Same." Avery looked at Josh and Piper, who were clearly itching to go. "Be careful!"

They nodded and slipped into the shrubs at the edge of the drive, shedding their clothes quickly and then shifting effortlessly into two beautiful wolves, Piper slightly smaller than Josh. In seconds, they had gone.

Alex followed their path into the shrubs, and Avery followed him. They edged their way up to the house, warily feeling their way, and slapping small branches aside. The wolves had disappeared.

"I don't like this," Alex whispered. "It's too quiet."

"The grounds are big. They'll have more protection closer to the house," Avery reasoned.

Her breath escaped in white clouds, and she wished she'd brought her gloves with her. Avery whispered a small warming spell, and felt her coat start to heat. She'd learnt that one from Eve, the witch from St Ives. *Thank the gods for weather witches.*

The attack was unexpected—the Devices had hidden it well.

As they came in sight of the house, a wall of darkness shot up from the ground, enveloping them completely. It felt sticky and cloying, and Avery quickly became disorientated. She dropped to her knees, pleased to feel the damp ground beneath her. She flared a light into her hands, but the blackness swallowed it. She couldn't feel Alex at all.

Shit!

She cried out, "Alex!"

Silence.

She tried again, this time grounding herself completely with the earth. She pulled its power into her hands and cast a lightning bolt ahead of her, hoping Alex was still to her left. The smell of magic and ozone was overpowering, but the oily darkness receded slightly.

She inwardly smacked herself. The air was still and heavy; what she needed was wind. She created a mini tornado, drawing the oily darkness into its centre. Within a few seconds it lifted and she sent the tornado away to the far side of the garden.

She turned to where Alex had stood only moments earlier, but he was gone.

For a second Avery panicked, and then she took a deep breath. *Smoke and mirrors. He was here somewhere.*

A wolf's howl broke the silence over to her right. After one final look for Alex, she turned, heading towards the sound.

A second howl followed the first, and her skin prickled. It was tempting to run, but that would be too dangerous. She broke free of the shrubs and the house appeared in front of her, on the other side of a lawn and large flowerbeds.

No one was in sight. She headed to the right, towards the sounds of the howl. There was another, much closer, and the large shape of a wolf came into view, its lips drawn back to reveal large teeth, a snarl building in the back of its throat.

It was Josh, she was sure. He had dark brown fur with a white stripe down his nose, she'd noticed when he'd changed, and he was bigger than Piper.

But something was wrong.

He advanced towards her as if he didn't know her, and Avery fell back into the shadows, watching him. She raised her hands just as he sprang at her, covering meters of ground in mere seconds. She sent a blast of energy at him and it struck him in the chest.

He rolled away, stunned, but quickly regained his footing. He howled again and Avery's blood curdled. She'd always wondered where that expression came from, and now she knew. A wolf's howl was terrifying.

He launched across the small space between them again and she struck, too, desperately not wanting to hurt him, but aware that one wrong move on her part would see her throat ripped out.

She was too slow. His paws landed on her chest, throwing her to the floor, and she was winded, crying out in pain as her injured ribs screamed in protest. Shocked, she struck out, sending out a wave of power so strong that it lifted him into the air and threw him back against a tree.

She staggered to her feet, ready to fight again. But then he looked at her, shaking his big, shaggy head with confusion, and she saw recognition flash into his eyes.

He bowed his head, whimpered, and then shifted. The very human Josh shivered and curled into a foetal position, and Avery ran over.

"I'm so sorry. Are you okay?"

He nodded. "I just need a minute. I don't know what came over me. I didn't recognise you at all. You were just someone—an enemy."

"Some weird spell. I plunged into one, too and have lost Alex."

Just then, another howl sounded behind the house.

"Time to go," Josh said. "Stay close."

He changed again, rose to his feet, and loped off around the house, Avery jogging to keep up.

The house was in complete darkness. There was no way anyone was here. These traps were to confuse and delay them, and they were working.

A sudden pain in her head made her stumble and fall, and Josh returned to her side, nuzzling her hand. A voice filled her head. *Avery, it's Alex. Can you hear me?*

Relief flooded though her, and she answered in her mind. *Yes! Where are you?*

Somewhere in the garden. It's dark. I can't get out, but I feel the earth beneath me, and can hear the trees. It's like I've been blinded.

Have you seen Piper?

I can hear howling, but that's all.

I'm coming. Stay with me.

She rose to her feet and sent out a witch light, illuminating the trees and a path that ran behind the house. She was sure now that no one was here. They had planned this to delay them, keep them here all night if necessary, all in order to miss the challenge.

Bollocks to them. They would not win.

She sent out light after light, floating around the garden, and then decided to cast a finding spell. Alex's scent was all over her, and she was wearing his scarf. She quickly cast the spell and a small, blue light appeared out of the air; she followed it across the garden.

She hadn't gone too far when Piper appeared, snarling on the path ahead of her. *Oh no. Not again.*

But this time, Josh intervened. As Piper leapt at Avery, Josh leapt at her, and the wolves collided mid-leap. They hit the ground, a snarling, tumbling mass of teeth and fur.

As soon as she had a clear shot, Avery sent of couple of blasts of pure energy at Piper, and like Josh, it seemed to shock her out of whatever spell had confused her. She whined as recognition flooded through her and both of them turned and headed off across the garden.

Alex. Can you hear us? Avery again communicated to him in her head. She could feel his presence, and his worry.

You're muffled, he replied. *As if you're overhead.*

You must be underground, she reasoned. They probably have a cellar or a basement. Can you see anything yet?

Something is binding my magic. I can't spell anything, other than to speak to you.

A howl disturbed Avery's attention, and she ran towards the sound. Josh and Piper were pawing at the ground, raking back dirt, and Avery joined them. They were at the back of the garden, next to an old shed, and Avery could see metal gleaming beneath the dirt.

"I hear you!" Alex shouted audibly from beneath her feet.

Relief flooded though Avery and she called to the wolves, "Stand back. I'm going to try something."

Avery used elemental air to move the earth, wielding it like a shovel to push it out of the way. As she dumped it to the side, she saw a hatch in the ground, like an old air raid shelter. Magic sang from it, crackling around the edges. "Alex, I've found a hatch. It's spelled shut. Bear with me."

She could feel a combination of Earth and Fire magic. The Earth must be giving Alex that suffocating blanket feeling that was blinding him, much like El's curse had. She tried a few different spells, attempting to break through whatever was holding Alex inside, but nothing worked. She sat back, thinking for a moment. El's sword wielded Ice Fire—maybe that would do it.

"Josh, Piper. I need the sword in the back of the car. Can you get it?" Josh nodded and loped off across the garden, returning within a couple of minutes, the blade between his teeth. Avery shouted, "Alex, if you can feel anything, make for the edges and crouch down."

She held the sword, activating its magic by sending a shiver of fire along its blade, and then pressed the point to the tin panel and felt the crack of magic. She cast a banishing spell at the same time as she plunged the sword through the tin as if it were butter. As soon as it punctured the metal, a *pop* sounded and Avery was thrown backwards several feet, leaving the sword in the metal. Josh changed form and took over, dragging the sword through the metal as sparks were thrown around them. An oily black cloud seeped out of the jagged tear, and he stepped back, coughing. Avery whisked it into the shed and sealed it in. Again she used her magic to peel the metal back and she peered in and saw Alex crouched on the floor about eight feet down, arms over his head. She called out, "Need a hand?"

He looked up and grinned. "I need many things right now, but getting out of here would be good."

"If it's all right with you," Josh said, shivering, "I'm changing back to wolf form. I'm freezing my ass off."

"No problem," Avery said. By the time she'd turned back to Alex, he was already dragging himself out of the hole in the ground, and Avery extended a hand, giving a final pull.

"Are you okay?" she asked, checking him over for injuries.

He tied his hair back in a half-ponytail, and rolled his shoulders as if ready for a fight. "Fine. Just pissed off. If they're going to throw stuff like that at us, we'll be in trouble later."

"We'll be fine," she said, giving him a big hug. "We just need to get more creative. We're a great team, remember?"

"I remember," he said, stealing a quick kiss. "Now, let's get out of here. I feel like Indiana bloody Jones."

Once they were safely back in the car and headed back into Ambleside, with the heating turned up full blast, they decided on their next step.

Josh was mulling over their options. "It's pointless going to Cooper's. We may well find the same problem, and we've wasted over an hour already. But, maybe I'll call my mate, Evan. I'd like to see what he thinks of all this."

"One of the Shifters who supports you?" Avery asked.

"And he fancies Holly," Piper said, raising an eyebrow. "You may find him more willing to help than you think, Josh."

He groaned. "He fancies her. It's not bloody Romeo and Juliet."

"You have no romance in your soul," Piper chastised him.

"Neither has he," he answered.

"I like this plan," Alex said, grinning. "Where to?"

"Keswick. The centre of all things Wolf in Cumbria."

"Is it?" Avery asked, feeling she was learning something new every second.

"That's where Castlerigg is, and where Cooper lives, as well as a few other Shifter families."

"But you're right, there's no point in going to Cooper's place," Piper said, adamant.

"Why's that?" Alex asked, twisting to look at her in the backseat.

"We may find ourselves trapped at Cooper's forever. He lives in what's near enough a bloody castle. We could end up in the dungeon."

"A castle?" Avery said, incredulous.

"Yep. With security."

With that, Avery's stomach emitted a large growl. "I have a small request. Before we do anything else, let's go to the pub. I'm starving, and sick to death of sitting in a car and eating motorway service food."

"My thoughts exactly," Josh said, finding a parking space on the side of a busy road. "And then we plan our attack."

17

The Unicorn Inn was a small stone building painted white, tucked in the middle of a row of shops along a one-way street.

They headed inside to find a cosy pub with a low-beamed roof, a long wooden bar, an array of local beers, and a gin display. There were a couple of spare tables, and once they had drinks and ordered food, they headed to the table in the corner, glad of the privacy.

Now that they were inside in the warmth, their experiences in the Devices' garden seemed like a nightmare.

"The good thing is that at Castlerigg, they won't be able to plant booby trap spells," Josh said, cheering up as he sipped his pint. "The whole pack will be there."

"But they could try to stop us from getting there," Piper pointed out. "The road is remote."

"Not if we time it right," he answered.

"How long to get there from here?" Alex asked. It was already nearing eight.

"Half an hour. But we'll leave as soon as we've eaten. Which reminds me, I'll call Evan." And with that, Josh slipped out to make the call.

"What's Keswick like?" Avery asked Piper, her expression already returning to her normal scowl.

"Busy, old, and full of tourists most of the year. It's popular with walkers."

"And Shifters," Alex added.

"Yeah, those too. There are forests, moors, lakes—all wild and remote, if you leave the towns far enough behind."

"And the stone circle is close?"

Piper nodded. "Just out of town."

They paused while the waitress delivered their food, just as Josh returned looking pleased. As soon as she left, Alex asked, "Good news?"

"Very," Josh said, grinning. "Evan and another couple of mates have decided to help."

Piper looked suspicious. "Who? And how?"

"Ollie and Tommy."

Piper frowned. "Tommy is a brawler! He just wants a fight."

Josh pointed his fork at her. "Exactly. And so do Ollie and Evan. I pointed out that Evan may actually stand a chance with Holly if he can get Cooper out of the way."

"You used Holly as bait?" she asked, outraged.

"No! Not like that," he said, looking equally outraged. "Will you shut up and let me finish?"

Piper grimaced and waved him on while Alex and Avery watched, amused.

"It turns out that in the last few months, Cooper's been pressuring them and a few others to support his business, whilst threatening theirs."

"What is his business?" Alex asked.

"Real estate. Don't ask me the details, because I have no idea. Anyway, they've had enough and with this latest incident with Hunter, and they have finally decided it's time to act." He turned to Alex and Avery. "If you can control the witches."

Avery looked at Alex with a smirk and then turned back to Josh. "I can't guarantee control, but we can probably work something out. But what's your plan?"

"Hunter will fight Cooper. I need to tell him he must submit once he's got a good way into the fight—we have to get to him to let him know—and then I will challenge, as will Evan, Ollie, and Tommy. All at once. We tell him we take him on, one at a time. He can't beat all of us. Whoever beats him becomes Alpha. He will have to capitulate."

Avery felt the faintest stirring of hope within her. "Until he capitulates to what?"

"Everything. Keeping his nose out of other people's business. His claim on Holly. His bullying tactics. He only remains Alpha if he agrees to those terms."

"And if he doesn't?" Alex asked.

"We fight," Josh said, shrugging. "And he will lose."

"Bullies don't like to be cornered," Alex said softly. "And he has the Devices to render you impotent."

"Not in the open, in front of everyone. Everyone knows they support him, but have never suspected them of manipulation using magic. The Devices have, in fact, sworn to us many times that they would never subvert our will or Cooper's leadership in that way." Josh was looking excited now as his plans began to take shape. "Wolves are swift and deadly. The Devices can't watch their backs all the time. They know they have to keep us sweet. They will need to agree. And you need to bind them to it."

"We need to what?" Avery asked, almost choking on her drink.

"Bind them. You can do that, right?"

It was Alex's turn to smirk. "We know all about binding."

A sudden memory of a spell flashed into Avery's mind as Alex spoke. "We can use a word binding."

"We can?" he asked, confused.

"Trust me. It's tickling my brain. I need to check my grimoire." She was itching to leave the table right then, but she forced herself to finish her meal and listen to what else Josh had planned.

"Excellent," Josh said, carrying on regardless. "We're heading to Evan's place in Keswick. We can leave the car there and walk to the stone circle when we're ready."

Alex asked, "Do we enter the stone circle with you, or loiter undercover nearby?"

"This fight will be witnessed by pack members and Devices only," Josh said, tucking into his pie and chips. "But the circle is surrounded by stone walls, so you should be able to hide behind one of them. At the right time, we'll call on you. Sound good?"

"And that means you can monitor them in case they decide to use magic anyway," Piper added, buzzing with anticipation. "But you'll need to disguise your scent, or stay a long way back. Wolves, even in human form, have a strong sense of smell."

"No problem. We'll think of something, won't we, Avery?" Alex said, winking at her.

"Nothing a cloaking spell won't solve," she answered. Despite her worry, she was curious to see a Shifter meeting, especially in a stone circle. Then she asked something that had been on the tip of her tongue all night. "Do you fight as wolves or humans?"

Piper answered, pushing her plate away. "Humans—most of the time. By mutual agreement, the last time Cooper and Hunter both shifted at the same time. It got ugly. That's why Hunter was injured so badly."

"Which brings me to my next point," Josh added, reaching forward for his pint. "For the last couple of days, he's kept a low profile. Rumours are he was pretty badly injured himself. We didn't see it because we fled. Only the ministrations of Rose Device have helped him so quickly. That's another reason he can't fight us all. He's not fit enough."

"So why fight now?" Avery asked, incredulous.

"Appearances are everything," Josh said. "Especially to an Alpha. And he thinks he'll only have one challenger to fight. He's in for a big surprise."

***

The group followed the A591 to Castlerigg Village, and then on to Keswick without incident. It was a small market town on the northern end of Derwentwater Lake. They passed through its quiet streets, and then scoped out the area around the stone circle before going to Evan's house, so that Avery and Alex could get a feel for the place.

The night was getting colder by the minute. Castlerigg Stone Circle lay at the bottom of Skiddaw and Blencathra hills. It was situated on raised ground, and the wind rolled across it relentlessly. A crescent moon rode high above them, and the sky was filled with stars. Dew lay heavy on the ground and soon it would frost. Already patches of white sparkled in the muted light, and snow speckled the hilltops above them.

The circle itself was large, formed by 38 tall, misshapen standing stones that went back millennia—at least 5,000 years. On the way, Avery had Googled it, fascinated by its history. There was a break in the stones on the left of the circle, indicating the possibility of a ceremonial entrance, and a small rectangle of stones in the centre. Like many stone circles, it was believed to have astronomical significance, as well as burial purposes.

Piper was right. Low stone walls edged the surrounding fields, including the one the stone circle was in. They discussed their approach and the best place to stand, and then Josh turned the car around, heading back along the lanes and snaking through the outskirts of the town, before finally drawing to a halt outside a small stone cottage at the end of a row of identical cottages. It backed into a small copse—the perfect place for a Shifter to live.

Josh bounded up the path, Piper behind him, but Alex and Avery reached into the boot for their magic supplies, and then stood for a moment, looking over the street. The air was crisp, and the hoot of an owl drifted across the still night air. Nothing else stirred.

"Are you sure we can do this?" Alex asked Avery, his hand resting slightly on her arm. "I don't want a war with the Devices."

"I'm sure. I don't want one, either. If I work this properly, we come to a truce. A mutual binding that will satisfy both of us."

"I don't think I want to be bound to *them*."

"It's not that kind of binding," she said, smiling up at him. "Come on inside and I'll explain. I'm really hoping there's some kind of hot toddy waiting for me."

The front door was still partially open, and they entered a small, narrow hall. Shutting the door behind them, they headed to the light at the end of the passage, and found five people clustered around a fire burning fiercely in a huge, old-fashioned range. A mismatched series of armchairs and an old, worn sofa battled for space around it. The other half of the room featured a very old kitchen that probably hadn't been updated since the 1950s.

Josh looked up and caught their eye. "Hi, guys. Let me introduce you to the troops." He indicated the three very large men in the room. *Now this is what I thought Shifters would look like*, Avery thought.

Ollie was tall with an athletic build, short-cropped hair like Josh, and pale hazel eyes. Evan was average height, wiry and lean. And well, Tommy was just huge. He looked exactly like what Piper had called him—a brawler. He had shaggy brown hair, a full beard, large muscular arms and legs, and piercing baby blue eyes, which were most disconcerting. Those baby blues were frowning, his sleeves were rolled up, and he looked ready to take on anyone.

After quick handshakes all around, Tommy resumed his conversation in a broad northern accent. "I swear I'll rip his head off, given the chance. I will not let Holly get trapped by that bastard. I've had enough of him. He thinks he's better than the rest of us, and I can put up with some stuff, but not this!" He banged his fist on the range, and Avery jumped.

"You don't need to rip his head off! Just threaten to. He won't want to fight you, Tommy. In fact, I'm surprised he's even attempted to rope you into his crap," Josh said, trying to calm him down.

Tommy looked slightly guilty and glanced away, into the fire. "He might have something on me."

Josh looked at Ollie and Evan, and then back to Tommy. "Like what?"

"Just a bit of under the table selling of building supplies."

"Don't tell me you nicked off Cooper's site?"

Tommy scratched his ear. "It was a small error on my part. It won't happen again."

"He's threatened you with the police?"

"Might have," he said sheepishly.

Josh frowned. "So why the change of attitude?"

"I don't like that bastard having something over me. This is one time when violence is the solution."

Ollie remonstrated with him. "The *threat* of violence, Tommy. The *threat* of him losing Alpha status. That's all!"

By now Avery had eased herself into a chair and was warming her feet and hands on the fire. Alex leaned against the wall behind her, arms crossed, an amused expression on his face as he watched the exchange.

Tommy caught him looking and said, "And what will you do, pretty boy? Here to tame the witches?"

"You don't tame witches," Alex said drolly. "They're not wild animals."

"Well, that Alice needs a leash. Mad cow. Interfering in our business."

"So are we, but I gather that's okay?"

"It depends what you're going to do," Tommy said, assessing Alex with an even gaze.

Avery could feel Alex's power building. If Tommy didn't watch his mouth, he'd find his tongue bound.

Piper intervened. "Oh, shut up, you great pillock. Alex and Avery are here to help."

He looked at Piper, frowned, and then laughed. "You've always got a big attitude for a little thing."

"And you're full of shit. Shut up."

Avery laughed out loud, and that set everyone off.

"So," Josh said, after wiping his eyes, "can someone give me a bloody drink before we have to traipse up to that place in the freezing cold?"

Evan grinned and headed to a cupboard in the kitchen, bringing out whiskey and glasses. He poured and handed everyone a shot, before turning to Alex and Avery. "So, what's your plan?"

"We're here to stop Alice from using her magic to either confuse or glamour you, or to influence the fight," Avery said. "We'd like to be there in the circle right at the start so they know we're there. It will make our life easier, and yours. They won't tamper because they know that we will know."

Tommy shook his head. "No way. The pack won't allow it."

"In that case, we work behind the scenes to prevent them from interfering in the fight. But at some point, we'll have to reveal ourselves."

"Why?" Ollie asked, speaking for the first time.

Alex explained. "Anything Cooper promises you could be subverted by the Devices at some point. You could have nasty *accidents*, your businesses might fail inexplicably..." He shrugged. "Anything might happen. If Cooper agrees to your terms, you need to demand proof the terms will be abided by, and that's when Josh or Piper have to invite us in."

Ollie looked suspicious. "And how will you manage that? They have influenced things for generations—we all know it. It's an open secret."

"We offer a reciprocal binding," Avery said. "We agree never to interfere here again, and they agree not to break their word by attacking you or seek revenge on us. They have violated Sanctuary already. Hunter can demand terms, and so can we. And the Cornwall Covens will support us."

"And that will hold how?"

"By magic. Binding spells are exactly that. They can be used in all sorts of ways—to bind someone's magic, tongue, actions—but also they can be used to maintain trust. And we will bind their whole family, No loopholes."

"I don't like magic," Tommy said suddenly, glaring at them. "I don't trust it."

"So trust me," she answered.

"How will we know you're there?" Evan asked.

"We'll be cloaked, but I promise you we'll be there. We won't let you down."

Ollie sipped his drink. "Tell me about the binding. Can anyone do one?"

Alex frowned. 'What are you thinking?"

"If something goes wrong. Can we do one?"

He nodded. "A blood oath. All witches will abide by that. It's the oldest and strongest binding there is—outside of actual magic. But you must make your terms very clear."

"Good to know," Ollie said, nodding thoughtfully.

Avery stood and knocked her drink back, shook her head at the sharpness of it, and then turned to Alex. "Let's get out of here and prepare. Can we use another room, Evan?"

Evan ushered them to a small front room, muggy with central heating, and as soon as they were alone, Alex shook his head. "I don't like this. There are too many variables."

"I know, and obviously Ollie thinks the same. But what other options do we have?"

"We can get in the car and leave them to it."

"You don't mean that," Avery said, looking incredulous.

Alex sighed. "No, I guess not. But I want an advantage. I have another idea."

Avery raised an eyebrow. "Go on."

"We protect these guys with a charm, so they can't be influenced by Alice."

"That's a good idea."

Alex grinned. "And I think we offer them a strength potion."

"Really? Isn't that a bit, well, cheat-y?"

"Do we trust *them* to allow a fair fight?"

"No."

"So we really are just evening the odds," Alex pointed out.

Avery grinned, too. "Well, when you put it like that… And we need something strong for the binding."

Alex nodded. "Bindings like this work best with something sympathetic. This place backs on to a wood. What about using ivy?"

"Excellent. You get it, and I'll start preparing the rest."

18

It was close to 11:30pm and Avery stood with Alex overlooking Castlerigg, cloaked in shadows. They had left Piper and Josh in Keswick so they could make their own way to the circle with the other Shifters.

Avery looked up at Alex's strong profile that at the moment, only she could see. His hair was tied back in a half-ponytail, and his jacket collar was high around his neck. It was freezing, but she had once again whispered the warming spell that enveloped both of them. It felt like they were the only people in the world.

She thought back on what he told Josh in the car, when he said he'd do anything for her and anybody else he loved, and she desperately wanted to ask him if it was true. She half-wondered if she'd imagined it, or if she'd exaggerated what he meant, because she realised now, looking at him under a huge sky full of stars and the faint crescent of the moon, that she loved him and needed him to love her. Desperately so.

Just as she was summoning her courage to ask, a sweep of car headlights in the distance caused Alex to look away, and she followed his gaze. Two men made their way to the stone circle. They were just barely visible as black shapes against the grey of the night sky and the faint line of the stone walls. One raised his nose to the sky and turned in their direction for a second, and then turned away.

Alex stiffened next to her. "They can smell us."

"No, they can't," Avery reassured him. "We cloaked sight, smell, and sound. And we're downwind. He can smell something, but it's not us."

The men walked to the very middle of the circle and huddled together, talking. Alex pulled her arm. "Let's get closer, then."

They edged away from the stone wall and trod silently across the grass, stopping when they were a few meters away. The wind carried the gruff male voices to them, and for a moment, Avery struggled to understand what they were saying. Their accents were so strong, but as she got used to the cadence of their tones, she started to understand the conversation.

"Alice will be sure they arrive last," an older man said. "She doesn't want him to get sympathy from the others."

"And Holly?" A younger man spoke, but he was bearded and had a wool hat on so Avery couldn't see his face.

"She'll be here. She needs to understand this is the way of the pack."

The younger one laughed unpleasantly. "She should know that already. That's why she ran."

"She won't run tonight. Alice will see that Cooper wins, and that Holly promises herself to him."

"What has Alice arranged?"

"Some potion or another." The older man shrugged. "Nothing too obvious, but it will give him the edge. Hunter injured him badly the other night, though he's kept it quiet. But he has to act now. Others are restless. Hunter has been busy on the phone, seeking support, and he's getting it."

Ha! Vindicated. Avery turned to Alex with a sly smile.

More voices broke the silence, and they retreated quickly, watching as others arrived in groups of twos and threes. They all gathered in the centre of the stone circle, until eventually—over the next ten minutes, Avery estimated—there were about 30 Shifters present, and other than three or four women, including Piper, they were all men.

The clear, ringing tones of a bell sounded from beyond the stone circle, and a tall man led a group into the middle. It must be Cooper. He carried himself with arrogance and command, and everyone turned to him as he arrived. The change in the energy was interesting. Avery sensed both excitement and dread.

Behind Cooper, Hunter and Holly were escorted between Alice and Jeremy, and behind them were another woman and three men all carrying long poles. The woman bore a distinct resemblance to Alice, and Avery guessed it must be Rose, her daughter, the one who'd been helping Cooper to heal.

As soon as everyone was present, Cooper turned to Alice. "Please seal the circle."

Immediately, Alex and Avery realised what was happening. They were watching from the walls at the edge of the field again, and if she sealed it before they reached the stone circle, they would be locked out and unable to help in any way.

Alice acted quickly, drawing her Athame out, and went to the ceremonial entrance, where she started to walk around the back of the standing stones, chanting the spell to consecrate the ground.

Alex and Avery raced to the far side of the stones, stepping inside far enough to remain away from the Shifters, but also well enough inside that Alice wouldn't stumble over them. *Thank the gods Castlerigg was big.*

Alice passed them by, her expression calm with a hint of triumph, as if she had already won.

Within another minute the circle was complete, and with the sound of wind through grass, a veil fell on the outside world. Josh looked around nervously, as did Piper, clearly worrying about whether Avery or Alex had made it, but there was no way to reassure them right now.

The three men who had entered last walked around the perimeter, placing out the torches they had brought with them. Once they were all in place, Alice lit them with a clap of her hands, and they flared into flames. Everyone's features came into focus, revealing expressions of worry, confusion, or excitement. Avery's unease heightened. She felt she had stepped into some kind of primeval gladiatorial arena.

Cooper spoke, his deep voice carrying in the clear night air. "Welcome. Tonight we finish what began two weeks ago, before Hunter was dragged from our midst before the fight was complete."

A rumble of laughter came from a few members, but not many. Most just watched Cooper with stony gazes.

He continued, "The rules remain. Hunter must defeat me to become the new Alpha. I will not yield. I want to make it clear to everyone that he has to kill me to do so. I, however, will not demand death." He turned to Hunter, his eyes cold. "You only have to yield to *me* and promise fealty."

Hunter was bristling with anger and determination, and he didn't flinch as he looked at Cooper. Avery wouldn't have imagined he was recently so grievously hurt had she not seen it herself. He looked fit and eager to fight. "And if I don't yield?"

"Then it will be a fight to the death," Cooper said, smiling unpleasantly.

Josh stepped forward from where he had been hidden within the circle of his friends, Piper behind him. "I would like to speak to my brother before the fight."

Cooper looked at him, surprised, as did Alice and the other witches. "I was not sure you would return after running away," Cooper sneered.

"And miss watching my brother win?" Josh said, baiting him. "No chance. Now, I believe I can speak to Hunter."

Hunter's hands had been tied up until now; Cooper leaned forward, pulled a large knife from a sheath on his belt, and cut the ropes. "You have two minutes to talk some sense into him. And don't think you'll be able to pull the same stunt as last time."

While the rest of the pack formed a circle around what Avery presumed would be where they fought, Josh and Piper took Cooper and Holly aside.

Alex pulled Avery up on one of the smaller standing stones that formed the inner square, well away from the edge of the circle, allowing them a view of the fight. Alice and Jeremy looked around Castlerigg with narrowed eyes. They might suspect they were there, but they didn't know for sure, and there was nothing they could do now.

Within minutes, the mutter of conversation fell silent, and Hunter and Cooper stepped into the makeshift fighting ring, both wearing only jeans. Their feet and chests were bare, and the flickering light revealed that both had livid red scars. After formal bows from each, the fight began.

It was bloody and brutal, a mixture of punching, kicking, and martial arts. The pair were evenly matched. They traded blow for blow, and several times it looked as if Hunter had the upper hand, with Cooper stumbling back over uneven ground. But he always got back up again.

By now both were bloody, lips were split, and one of Hunter's long scars, barely healed, had already opened up and was bleeding again. The smell of blood was thick in the air, and Avery noticed that several Shifters had taken on distinctly wolfish features, their eyes ringed with yellow fire.

Avery grimaced as Hunter sustained his biggest beating yet, and as he fell to the floor, Cooper kicked him in the ribs before he could roll away.

"Submit?" Cooper asked with an evil grin.

"Never," Hunter grunted before launching at Cooper again.

Avery whispered to Alex, "Why doesn't he submit now?"

"Because he's trying to wear Cooper out. If he takes him right to the edge before submitting, he'll struggle more in the second challenge."

Avery nodded and looked away. This was horrible and brutal.

The fight went on and Avery could hear grunts, thumps, and brutal cries, and then a gasp from the Shifters as a crack resounded.

Avery reluctantly looked, and saw Hunter lying on the ground, more blood than man, holding his left arm.

"Yield?" Cooper asked, triumphantly standing over him, and also dripping with blood.

It was clear that Hunter could not continue to fight.

Hunter nodded, pain visible in every movement, and someone ran forward, helping him to his feet to hobble away.

Cooper surveyed the crowd. "Is anyone foolish enough to challenge again?"

Despite being bloodied and bruised, with a thick lip and cuts to his face and the rest of his body, Cooper looked like he could keep going, and the crowd fell silent long enough for Cooper to grin as if he'd won. But then Evan stepped forward.

"I challenge. Same terms, same conditions—which means that if I win, you relinquish your claim on Holly."

The light in Cooper's eyes dimmed for a moment. He risked a glance at Holly's mutinous face, and then he nodded. "It seems like some people don't know when they're beat."

"And it seems you don't know when you've been rejected," Evan shot back, fists clenched at his side and a snarl starting in the back of his throat. "Why don't you act like a gentleman for once in your miserable life and revoke your claim on her?"

"I'll revoke my claim when she has the nerve to reject me." He looked at her once more, but she remained silent, and once again he looked triumphantly at Evan and the other Shifters. "Anyone hear a rejection, then? No, I thought not. Now, let's get this over with."

Cooper wiped the blood from his face with the back of his hand and stepped back, inviting Evan in. And then the next fight began.

Evan was shorter than Cooper and Hunter, and his fighting style was different. He was wiry and fast, and managed to get a few quick punches and throws in. But Cooper drew on an inner strength, and soon had the upper hand. But he was tiring, that was obvious. He took a second longer to recover after blows, and a second longer to stand, and his wounds opened up even further.

Avery watched for only a short while before turning aside. "How can you stand to watch?" she whispered to Alex.

"Because one of us has to. I'm making sure the Devices aren't using anything, and so far, so good. Just the potion."

But Evan didn't push his luck too long. He made sure he was bloodied and bruising too, and that Cooper was breathless, lasting just long enough to look convincing before he yielded.

Cooper's victory stance was more unsteady this time, but he threw his head back as he snarled out, "Anyone else?"

Cooper's supporters were moving through the crowd, and heads were dropping. It was clear some were intimidated, despite Cooper's weakness, and were genuinely terrified of him. Others, however, had clearly had enough, and some of the older Shifters who were too old to challenge successfully looked around with an anticipation that wasn't lost on Cooper or the witches.

"Do you think my time has come?" Cooper asked defiantly. "Because I don't think anyone else has the nerve."

Ollie stepped forward. "I do."

Cooper narrowed his eyes at him, and then at the half a dozen Shifters gathered behind him, and he looked wary.

"Taken leave of your senses, Oliver?"

"Come to them, more like," he answered as he peeled off his shirt to reveal a muscled physique covered in tattoos.

Alice stepped forward. "Cooper should have a break first."

"No, he shouldn't," Ollie said, glaring at her. "These are the terms of challenge, Alice. You know that. Don't interfere."

Avery felt her magic start to manifest as Alice prepared to retaliate, as did Alex next to her, but Jeremy laid a hand on her arm.

"We will not interfere," he agreed, and shot Alice a warning glance as he pulled her back to the edge of the watching crowd.

At this point, Avery expected Tommy to step forward, too, to warn him that he would challenge next, just as they had planned, and offer Cooper a chance to release Holly now, but that didn't happen. They were going to push him to the brink.

By now the atmosphere in the crowd had shifted, and it was clear that whatever the outcome many had thought there would be tonight, it actually might prove to be very different. It was as if a thrill of electricity ran through everyone, and the energy in the circle spiked in anticipation.

One of Cooper's supporters rounded on Ollie, and Avery recognized him as being one of the two men who had arrived first. "Ollie, you don't want to do this. We'll all have much to lose if you win—yourself included."

The threat was clear, and if some had forgotten Cooper's influence in the excitement of the challenge, they all remembered now.

Ollie smiled slowly. "It's threats like that, Garret, which remind me why change is good." He rolled his shoulders, and started to turn away.

"If you win, I will challenge *you*." Garret's voice was low and threatening, and once again the mood changed.

Ollie grinned and his eyes lit up. "Is that so?"

At which point, Tommy shouted, "And if you win, I'll challenge *you*, Garret, you little prick. And I promise to break your scrawny little neck, and then I'll take on the next." He swung around to face Cooper and pointed. "I'd love for that to be you, but anyone will do."

Cooper snarled, and the pack dissolved into shouts as small fights began to break out.

Alex looked at Avery. "I think our plans have gone awry."

Alice shook free of Jeremy and raised her hands as if to use magic, but someone shouted, "Beware the witch!" She turned abruptly as a dark shape launched from the crowd and took her down, landing on her chest and snarling in her face.

Alice lay frozen, understanding dawning that everything hung in the balance of this moment, and Cooper looked panic-stricken as he realised he was losing control.

A shout broke through the air. It was Holly. "Enough!" She threw back her head and howled, and every hair on Avery's body stood on end.

Silence fell, thick and heavy, as all eyes turned to her. "If you want to remain Alpha, you release me right now, Cooper Dacre, from all commitments, with no repercussions for anyone who has helped us. I reject you, and I expect you to comply."

He glared at her, snarled, and then despite everything he had to lose, leapt at her. But before he could get near her Ollie charged, tackling him to the ground, and all hell broke loose.

Avery and Alex leapt down, fighting their way to the witches, who were now casting spells in any way they could to aid the fight. Alice had thrown the wolf off her chest and was back to back with Rose and Jeremy.

Despite the torches flickering within the standing stones, the light was low, and long black shadows stretched across the ground. Alex and Avery cast their shadow spell aside, deciding it was too hard to maintain, and went head to head with the Devices.

Alice shrieked. "You! How dare you interfere with this?" She sent a fireball at Avery that she caught and threw back, and then threw flashes of bright white energy in rapid succession, knocking Alice off her feet. She heard a snarl as a wolf leapt at her throat, and she pulled the sword free of its scabbard. Flames licked along its length as she slashed at the wolf, sending it rolling past her.

Alex was fighting his own battle with Rose and then Jeremy, as both ganged up on him.

Josh came running to her aid. "She's with me!" he yelled, as an unknown Shifter turned to her, fists raised.

And then there was another howl, this time guttural and vicious.

Most fighting came to a halt as Ollie triumphantly lifted Cooper's head—and only his head—above the watching pack. A gasp rippled around the crowd, and Alice visibly paled.

"Does anyone want to challenge me?" Ollie roared.

A small spat broke out as Garret, Cooper's clear second in command, struggled to rise from the ground. Tommy was sitting astride him. "You move one more muscle, and I will end you now."

"Screw you!" he shouted in Tommy's face, and without hesitation, Tommy ripped his throat out with his bare hands, and Garret fell back, dead.

"Anyone else?" Ollie yelled again.

The silence was deafening.

"Are you accepting me as your Alpha?" he shouted as the crowd drew back, revealing him to be covered in blood and gore and standing above Cooper's now headless body.

Josh answered first. "I do. If you agree to run the pack *without* the Devices."

Ollie looked at the others and shouted, "Is this what you all want?"

The muted rumblings of "yes" became louder and louder as the Shifters realised the position of power they were in, and then the cries of agreement were deafening.

Ollie nodded and turned to Alice and her children. "From this moment, you no longer have any affiliation with us. I demand your word that you will agree to this."

Alice stuttered, "But we have been loyal to this pack for generations!"

"You have been loyal to the Dacres. They are gone now. Do you agree? If you do not, you will not leave Castlerigg alive, regardless of your magic."

Jeremy and Rose looked to their mother, and Alice nodded, knowing they were defeated.

"Swear it," Ollie demanded. "No repercussions. I will allow you to remain in Cumbria, but our business is separate."

Alice's eyes were hard, but she nodded reluctantly, and Jeremy and Rose nodded as well. "I agree. No repercussions."

"Then swear it on a blood oath," Ollie demanded.

Alice's voice was harsh. "We need to do no such thing."

"Yes, we do."

Ollie held his hand out, and Avery passed him El's sword, the flame now quenched. He ran the blade along his palm, and blood dripped onto the grass. He passed the sword to Tommy, who now stood next to him, and then to Hunter, who stood supported by Piper and Josh. Each cut their palms, and then passed the knife to Alice.

All swore the oath, palm to palm, repeating, "From this day forth, all Devices, from generation to generation, swear that they will leave the Cumbria Pack to manage their own affairs. The pack in return swears not to interfere with the Devices. To break the oath invites death."

Once it was done, Ollie roared to the Shifters, "You are witness?"

"We are witness," they agreed as one.

"And now we must also swear an oath, Alice," Avery said, determined to protect herself, Alex, and the others. She didn't trust Alice at all. "We promise not to interfere with your business here, and you promise not to pursue us in White Haven." Alice narrowed her eyes as if she was about to complain, but Avery pressed on. "You broke Sanctuary. I demand your oath."

Jeremy and Rose shuffled in discomfort, but Alice held her gaze. "A blood oath?"

"A witch-binding oath," Avery answered.

Alex reached into his backpack and brought out the spell's ingredients. Watched by the Shifters, all five witches repeated the spell Alex and Avery had prepared, and while saying it, Alex wrapped the long piece of ivy around their wrists, binding all of them together. As the spell finished, the ivy ignited and then turned to ash, leaving a sooty mark.

Alex smiled, but it didn't reach his eyes. "It is done." He turned to Ollie and Hunter. "You are witness?"

"We are witness," they agreed.

Ollie addressed Alice, his eyes alight with victory. "Leave now, Alice. Dissolve the circle and be gone."

He didn't speak again until Alice lowered the protection spell, and the normal night noises flooded into Castlerigg as the witches walked across the fields and left.

One of the other Shifters looked at Alex and Avery, and then back to Ollie. "Care to explain who these are?"

A ripple of curiosity and fear ran around the crowd, and Avery wondered if they were going to have to fight their way out. Over half the pack had changed into wolves, and as she looked around, she realized some of the wolves were grievously injured. Cooper's supporters, she hoped.

It was Josh who answered as he stood next to them. "They gave Sanctuary while we recovered. Alice defied it, taking Hunter and Holly hostage for Cooper. They came here to see that Alice did not interfere in tonight's meet."

The Shifter nodded. "Fair enough. But it's time for you to leave now. We have much to discuss."

Alex and Avery nodded their agreement, and Avery said softly to Josh, "See you later."

He smiled a silent thanks as they headed to the road. Alex shook his head in disbelief. "So much for us needing to do a binding spell for them."

She laughed. "I prefer their version, although it was hideously bloody. I knew they'd be stronger than the average man, but to rip someone's head off..." She shuddered at the memory of Cooper's bloody head.

"I like this Ollie guy. He'll make a good Alpha!"

Avery stroked his cheek and smiled. "Let's head back to Evan's place and await their return. If I remember correctly, there's a bottle of whiskey and a fire to keep us company."

***

It was at least another hour or two before the others returned, and Alex and Avery were dozing on the sofa, full of the comfort of whiskey when they heard the key turn in the lock and the others come in.

Evan led the way, a bounce to his step, and he grinned to see Alex and Avery in front of the roaring fire. Hunter was walking behind him with a limp, leaning heavily on Piper. He was bleeding from at least half a dozen cuts. His right eye was swelling, and he held his left arm carefully.

Josh and Holly followed, and Josh wasn't looking much better than Hunter. Holly, however, was grinning like the Cheshire Cat.

Alex and Avery scooted out of the way to allow Hunter to sit. He gave them a weak smile. "Do you think Briar will fix me again?"

"I think she'll give you an earful of abuse," Avery said, bending to look at his many wounds. "But yes, she'll fix you. As long as you promise no more fighting, at least in the near future."

He winked, leaned back, and closed his eyes.

Holly hugged Avery. "Thank you for helping, both of you."

Alex shrugged. "We really didn't do much in the end. Looks like Ollie had a better plan."

Evan topped their drinks off as he said, "It was a very last-minute change of plan when we realised we could actually win if we kept pushing."

"What happens now?" Alex asked, sitting and pulling Avery onto his lap to make more room for everyone else.

"Ollie has plans," Josh said, sitting with relief. "I didn't realise he wanted to be Alpha."

"I don't think he did until seconds before it happened," Piper said. "At least now we can stay here."

"Not right away," Hunter grunted as he opened half an eye. "I'm heading back to White Haven to heal, and you're coming with me."

Piper looked outraged and appeared as if she might complain, and then she thought better of it. "All right."

"What about you two?" Avery asked Josh and Holly.

"We'll head back to our house," Holly said, smiling. "Resurrect our business! Do you think the Devices will retaliate?"

"No. Not after a blood oath," Alex said with certainty.

Avery added, "Not unless they're insane. There'd be huge repercussions, and they know it." She frowned, remembering the deaths of Cooper and Garret. "Er, what are you going to do with Cooper and Garret's bodies?"

"Their bodies have been dragged a long way away and hidden. They'll be found eventually, but not before the local wildlife has picked over their bones."

Avery paled as she realised that probably, hopefully, no one would know what had really happened. *What was she thinking? She was becoming a monster.*

"Great," she said weakly.

"So now you just have your rogue witch to worry about," Holly said, as if hiding bodies was an everyday sort of thing. She cradled a drink as she huddled in front of the fire, and every now and again she cast shy glances up at Evan.

"Yes, we do." Avery said thoughtfully. "And it won't be easy."

"But we'll help if we can," Hunter said earnestly. "We owe you."

19

Everyone arrived back in White Haven late on Friday night after what seemed to Avery like the longest car journey ever.

They'd had a few hours of sleep at Hunter's house in Chapel Stile before they headed out in the late morning, each of them taking a turn at driving. Avery had phoned Reuben to let the others know when to expect them, and they'd dropped Hunter and Piper off at their rental house, promising to visit the next morning with Briar. Whatever injuries needed fixing would have to wait, and once again, Hunter had refused to go to the hospital.

By the time they arrived at Reuben's house, Avery was exhausted. Fortunately, the aroma of food hit her, and they walked through to the back of the house to find all three witches and Newton in the snug, snacking on chips, drinking beer, and keeping half an eye on the TV, which flickered quietly on the wall. For the most part, they were surrounded with spell books, history books, and Avery recognised some of Anne's papers. They looked up and grinned as the weary travellers entered, and Avery's cats emerged from their hiding spots around the room, meowing loudly and rubbing her ankles.

"Circe and Medea," she exclaimed, reaching down to give them a big fuss. "I've missed you."

"You're back!" Briar said, leaping up. "Sit down, you look dead on your feet. I'll bring through some food."

Avery looked at her gratefully. "You don't have to," she said, trying to protest, but Briar shushed her away.

"It's pizza, won't take two minutes."

"Had a fun two days, then?" Reuben said sardonically.

"Yes," Alex said dryly, as he dropped into a large, squashy armchair. "Mutiny in Shifter packs, wolf fights, interfering Devices, and lots of blood. Loved it!"

Newton held his hands over his ears in mock protest. "I don't want to hear if anything serious happened."

"Like decapitations?" Alex asked, sipping his beer.

Newton glared. "I'm bloody serious! I'm a policeman!"

"Cornwall's finest *paranormal* policeman, too!" Reuben added with a smirk.

El laughed. "Leave him alone!"

Newton scowled. "Piss off, all of you."

Briar came in with two plates loaded with food and passed one each to Avery and Alex. She looked at Newton's grumpy face and grinned. "Oh no, I think we're baiting Newton again."

"If it's any help," Avery said before she took a bite, "the two affected Shifters were pretty vile people."

Newton held a hand up. "Stop right there."

Briar sat on the rug in front of the fire. "Are you talking about Hunter? Is he okay?"

Alex nodded. "Beaten to a bloody pulp once more, but he's okay. He's back here and wants your help to heal again." He raised a quizzical eyebrow at her. "Interested?"

Briar flushed. "Of course I'll help. But he better stop fighting. I'm not a miracle worker."

"Are you any good at healing broken bones?"

"Are you kidding?" She looked horrified. "Not particularly, but I suppose I'd better learn."

"Good." Alex pushed his plate away with a satisfied look. "Because there's no way he's going to a hospital." He filled the others in on their trip and the outcome of the fight. "And now that they're back, Hunter wants to help us—well, once he's healed."

"So, how are things here?" Avery asked. "How are you, El? You look better than when we left."

She smiled. "I am, thanks. The curse left me pretty weak for a while, and it really knocked my mood. I couldn't shake off this horrible feeling of oppression and sadness, but it's going. I went into work today, which gave me something to focus on."

"No attacks on anybody else?" Alex asked.

El shook her head. "No, and the protection spell on this house is working well."

"Any updates on Old Haven?"

"Bloody Halloween horror hunters are flooding up there," Newton grumbled. "Gabe has his work cut out."

"Really?" Avery said, astonished. "I didn't think that many people would actually bother to go."

Reuben threw his head back and laughed. "It's the latest attraction! Stan's really excited. Thinks it will be the best celebration we've had yet." He was referring to their resident occasional Druid. "He's contemplating moving the bonfire."

Avery gasped. "Please tell me you're joking."

"No. But James has put his foot down, and so has Gabe, who, as you can imagine, is very firm when he wants to be."

"Thank the gods," Avery said, relieved. "That could have really complicated things."

"But there's a change up there," El said. "The witch has cast another spell around the area again. It's a sort of revulsion spell, makes your skin crawl just to get close. It's very effective—we couldn't make a dent in it. But the good thing is, it's putting off our Halloween hunters."

Alex frowned. "She got past Gabe and the other Nephilim?"

"She can do witch flight, remember?" Avery pointed out.

Reuben nodded. "I went up there today. The whole place is bristling with power, and it's still building."

"Less than a week to go until Samhain," Avery said thoughtfully. "Have you found any new information?"

"Yes, we have," Reuben said, pleased with himself. "Have you heard of Ley Lines?"

"Sure. They're hidden lines of supernatural energy that connect across the Earth, and where they cross, their power is amplified."

"Exactly." Reuben gestured at the papers around him. "And on them we find ancient places of power, such as stone circles, cairns, mounds, dolmens, henges, hill forts, long barrows."

Newton scoffed. "Sounds like hocus pocus to me."

Briar just looked at him. "After all you've seen, you'd dismiss this?"

"Well, hidden lines of power. Sounds loopy."

Her gaze hardened. "And yet you've seen us wield magic. Seen Shifters, Nephilim, Mermaids… Why wouldn't these lines exist? Just because you can't see them!"

Newton looked away, slightly chastened.

"Anyway," Reuben continued, "Cornwall has a Ley Line running directly through it, right from Glastonbury and Stonehenge to St Michaels Mount. And a small line runs off it to Old Haven."

Alex and Avery looked at each other and back to Reuben. "Really?"

"Really. And in this book," he gestured to an old history book on Druids at his feet, "are listed places where Druids were known to be more prevalent. This area is one of them. Druids liked their groves of trees. They were natural places of worship and magic. Old Haven is one of them. Or rather, the grove of trees with the yew tree at its centre is one of them."

"What better place," Briar said, "to build a church than in one of the old pagan places of worship?"

El smiled. "The usual tale. We all know it. Buy good will off the pagan community who follow the old gods by co-opting their place of worship."

"And their celebration dates on the calendar," Alex added.

Avery frowned. "Isn't there another name for Ley Lines? Spirit ways or death lines?"

"Death roads," Reuben corrected her. "The roads that the dead were carried along. People were very specific about how they were walked and how you would carry your dead. And they're also called Faery paths—you have to respect them, or bad things happen." He rummaged through the books around him, pulled one free, and passed her a page with a map on it.

The map showed Britain with lines running across it, many intersecting. On these lines, and particularly where they crossed, were places of historical and supernatural significance. Stonehenge, Glastonbury, Anglesey, and the Lake District in particular were places where many of these lines intersected, as if they were hot spots of power.

"Strange," Avery mused. "We spent last night at Castlerigg Stone Circle in the Lakes. It was ancient and powerful. It's the Shifters spiritual home—I think that's what Piper called it."

"I would say it's had a lot of blood spilt there over the years," Alex mused. He'd moved behind Avery so he could see the map.

Reuben continued. "Anglesey, as you can see, is another hot spot, and well known for its Druid worship. It was supposedly covered in trees at one point, but the Romans cut them down as they executed the Druids and destroyed their religion. It's another place that is believed to be have been a source for Avalon—the island out of the King Arthur tales. Its ancient name was Ynys Mon."

Newton had been listening silently to all of this new information. "Were there Druids in Cornwall?"

"Yep. Where do think Stan gets his ideas from? Cornwall was a Celtic nation once, and Celts and Druids go hand in hand."

"Wow." Avery leaned back, deep in thought. "So the grove at Old Haven is on a Ley Line, and was a Druid centre of power?"

El ran her hands through her white blonde hair, ruffling it thoughtfully. "Looks like it. And maybe a gateway to the Fey."

"Hold on a minute," Newton said, looking confused. "Fey? As in Faeries? You're talking like these really exist!"

"We keep talking about gateways for a reason, Newton," Briar explained patiently, as if she was talking to a child. "Faeries live in another reality—supposedly—one that runs parallel to our own, but used to be accessible years ago, when the paths between worlds were thinner. The Druids and Fey exchanged knowledge."

"Druids and Fey have always been linked," Reuben added. "Druids worshipped trees and nature, and were connected spiritually to the Earth, just like the Fey. There's nothing more magical than the Faeries and their mounds, where the myths suggest they live beneath the visible world."

"Heard of Merlin?" El asked Newton.

"Of course I bloody have. I'm not an imbecile."

"Merlin was a Druid, and all of the King Arthur tales were linked with the Fey. Arthur's half-sister, the dreaded Morgan Le Fay, was half-Fey and a witch—hence the name."

Reuben continued to explain, "The yew, remember, also represents—" He held his fingers up one at a time. "Death, rebirth, a guardian to other worlds, a symbol of the Triple Goddess, and is linked to Samhain, the time of the year when the veils between worlds are at their thinnest. That's a pretty powerful combination."

Briar shivered and wrapped her arms around herself. "Well, now we know why she picked that place."

Alex exhaled heavily. "Well, we guessed it must be something of the sort, but it's good to have some tangible evidence. But this doesn't really tell us why."

"And we still don't know how to stop it or close it," El pointed out.

"Or how bloody big it might get!" Newton said. "What if this thing blows up and takes over most of White Haven?"

"It's not a bomb, Newton." Briar looked at him, exasperated.

"How do you know that?" he said angrily. "It's a big hot spot of concentrated energy up there, and it's building by the day. And what's going to come out of it?"

"We have to find out who she is," Alex said, looking around at them all. "I know it seems impossible, but it might help."

"I don't give a crap who she is," Newton answered, popping the cap on another bottle of beer. "I just want you to stop her. The last time a doorway opened, we ended up with the Nephilim. I don't want some raging Goblin King like David Bowie coming out of it next."

The room erupted in laughter, and even Newton sniggered. "Well, you never know."

20

After the best night's sleep she'd had in a long time, Avery headed to Happenstance Books, looking forward to catching up on work gossip.

Saturdays were always busy, and she was hoping for a welcome distraction from Old Haven. In the end she hadn't gone to see Hunter. Briar was happy to go on her own, and Avery wondered if she liked Hunter more than she was letting on. It was hard to know with Briar; she liked to keep things to herself. She did notice, however, that Newton was very grumpy about Hunter being back, which she thought was pretty funny. Maybe he'd changed his mind about pursuing a relationship with a witch.

The shop was still closed when Avery arrived, but she found Dan and Sally in the backroom, starting on their first coffee of the day. Sally ran over and hugged her.

"So glad you're back! I've been worried sick," she said, looking at her carefully for signs of injury.

"Things were weird, but I'm fine, and the Devices are neutralised, for now," Avery said, trying to reassure her. "How have things been here? Did the story time go okay?"

Dan preened himself. "Brilliantly. The kids loved it, and there's another session this afternoon. Sold oodles of books, too, you'll be pleased to know."

"And were the costumes a success?"

"Of course! Looking forward to seeing yours, Avery." He grinned as he passed her a coffee.

"Can't wait, either," she grumbled into her drink.

"Excellent, I'm going to get changed." He grabbed his costume off the back of the chair and headed for the staff bathroom.

"I'm so relieved things have been okay," Avery said, sinking into a chair. "I was worried something might happen."

"All good so far. Just Stan and his niece waxing lyrical about our shop and costumes. The local press is visiting at some point today."

Avery groaned. "You're kidding."

"No. It's good for the town, promotes tourism, and very good for the shop, too," she pointed out. "They're visiting a few places. The Witch Museum is first on the list, I think."

"I suppose you're right," Avery answered.

Sally looked nervous. "Oh, and before I forget, I need to warn you that Stan's niece, Rebecca, is coming back today. She loves this place, loves everything about it, especially the tarot cards, and Dan accidentally let it slip that you read them."

"He did *what*?"

"Nothing witchy mentioned," she said, trying to reassure Avery. "Just tarot. So she's coming back for a reading. We said she'd have to ask nicely."

Avery groaned and stood up. "I suppose I could do one." She headed to the door of the shop with her coffee. "In the meantime, I'm going to try to cheer myself up by spelling us up a little Halloween magic."

"And then your costume!" Sally wagged a finger at her at her retreating back.

Avery smiled with pleasure as she spelled the lights on in the shop. The place really did look magical, and that was all Sally's doing. Halloween-themed strings of lights were festooned over the shelves and walls, and pumpkins, grinning skeletons, witches, and ghouls were propped everywhere. The reading corner looked especially good, with rugs and cushions spread over the floor.

Avery reinvigorated her special spell that helped her customers find the book they never knew they'd always wanted, and lit incense and fake candles as she progressed around the shop. She took a deep breath as she glanced around. Today was going to be a good day; she just had this feeling, despite the fact that she was going to have to dress up.

Her thoughts were disturbed by the arrival of Dan in a sweeping black cloak, black suit, and slicked black hair popularised by film Draculas. "Oh, nice! You look good in a suit, Dan. You should wear one more often."

He winked. "Thanks. And the cloak?" He picked up one side and held it dramatically over the lower half of his face.

"No. Not the cloak."

"I'm crushed. Now, off you go to get changed." He shooed her out and she headed back to the kitchen to see Sally emerging from the bathroom in a long, empire line gown with the beginnings of zombie make-up on her face.

"That's not a zombie costume!" Avery said, looking with bewilderment at her dress.

"Er, yes it is! *Pride and Prejudice and Zombies*! Come on, Avery. Know your popular culture, please. This is a book shop, and *Pride and Prejudice* is a national classic."

"Ah! Very good. I stand corrected. Give me five minutes to join the fun."

Avery's costume was where she'd left it on the bed in her flat, and she changed quickly, laughing at herself in the mirror. Despite her misgivings, it looked good, and as she strode through the attic swishing her long skirt, Helena appeared in front of her, a wry smile on her face.

Avery smiled and twirled. "Morning, Helena. Like it?"

Helena reached out, and Avery felt Helena's cool hand stoke her cheek.

Holy crap, what was that? And was Helena being affectionate?

She stepped back. "You shouldn't be able to do that!"

Helena shrugged and smiled mischievously.

"Is this a Samhain thing?"

Helena shrugged again.

"Any other surprises?" Avery asked warily.

Helena merely smirked and disappeared.

With chills running down her spine, Avery picked up the large, pointed witch's hat with a broad brim and headed back downstairs and into the shop, stopping to grab an ornate fake wand from a display shelf. Witches didn't really need to use a wand, she never had, but popular convention liked them, so she decided to add one to her costume. If she was going to do this, she may as well commit to it.

Dan howled with laughter when he saw her. "I love it!"

Avery pulled the hat on and posed. "Do I look the part?"

"And then some!"

"Where's Sally?"

"I'm here!" she yelled from behind a large bookshelf. She emerged, fully made up as a zombie, fake blood artfully placed on her face and arms.

Avery laughed as she unlocked the front door. "What we must look like! Come on, let's get this show on the road!"

The customers started arriving early, and kept coming in a steady stream all morning, lingering a long time. Sally had placed bowls of Halloween sweets around the shop and on the counter, and these encouraged loitering and chat, so that when the press arrived, Avery was shocked to find it was already late morning.

Stan beamed as he shepherded them in, greeting them all with hearty hellos. Avery was surprised to see the blonde news reporter who'd been at Old Haven. She was accompanied by a middle-aged man who carried camera gear, and a young girl bringing in lighting equipment. Avery struggled to remember the reporter's name, but she introduced herself anyway as she extended her hand. "Sarah Rutherford. So pleased to meet our resident witch!"

Avery stuttered, "What?"

"Your costume! You look fantastic!" She turned on a wave of perfume. "And Dracula and a Zombie Miss Bennett! Perfect!" She gestured towards her cameraman. "This is Steve." He waved a silent hello, pre-occupied with setting up the camera and scanning the room.

A young voice said breathlessly, "I'm Becky, and I'm so excited to meet you!"

Avery turned in alarm to see the girl who'd arrived with them at her elbow, gazing up at her in admiration.

"Hi!" Avery said, slightly bewildered at this young, breathy creature who looked so excited.

Stan swooped in. "My niece, Becky. She's been dying to meet you after hearing about your skills with the tarot. And she just loves your shop, don't you, Becky?"

"I do! And I love your costume, too!"

Faced with this enthusiastic teen who could barely be older than 14, Avery blinked and tried to be polite. "That's lovely, thank you." She reached for a bowl of sweets. "Would you like an eyeball?"

"Yum!" she said, reaching in and grabbing a couple. "I love these." She lowered her voice and pulled Avery aside while the news team decided where and what to shoot. "Dan said you might be willing to read the tarot for me later. Would you, please?"

Avery hesitated for a second, having rehearsed all morning ways to say no, but found in the face of such pleading it was impossible. "Of course. We'll go into the back room after the news team has finished. But I'm not that good, really," she said, lying horribly. "I wouldn't get too excited."

But it was as if she hadn't spoken. "I can't wait. Dan said you're the best."

"He's being polite because I employ him." She looked up and caught his amused glance with a glare that said, I will kill you. She turned back to Becky. "You know, lots of people do tarot reading around White Haven. You could try some of them if you like."

"But none of their shops are as cool as this. I'd like to buy my own cards too."

Avery smiled. "You should never buy your own cards. They should be given as a gift."

Her face fell. "Oh, why?"

Avery lowered her voice. "It's the rules of magic. They work better that way."

Becky widened her eyes with surprise, but Avery turned away, caught by the commotion by the till.

"So," Sarah was saying, "who's best to interview?"

"Sally!" Avery said, heading over. "She's my shop manager, and is the one responsible for all of these amazing decorations. Without her this wouldn't be anywhere near as good."

Sally looked surprised but actually quite pleased, and Avery smiled. She deserved it. And besides, she didn't want to be interviewed at all.

Sarah seemed happy. "Excellent. I've never interviewed a zombie Miss Bennett before."

Avery hated to tell her Miss Elizabeth Bennett was never a zombie, she was a zombie hunter, but decided to let it go and kept out of the way while the news team did their shoot. They didn't take long, and Sally was a natural.

While the cameraman set off around the shop to take some more footage, Sarah warned them that only a snippet might make it onto the news. "We've got a few other places to visit, so we'll see how much time they give us. It will all probably be edited down to a few minutes at the most. But all this activity at the church has created a lot of interest in Halloween and White Haven. The story might even go national!"

"Really?" While Avery thought that sounded horrible, Sarah looked pleased at the thought.

"Yes. It will be great for me, and you'll get more tourists. Good all around, don't you think?"

"So, you think everything happening at Old Haven is a hoax?" Avery asked, feigning ignorance. "You were the reporter up there the other day, weren't you? I think I saw you on TV."

For a moment, Sarah looked worried. "It was odd, if I'm honest. The vicar just flew off those ladders, and the camera was already playing up. It gave me a hell of a shock, too." And then she laughed. "But of course it was a hoax! A good one, I admit, and we couldn't work out how they'd done it, but—well, what else could it be?"

Stan had been listening with interest and he joined in. "White Haven is well known for its old religions and witch history. Someone's just decided to take it a step further." He turned to Sarah. "I agree with you, it just adds to the fun of Halloween in White Haven. Fortunately James is okay, so no real harm done."

"Well, Steve had a few burns, and our camera was destroyed, but the insurance will cover that," Sarah added brightly, as if Steve's burns didn't matter at all. "And of course the place is well protected now by that lovely Gabe and his team."

Avery nodded. "So I saw. Have you been back?"

"Not yet, but I'm hoping to go later this week, just to report on updates before Halloween, talk to some of the locals who are staking out the place, and interview Gabe. Anyway," she said as Steve returned. "We better get to the next place. Where's that, Stan?"

"Angels as Protectors," he said, mentioning one of the many new age shops closer to the quay.

"Okay. Lovely to meet you all," she said, heading for the door.

"Uncle Stan," Becky said quietly. "Can I stay here and I'll meet you later?"

"Sure thing," he said, patting her head like she was a dog. "See you at Cakes and Bakes in an hour."

As soon as he'd gone, Becky turned and looked expectantly at Avery, and Sally smiled.

"Come on, then," Avery said, leading the way to the back room. "Let' see what your future holds!"

Avery sat Becky down at the small table with a cup of tea and headed up to collect her own tarot cards from the attic. She'd been tempted to use a fresh pack, but the results wouldn't be as good, and she felt she owed it to the young girl to give her a proper reading since she was so excited.

By the time she returned, Becky was already looking at some of the tarot packs they kept as stock. Avery asked, "Is there a pack that speaks to you?"

Becky frowned. "What do you mean?"

"Well, usually as you look at or handle a set of cards, you might get a warm feeling, or a sense of familiarity with one. That's the one you should work with."

Becky was wide-eyed. "Really? I don't know! I need to check them again."

Avery smiled. "That's okay. We'll do the reading now and you can do that later." Avery lit a small white candle on the table and unwrapped her cards from the square of silk she kept them in. She fanned them out, blew on them gently to cleanse them, and then gathered them back together and knocked on the top of the pack. She handed them to Becky. "Now shuffle them for me."

Still wide-eyed, Becky did as instructed and when she'd finished, Avery split them into three piles and placed them on the table. "Choose a pile." Becky tapped one and Avery placed it on top of the pack and started to lay them out in the Celtic cross.

"This is so exciting," Becky said, watching her every movement.

"What do you want to know?"

"Anything. Will I travel, will I meet a handsome man? You know, stuff."

"A specific question sometimes works best," Avery advised her. "But that's okay, I can do a general reading today."

The first few cards seemed fairly straightforward, and Avery talked through them as she placed them. Avery saw a strong male influence, some chaos in her past, and Becky nodded. "My parents have split up. Uncle Stan has been really sweet. Will they get back together?"

"Your parents? I can't really see what will happen for them, this is about you," Avery said, smiling.

As Avery turned the cards, preferring to see all of them before she made predictions, a heavy feeling flooded into her, but she kept her face neutral. This was not a nice, light reading for a teen; it was edged with darkness. The Wheel of Fortune sat poised on her outcome at the top of the ladder, below it the reversed High Priestess, and beneath that the Queen of Swords, and below that the Moon. There was a powerful woman in this girl's life, and she did not mean well. But there was also a protector, Avery's own card, the Queen of Swords. As Avery concentrated on the cards she had a vision of blood, and she closed her eyes for a second, trying to see it more clearly, but it went as quickly as it arrived.

"What can you see?" Becky asked, watching her closely. "Is it bad?"

Avery looked up, schooling her face into calm neutrality. "No, of course it's not bad, but there's a strong woman in your life, see here, The High Priestess?"

"She's upside down."

"Yes, someone maybe who is a negative influence on your life. Is someone pressuring you at the moment?"

Becky looked alarmed. "No. No one. Maybe my teacher at school? She says I should concentrate more—stupid cow."

Avery shook her head. "No, that's not it. How's your relationship with your mother?"

"It's fine, I suppose," Becky said, shrugging. "She's left my dad, which is crap, but you know…"

Avery fell silent. It wasn't her mother, she just knew. She had an intuitive feeling for the cards. Why would Avery need to be her protector? She didn't even know Becky. A horrible thought kept returning.

"Have you met anyone recently? A new female friend?"

Becky shrugged. "There's Uncle Stan's new girlfriend. She's pretty cool, I guess. A bit weird sometimes—intense, you know? But he likes her."

"How long has he been seeing her, Becky?"

"Couple of months, I don't know." Her enthusiasm was wearing off. "What's this got to do with my reading?"

"Absolutely nothing," Avery said, lying through her teeth. "Let's get back to your reading. The cards say that you have been through some unsettled months, and you have some difficult decisions to make. These decisions are blocking a long-term reading, sort of clouding your future. I think in another month your reading will be much clearer."

"So it's a short-term reading, no plans for the future, a hot man, travel?"

"Not that they reveal yet." Avery could feel disappointment coming off her in waves. "The cards reveal what they want to. It's my job to interpret them. Sometimes that's tricky." And dangerous. Becky might not even have a future. "But you also have a powerful woman on your side. That's cool—someone mysterious. Call her a guardian angel. She's telling you to choose wisely and listen to your intuition. If something feels bad, then it is bad."

"A guardian angel is cool, I guess."

"Better than cool," Avery said, leaving the cards on the table for her to examine at her leisure later. She placed out the half dozen new packs of tarot cards on the table. "Now. Have another feel of these and see which one speaks to you. I will give you whichever you choose."

Becky immediately brightened up. "Wow. Will you? That's great." She returned to the cards and examined them all in silence for the next few minutes, closing her eyes as she concentrated.

Avery waited, quietly examining the spread. Could the High Priestess be their mysterious witch? If she was, she was close to Becky. Too close. What did she want with her? Why did she see blood?

Becky chose her pack, sliding it in front of Avery. "This one, please."

"The Aquarian Tarot Deck. Nice choice!" Avery took it from her, blessing it quickly, and then wrapped it in a bag. "Just spend some time getting to know them," she suggested as she headed back into the shop. "I'm sure you'll have lots of fun with them. By the way, Becky, I'm wondering if I've met Stan's girlfriend. What does she look like?"

She shrugged. "Oldish, like him—well, older than you anyway, and long, reddish hair. Darker than yours. Pretty tall, really."

"Does she live with him?"

"Nah. I don't know where she lives." She grinned at Avery suddenly, making her look even younger. "Thanks for the cards and stuff." And then Becky headed out of the door, leaving it swinging behind her.

By three that afternoon the children's area was full of excited kids and parents ready to hear another spooky Halloween tale. Sally had handed around fairy cakes with icing made to look like witches and grimacing pumpkins, and they had disappeared in minutes.

"What are you reading today?" Avery asked Dan, as he pulled a book from his bag.

"I thought I'd keep it local, by popular request. The kids want Cornish tales, so we've got a doozy. It's very Halloween!"

"Go on," Avery said, intrigued.

"I'm reading a story about the Devil's Dandy Dogs."

"The what? Doesn't sound that scary. What are Dandy Dogs?"

Dan grinned. "Avery. You should know this. It's what our Shifter friends do." He looked at her expectantly.

Avery looked at him blankly. "Change to wolves?"

"Hunt! It's the Cornish version of the Wild Hunt. You know, unearthly warriors summoned from the Underworld to come and claim more souls. It used to be seen as a way to cleanse a place—clear out the bad folk." He looked up dramatically. "If you look up at the sky on Halloween, you can see the Wild Hunt racing across the night sky—mad horses and wild dogs!"

Avery frowned. "I've heard of the Wild Hunt, but never the Cornish version. Who leads it?"

"Odin, Herne the Hunter, sometimes Diana, sometimes Hecate. It varies depending on the tale. But essentially they cross from the Underworld," he shrugged, "or Otherworld. The Fey come to hunt humans as sport—and hunt until dawn. Lots of bloodshed, death, vanishing people, and mayhem. Fun, eh?"

But Avery wasn't grinning. She'd just had a horrible idea.

21

After work, Avery headed to The Wayward Son, and found Alex hard at work behind the bar.

It was almost six, and the pub was busy. Zee was also working, and he headed over as Avery sat at her usual corner of the bar. She hadn't spoken to him often, and still couldn't place which of the Nephilim he was from her first impression in the mine.

He spoke softly for his size. "Hey, Avery. What can I get you? It's on the house."

"Hey, Zee. A large glass of the house red, please."

She settled herself comfortably and waved to Alex when he looked up and saw her. He winked and continued to pull pints. She'd left him in bed that morning, and was looking forward to having a lie in with him tomorrow.

Zee slid the glass in front of her and before he disappeared, she asked, "So, how's life in the twenty-first century?"

He smiled, revealing gleaming teeth. "Pretty good, if different."

"I bet. Do you like it?"

"I'm getting used to it. Humanity has progressed in interesting ways. Not always good, I have to say, but to be quite honest, humans often indulge their baser instincts."

She lowered her voice. "So you don't think of yourself as human at all?"

"No. I have wings. Do you?"

She smirked. "What? Think of myself as human, or have wings?"

He laughed. "Have wings."

"No. Your perspective is interesting."

"So is yours, witch," he said quietly.

"What do you think of Old Haven?"

"It is steeped in old magic and ancient rites. Blood rites. The ground is soaked with it."

Avery put her glass down in alarm. "Is it? How do you know?"

"I feel it. We all do." He glanced up and saw a waiting customer glowering at him and called over, "One second." He lowered his voice even more. "Old magical places are often built on blood. It creates power, but you know that. Druids loved their blood sacrifices."

"You knew Druids? I thought that they were too recent for you."

He shook his head. "They have been around for a long time, only their name changes. They believed the Earth demanded sacrifice—she does sometimes, that is true—and so they gave it. The grove was once a dark place. The magic that's up there now was started with blood and will end with blood—if that doorway is to open properly."

"Have you seen the witch who has triggered it?"

"No. We feel her sometimes. She passes like the wind and feels like the Carrion Crow. We cannot stop her or follow her. But that's not what we're there for. We keep the locals back, and they are safe while we are there. For now."

And with that ominous warning, he returned to his job.

Avery sipped her wine, thinking on what Zee had said. He must have discussed this with Alex, so she'd be curious to know what he thought of it. And she wanted to share her tarot reading.

As soon as Alex was free he came over, his dark eyes warm and admiring. "How's my gorgeous girlfriend?"

"Feeling better by the moment. How's my gorgeous man?"

"Missing you." He leaned over the counter and kissed her. "Why aren't you wearing your costume?"

"Funny! It's back in the shop where it belongs."

"Shame, I'd have liked to peel you out of it later."

She blushed. "Alex! You're very naughty. You can peel me out of this instead." She gestured to her jeans, top, and boots.

"That will be my pleasure," he said with a grin. "You want some food while you're here?"

"It depends, could do, but what are the others doing back at Reuben's?"

"No idea. Why don't we go out for a meal and then head back?"

"Sounds great. I'll let him know."

But no sooner had she said that than Briar breezed in and sat next to Avery. Her cheeks were flushed and her dark hair tumbled around her shoulders, complimenting her dark red coat. "You beat me to it, Avery. I've been hanging out for this all afternoon." She eased her coat off and waved at Zee, and within seconds a glass of wine appeared in front of her. There were definitely perks to knowing the owner.

"That bad?" Avery asked.

She sipped her wine. "Just busy. Stock is flying off the shelves, which is great, but it means I'll have to spend all day tomorrow making new stock and filling the shelves. Eli said he would help. All this healing has drained me and sucked my time." She looked guilty. "Don't get me wrong, I'm happy to help, but I need to spend time in my shop, and although Eli and Cassie are great, they can't do what I can."

"I get it. You've been great though this week. We're lucky to have you. So is Hunter. How is he?"

Briar sighed. "Charmingly dangerous, and in need of a lot of healing."

Avery leaned on her hand, watching Briar. "Charmingly dangerous? Sounds interesting."

"He keeps asking me out. He's covered in bruises with a broken arm, and that won't keep his libido down." She giggled. "Imagine what's he like when he's fit?"

Avery almost choked on her drink. "I'll leave *you* to imagine that."

"That's not what I meant! Anyway, he wants to take me out to dinner later."

"Why not go? You said yourself you'll be hard at work all day tomorrow, and have been all week. Take a break tonight and have some fun. It's just dinner. And it's Saturday."

Avery glanced up and saw Newton come through the door, and Briar followed her gaze. "I think he's still interested, too," Avery said.

Briar rolled her eyes. Just then, her phone rang, and she glanced at it. "It's Hunter."

Avery mouthed, "Go on!"

As Newton grabbed a stool, Briar said brightly, "Hi, Hunter. Okay, sounds good. Where?" She looked at her watch. "Sure, I'll meet you there. "No. No lifts. Bye."

"Plans?" Newton asked Briar.

"Yes. Dinner with Hunter." She stood up, knocked back her wine, and grabbed her coat and bag. "See you later, Avery."

"Have fun," Avery said, grinning as she turned back to Newton.

He scowled. "I don't know what she sees in him."

"He's single, hot, and fancies her. And she needs some fun in her life right now."

"Is he staying In White Haven?"

"Don't know. Does it matter? Didn't think you were interested anymore."

Newton shrugged and ordered a pint.

Avery took pity on him and changed the subject. "So, what else have you been up to, Newton?"

He let out a world-weary sigh. "This old guy, a tramp who used to sleep rough around Truro, has disappeared. It's a bit weird. Everyone knew him—the shop owners, locals, police, local services, you name it. We all spoke to him, checked in on him, encouraged him to go to the night shelter, but he was a law unto himself. He sat outside shops, begged, slept in alleyways, drank." Newton looked into his pint. "You know, he had a job once, a wife, children, a life. And then—poof! Gone. Just like him."

"You can't find him at all?"

Newton shook his head and looked at Avery, sadness filling his eyes. "No, and he's been gone a couple of weeks. He couldn't have moved to another town, because we've asked—he's done that before. He has literally disappeared. We can't even find his dead body."

"I'm sorry. That sucks. Poor old guy. Maybe someone took him in?"

Newton shook his head. "He stank. No one would take him in. And he wouldn't go, anyway. Hundreds of people have tried to help him, and everyone has failed, because he didn't want help. So, I can only conclude that we'll find his body somewhere—rotting, probably, in a few months' time."

Time to change the subject again. "Well, let me tell you about my day, because I bet you didn't have to wear a costume for Halloween!"

***

Over dinner at a local Thai restaurant, Avery told Alex about Becky's tarot reading. "I think we need to find out who Stan's girlfriend is."

"You think she's our witch."

"Don't you? The timeframe fits—after all, she must have only arrived here recently. She's the right age and description, and I just get bad vibes about her. And she's intense."

"Maybe," Alex said thoughtfully. "She could also be a regular intense person who is dating Stan. I would imagine he'd make you intense."

Avery laughed. "Really? You think about Stan often?"

"All the time," he answered, deadpan.

"Well, I think we should try to see if she's the same woman who appeared in your lounge. If she's not, then back to square one."

Alex frowned. "It's just that I find it hard to believe our time-walking witch would shack up with Stan, of all people."

"Why not Stan?" Avery was slightly affronted on his behalf. "He's a nice older guy with a good job, and he's open-minded and culturally sensitive. He's grown on me recently. He was very sweet today with Becky." She thought for a second. "What if it's the fact that he's our town's pseudo-Druid that led her to him?"

"Maybe. And I guess at the moment we have no other leads. But why take up with anyone? Why not just keep her head down, know no one, and talk to no one? This way she has tangible links. She's traceable."

"Maybe she needs him for something." Avery had a horrible thought. "Have you chatted to Zee about Old Haven?"

"Not really. He's had a couple of days off, and today's been busy."

"He said that blood had opened the spell in the grove, and that blood will close it. Maybe she needs Stan as a sacrifice." And then Avery gasped. "Maybe it will be Becky? She's younger, easier to handle, more impressionable. That fits my reading!"

Alex looked at her, astonished. "A blood sacrifice! As in, she's going to kill someone?"

"Yes. That's what Druids did. We know that. They believed in it. But if you were desperate enough…"

Her words hung on the air and Alex sat back, perplexed.

And then things dropped into place as Avery remembered her conversation with Newton. "And a tramp has disappeared. Vanished. What if he was the sacrifice that started the spell?"

Alex just watched her for a second. "That's quite a leap! Anything could have happened to him!"

"I know, but it's unusual. And as Newton said, if he'd died, they'd have found his body by now."

"Human sacrifice is pretty old school—and extreme!"

"So is she. She cursed El. She could have died! She would have, without Caspian's help! So could you if I hadn't been there! This woman is a killer. She will do anything to open that gateway to wherever it is!"

Alex had finished his meal and he pushed his plate away. "I guess it makes sense. Horrible, gruesome sense."

The more she thought about her theory, the more sense it made to Avery. "Think about what we found under Reuben's mausoleum—evidence of demon traps and blood sacrifice.

There are spells involving blood magic in our grimoires, and you had to use it just to get to your grimoire. This is in our past, too!"

"There was no evidence of human sacrifice," he pointed out. "Just blood magic, which is very different."

"True, but it indicates a different mindset—a different way of approaching magic."

Alex exhaled heavily. "So, you want to check her out tonight?"

"Yes. We have to. And if she is Stan's girlfriend, than I am willing to bet that either he or Becky is the next planned sacrifice."

"If that's her plan—we don't know that, remember?"

"As much as I hate my theory, I'd put money on it. And Dan said something today that made me think about what our witch could be summoning. Have you heard of the Wild Hunt?"

"Yes, vaguely."

Avery gave him a brief summary. "What if that's what she's trying to do?"

Alex took a long drink of his beer before looking at her. "I think your imagination has gone nuts."

"I know how it sounds, but it feels right."

"Why would she want to summon the Wild Hunt?"

"I don't know."

"For just some random weirdness?"

"No. There'll be a reason. We just have to find what it is."

***

After some Googling and looking through a phone directory, Avery found Stan's address. He lived in a large Victorian semi-detached house in a small suburb of similarly-aged houses, and they drove slowly down the street, identifying his, before parking several doors down.

It was an average suburban road, lined with trees and with cars parked along the kerb. Like most houses of that age, there were no garages, and everyone had to park on the road. The houses all had three floors, with small front gardens and large back gardens. Tonight the road was busy, and they were lucky to squeeze into a small space. Fortunately, they were in Alex's Alfa Romeo.

They cast Avery's favourite shadow spell and settled in to watch the house and the road. It was after nine and cold. Stray leaves whirled past on the biting wind that set the bare branches skittering together. Some of the houses were well lit, and they could see TVs on in the front rooms of some houses where the curtains hadn't yet been closed. Stan's house was in darkness, other than a light over the front door and in one of the third-floor dormer windows.

"Maybe they're in a back room?" Avery suggested.

"Or, maybe Becky is in and Stan's out with his girlfriend? Or Stan and his girlfriend are snogging on the sofa and Becky's left them to it. I bet that's Becky's room." Alex pointed to the third floor room.

"They might all be in watching Strictly."

Alex grimaced. "Ugh. Sounds hideous."

She sniggered. "I bet you're a great dancer."

"Well, of course! But I wouldn't sit and watch Strictly, thanks very much."

Avery laughed again, and then wriggled further down in the seat to get comfortable. For the next half an hour, nothing much happened. A few people walked down the street, a few more lights went on, some went off, and then, close to ten, Stan appeared at his front door with a woman. It was difficult to see her at first. The light from the hall was behind Stan, and she was in his shadow.

"She looks tall," Avery observed.

"There are a lot of tall women in the world."

Stan leaned forward and kissed the woman on her cheek and then she turned and walked down the path to the road and turned right, away from them, walking to an old, black VW Golf. As she walked beneath a street light they could see her long, auburn hair and slim figure. She was wearing a stylish woollen coat and leather boots. For a second she hesitated, and then turned to look down the road. Instinctively, Avery and Alex hunched lower in their seats, even though a spell cloaked them completely.

The light showed the arrogant expression of the woman who'd appeared in Alex's flat. She narrowed her eyes as she looked around, and then turned back to her car and got in.

"Well, that looks like her." Alex looked annoyed. "Why did she have to be Stan's girlfriend? That sucks."

The car's headlights flashed on as the engine started, and she pulled out, driving towards them. They had a glimpse of her as she passed, a malicious, satisfied expression on her face as she accelerated away.

As soon as she passed, Alex started his car and he pulled out, with the intention of following her. "Crap, there's nowhere to turn around." He sped down the road looking for a gap to turn in, but reached the intersection. He turned right. "I'm hoping we can pick her up this way."

Avery fell silent for a moment. Something was troubling her, and she couldn't quite place it.

Meanwhile, Alex kept driving, turning once and then again, hoping to find her on another side road, but after a few minutes of cruising up and down, he slammed the wheel in frustration. "Bollocks. She's gone."

Crap! "Oh, no. I know why I recognise her."

"Er, she was in my flat!" He looked confused.

"No. I mean she looks like someone. The look on her face as she drove away. She looked like Helena. That's her expression when she's malicious and sneaky."

"You have to be kidding."

"I'm not."

"What are you suggesting? That Helena has possessed her?"

"She looked so pleased with herself this morning. What if she has?"

"You really know how to ruin a perfectly good night out," Alex groaned.

22

Avery woke on Sunday morning wrapped in Alex's arms, and with the weight of a cat on her stomach and one between her feet.

She smiled in satisfaction as Alex stirred next to her, and she stroked his bicep, her fingers tracing his tattoos. He is so delicious. Medea and Circe stirred too, meowing softly, and then Medea padded softy up to her chest and began to lick her face and then Alex's.

He groaned. "Avery, don't lick my face."

She giggled. "Idiot. It's the cat."

He nuzzled her neck. "Ah. I didn't think your tongue was that rough."

She giggled again. "You're a silly bugger."

The house was quiet, and the outside world seemed a million miles away. She stretched luxuriously and the cats meowed, demanding food, so she wriggled out of the bed to feed them. She'd set up their bowls, bedding, and litter tray in the corner of their large bedroom, so the cats would have a safe space. Not that they seemed to care; they both wandered all over the house and congregated where people were, mainly in the snug.

Alex roused, too, and they pulled on jeans and t-shirts and padded down to the kitchen where they found El and Briar sitting at the large wooden table, sipping coffee. Outside the sky was a leaden grey, and the sea beyond the garden matched it.

"Morning guys," El said, her eyes sleepy. She was wrapped in a large bathrobe that dwarfed her, and Avery presumed it was Reuben's. "There's a fresh pot of coffee over there."

"Awesome, I'll get it," Alex said as he fished two mugs out of the cupboard.

Avery sat next to the others. "You look loads better, El!"

She smiled. "Feeling loads better, too. I finally feel like my magic is surfacing again. I think your potions are helping, Briar."

Briar nodded, looking bright-eyed and alert, which made Avery feel even more knackered. "It's one of my favourites, and very effective."

"How was your night?" Avery asked her with a grin. "Have fun with Hunter?"

"Fine, thank you," Briar said primly. "We had a lovely meal."

El grimaced. "She's giving nothing away! Spoilsport."

Alex joined them, plonking a coffee in front of Avery. "Good for you, Briar. I think Newton's jealous."

"I don't care what Newton thinks! And I didn't do it to make him jealous." She looked at Avery. "You were right. It was just a meal, and why not? He wants to help us find our witch."

"We have found her—sort of," Avery said, and she updated them on what they'd found.

"Stan's girlfriend?" El looked perplexed. "And blood sacrifices? What does she want up there?"

Alex sighed. "Avery has had another crazy idea. Tell them about the Wild Hunt, and the fact that you think she's been possessed by Helena."

"Dan gave me the idea," Avery said, as she told them about his storytelling, and then the strange witch's expression that reminded her of Helena.

El raised an elegant eyebrow. "Did you guys do some serious drugs last night?"

"No!" Avery said, affronted.

"It's quite a leap," Briar added. "You actually think Helena has possessed someone again?"

"She liked it last time. What if she's found a way to do it again?" Avery felt panic starting to bubble up inside her as she talked it through. "Crap. She really could have! What am I going to do?"

"We are going to calm down and think about this logically. After breakfast." Alex rose from the table and headed to the fridge. "I can't think on an empty stomach. Where's Reuben?"

"Surfing, of course." El looked outside and shivered. "Looks freezing, but you can't keep him away when it's calm like this. But he went really early, so he might be back soon."

"I'll do enough breakfast for him, then," Alex said, starting to gather bacon, eggs, tomatoes, and bread.

El sipped her coffee. "Yeah, let's park this discussion until Reuben is back and I've had a least a gallon more coffee."

Avery felt slightly put out that everyone thought she was mad, but she sighed in agreement. "All right. So what did you and Reuben get up to last night?"

"We had a thrilling Saturday night looking at our family histories. We had this theory that maybe the reason the witch is here is because she knew the town well at one point."

"Interesting," Avery said thoughtfully. "You think she's one of our ancestors? Did you find anything?"

El shook her head. "No. Not yet. It's just a theory. I prefer it to yours, if I'm honest."

Avery grinned. "So do I. I want to head to Old Haven first though this morning, and then I'll help with research this afternoon."

"I have to work," Briar said. "But remember to call Hunter. He wants to help."

***

Full of English breakfast, Avery headed to Old Haven where she'd agreed to meet Hunter. The Old Haven car park had half a dozen cars parked on there, including Gabe's big shiny SUV, and within seconds of her arriving, Hunter pulled up in his old Volvo.

Hunter winced as he got out of the car, but nodded at the SUV. "Nice ride."

Piper exited from the other door, and gave a half-smile of greeting towards Avery.

"Yeah, I have no idea how he can afford that," Avery said, inwardly marvelling at Gabe's enviable resources and negotiation skills. "Are you sure you shouldn't be resting? You look like you're in pain."

"No. I'd just get bored. Besides, Briar's healing skills are great."

"But you look terrible," she said, looking at his split lip, black eye, scratches, and his arm in a sling. "Did you get a proper plaster on that arm?"

"No. It would mean I couldn't shift. Briar's not happy."

"She's the only one he'll listen to," Piper said, annoyed. "But not even she could persuade him to do that."

Hunter grinned. "I like it when she shouts at me."

"You're gross," Piper said, leading the way across the car park and along the path to the church.

Gabe was standing at the end of the path, dressed in black fatigues with dark shades on. He nodded in recognition as they approached. "Hey, guys. You come to see the freak show?"

"Just like everyone else," Avery told him. She was glad she sort of knew him, because he looked really intimidating. She looked past him where she could see a few people milling around the graves. "Are they here for the cemetery or the grove?"

Gabe grinned. "They say the cemetery, but they just keep prowling around, taking lots of photos."

Hunter narrowed his eyes. "You don't throw them out?"

"Makes it too interesting not to let them in at all. We let them wander around, but the new spell the witch has put on the place means no one wants to venture beyond the trees. Dread creeps into your bones when you get too close. But there's another couple of my guys closer to the grove, just in case. You'll see when you get there."

Avery frowned. "A protection spell, is that right?"

"Of a sort," he said enigmatically.

Intriguing. "Okay. I have to see." Avery headed down the path, followed by Hunter and Piper. Her breath caught as she saw the grove in the overcast autumn light, and her blood chilled.

A line of witches-signs hung from the trees on the edge of the grove, twisting in the biting wind that blew in off the sea, and marking a very distinct boundary. She could see dark red marks daubed on some of them, and close up her suspicions were proven correct. It was dried blood.

Hunter and Piper lifted their heads and inhaled deeply, and both recoiled.

And then Avery felt it. A wash of dread and creeping terror that made her want to turn and run. She stepped back and shuddered. *What was that?*

One of the Nephilim strolled over. "Avery. You've brought friends."

"I have. Hunter and Piper. I'm afraid I don't know your name." She held her hand out and he engulfed it in his large one.

"Othniel. Niel for short." He turned and greeted the other two.

Niel, like the other Nephilim, was tall, broad-shouldered and olive-skinned, but unlike the others, he had white-blond hair and bright blue eyes. He'd kept his hair long, but had tied it back, and he had long sideburns and stubble.

Avery asked, "Have you been in the grove beyond the witch-signs?"

"Once or twice when I thought I heard someone in there. I wouldn't advise it."

"Why not?" Piper asked.

"Because, small wolf, it affects you here." He pointed to his head and his stomach.

"I can take that," she said, lifting her chin.

"I doubt that." His blue eyes bored into hers.

Piper pouted in annoyance. "How do you know what I am?"

He smiled with a predatory grin. "I have many special skills."

"Did you find anyone in there?" Hunter asked. "The noise?"

"Just the rustle of dry tree branches and the scent of Carrion Crow. It was her, I'm sure. She comes with the wind and adds to her spell."

Avery took a deep breath, hating what she was about to suggest. "I need to enter. I'd like to try and work out what she's done."

"Be my guest, but I'll come with you."

"Is she there now?" Hunter asked, lifting his head and sniffing again.

The Nephilim shook his head, turned, and ducked beneath the rattling bare branches, into the trees.

Avery followed him, yet every instinct she had urged her to run. Dread settled into her stomach as heavy as a stone and she started to shake. *This is a spell, only a spell,* she whispered to herself as she followed Niel further into the grove, Hunter behind her.

A small voice shouted, "I can't!"

They looked around to see Piper frozen in fear.

"It's okay," Hunter said, reassuring her. "Go back and wait, we won't be long."

She turned and fled, and they watched her until she was clear of the trees.

Avery fought down the desperate urge to follow her. "Are you okay?" she asked Hunter.

"No, but let's keep going."

With every step that brought them closer to the yew, the feeling of terror rose, and Avery cast a protection spell in a bubble around them. Immediately the sensation eased, and she started to breathe more easily.

Hunter sighed with relief. "If that was you, thank you."

She nodded and kept going, the bare branches clicking above them impatiently. Niel stood waiting in front of the yew, its huge trunk cracked like an open mouth, screaming in pain. Its gnarled branches loomed over them, one of the only trees still to have its dark green, needle-like leaves.

"This place has changed in the days since we were last here," Avery observed. "The magic is deeper and darker. The trees, the ground, the air—it's all saturated with growing power." She cast her awareness out, seeking the magic beyond the spell, and all of a sudden felt their own magic they had released from the binding spell. She was drawing on it; it was subtle but unmistakable. She looked at Niel. "You can feel her spell?"

He nodded, his eyes wary. "It chills my blood, too. *She* chills my blood. She is not like you."

Hunter had been looking suspiciously around the small clearing surrounding the yew, but he now looked at Niel. "You look human, but you obviously aren't. You're a bit like the witch—there is something ancient about you."

Niel was silent, so Avery answered for him. "You're right there, but I'm not sure Niel wants to share." She turned to him. "You called her the Carrion Crow earlier, so did Gabe. Why do you call her that?"

"She reeks of death, feeds on death, and rejoices in it." He pointed across the grove to a bundle of feathers on the ground. "Every day for the last few days she kills a small creature, mostly birds, but it could be other woodland creatures. And always there."

Avery stepped a little closer, trying not to gag as the smell of decay grew stronger. Small animal bones and the rotting bodies of birds lay in a pile next to a cairn of stones covered in blood. The Carrion Crow. *The Crone.* She frowned. The Crone was an aspect of the Goddess, associated with age and death, but not necessarily cruelty. But there were other aspects of her nature, such as Hecate the Goddess of Death. *Was that what she could sense, what the Nephilim could sense?*

Avery retreated from the bundle of death and turned back to Niel. "The Mermaids' call did not affect you, their Siren call. Why can you feel this?"

"We heard their call, but we could resist it, as we can resist this. Our uniqueness gives us added strength, but we are not impervious. I feel it well enough. The darkness invades my dreams. Have you seen enough?"

As he spoke, wind ripped through the trees, setting the branches rattling and the witch marks spinning, and the scent of decay intensified. "Yes." She turned and all three ran as if the Devil was at their heels.

***

Avery drove back to Reuben's place, and Piper and Hunter followed.

The snug next to the kitchen was warm and bathed in weak autumnal sun that struggled to get through the clouds, but Avery could still feel the sullied air of the grove clinging to her like a second skin. Only El was there, tucked into an armchair in front of the fire, and she looked up as they came in.

"What happened to you?"

"Why?" Avery asked. "Do we look odd?"

"You look haunted. What happened?" She uncurled and put her book down.

Avery sank on to the sofa, her legs suddenly weak. "The grove feels horrible. You're right about that spell. It spills out terror and dread."

Piper sat on the floor next to the fire, looking ashamed. "I couldn't even go in. I wanted to scream."

"There's no shame in that," Hunter said, looking at his sister fondly. "That's exactly what the spell is meant to do."

"But you managed to cope with it," Piper protested.

"Not for long," Avery said. "I had to cast a protection spell once we got close to the yew. It was the only thing that stopped us from running."

El leaned forward. "Is it just a spell, or is something else going on there?"

"Oh, there's plenty going on." Hunter ran his hands through his hair. "The stench of blood and decay was overwhelming, and with my sense of smell, I'm used to being more sensitive. But that was something else."

"She's making blood sacrifices now, daily. Killing small animals and birds." Avery shook her head. "I went in there trying to work out what spell she might be using, or just to try to detect what's happening, but the feeling of terror was so overwhelming it just drowned everything out—even with my spell as a buffer."

"Damn it!" El exclaimed, leaping to her feet and joining Hunter's pace around the room. "Who *is* she?"

"Gabe and Niel call her the Carrion Crow. She even scares them."

"That's not a good sign," El grumbled.

"You know, I think I'm wrong," Avery said thoughtfully. "I was worried Helena was doing this, but she isn't. I just know it. Maybe you're right. Maybe it's someone who knew the town well in the past. Have you found out anything?"

"Well, we've scoured our family trees and histories, but nothing particularly odd stands out. We considered Rueben's mad uncle, Addison, but he doesn't fit for many reasons, particularly because he's a man. But we thought maybe a descendant?" She shrugged and sighed. "Anyway, we realised the only family history we didn't have here was yours, so Reuben and Alex have gone to fetch them from your flat."

"It took two of them?" Avery asked.

"Research isn't Reuben's strong point," El said, grinning. "I think he needed a break. And they needed more beer."

At that moment, the front door slammed and their voices arrived ahead of them. Alex headed into the snug carrying a huge box, while Reuben stayed in the kitchen, yelling, "Who wants a beer?"

"Me!" a chorus of voices called back.

Alex took one look at Avery and his face fell. "What's wrong?"

"So many things," she said, groaning. "But I'm fine. I'll tell you both over a beer."

She headed to his side and helped him unpack Anne's files, placing them on the floor within easy reach of the sofa and chairs. As soon as Reuben came in with the beers and they were all settled, she filled them in on what had happened at the grove.

Reuben frowned. "This is all sounding very bad. The Crone and the Carrion Crow?"

"I keep coming back to the Wild Hunt," Avery said. "It just got stuck in my head, and I can't shake it."

"It's just a myth, surely," Hunter said. He'd finally sat down next to his sister on the rug in front of the fire, and he sipped his beer, listening carefully.

"So were Mermaids, until they attacked White Haven," Alex pointed out.

Piper looked shocked. "And I thought our life was weird."

"Stick around White Haven some more and you'll realise what weird is," Reuben said dryly. "What did your super noses pick up?"

"Blood, death, and decay. Always a winning combination," Hunter said.

"Pass me one of your books on myths," Piper said suddenly. "I'll look up the Wild Hunt."

"And I'll start searching my history, again," Avery said, settling back on the sofa with Anne's research.

For the next hour, the room was relatively quiet as they poured over papers and books, even Hunter helping as he looked at some of the maps of White Haven and histories of Ley Lines. She could hear him, Reuben, and Alex discussing where the lines fell across Old Haven, but she tried to block them out as she studied the tiny writing spread across several pages of her family tree. Although Anne had concentrated on Avery's main line from a couple of generations before Helena, there were lots of names to study.

And then she saw it, buried deep on a line in the centre of one big roll of paper. A name with no date of death—just like Addison Jackson. The name was Suzanna Grayling, and she was descended from Ava, Helena's older daughter.

Avery's pulse raced as she scanned the names above and below, but Suzanna was the only one not to have a date of death. *Why couldn't Anne find it? Was she their mysterious time-walker?* She looked up at the others. "I've found something. Suzanna Grayling, one of my ancestors, has no date of death."

El's mouth fell open in shock. "Wow. When was she born? I mean, age-wise would it fit?"

"She was born in 1780, and she married a David Grayling when she was…" Avery quickly did the maths. "Nineteen years old."

"Does it say anything about her?" Alex asked.

Avery fumbled for the book of notes Anne had made. "I don't know. Anne sometimes commented on certain people and anomalies, but often they were nothing much, just odd snippets she'd found out about what they did and where they lived." She shook her head. "Her research was phenomenal. Give me a few minutes and I'll let you know."

Anne's notebooks were carefully numbered and annotated, and Avery briefly wondered if she'd spent so much time on the other witches' history. She presumed Helena's special status as the only one to be burned at the stake made her more interesting, in a gruesome way.

It was another ten minutes before she found what she was looking for, and she lifted her head to tell the others. "Suzanna Grayling was the first of Helena's descendants to return to White Haven."

"No way!" El said, wide-eyed. "That has to be significant!"

"Who's Helena?" Piper asked. "You keep mentioning her."

Awkward. "She's my ancestor who was burned at the stake, and now haunts my flat as a ghost."

"Right." Piper nodded with a grim smile.

Alex asked, "What else does it say?"

"The man she married, David, bought the house that I now live in…" She checked the document. "In 1801. Two years after they got married. Well, he bought the middle house. The others were bought later."

Alex smiled. "So after two hundred years, your family returned to White Haven. That's amazing."

"Do any of you know when your ancestors returned here?" Avery asked thoughtfully.

"Well, mine never left," Reuben said, gesturing around him at the house.

El nodded. "True. Is there anything in your notes, Avery, that says anything about our families?"

"Not that I noticed, but then again, I haven't really looked for that."

"What was the date for your *new* grimoire?" Alex asked.

It wasn't a new grimoire, but Avery knew what he meant. It was the grimoire that wasn't Helena's. She hesitated for a second as she scrabbled to find her grimoire under the documents. "1795."

"And who is the first name in your new grimoire?"

Her gaze met his. "Suzanna Grayling."

"So, she was fifteen years old when she decided to assert her witch roots. That's pretty young. Who's the next name?"

"Ava Helen Grayling." She looked at the others in shock. "Her daughter, who she named after Helena's oldest child and Helena herself!"

Piper had watched their conversation with interest. "She was a woman on a mission. She obviously knew her own history very well. "

El agreed. "Your family might not have been living here, but they certainly passed down their heritage. And Suzanna was keen to practice the craft again. She started the book before she moved here with her husband."

Alex sat next to Avery and pulled Anne's notebook from her hands. "Didn't Helena say that Ava was already strong as a child, and that's why Octavia wanted her?"

Avery narrowed her eyes as she looked for the original grimoire, and quickly thumbed to the back where the note had been written next to the binding spell. She read, *"Ava already shows signs of power well before one would expect it."*

"So," Alex said softly, "it would be reasonable to assume that Ava's strong abilities passed down to her descendants, and that Suzanna had been honing her magic for some time. Maybe she even pushed her husband into coming here."

"It must have been a wonderful feeling to have finally come home," Avery mused. "Maybe though, once she was back, she got annoyed and wanted to make White Haven pay for Helena's burning all those years ago. I mean, it wasn't really the town's fault, but I guess they didn't stop it."

"They couldn't," El pointed out. "Our families fled, too, except for Reuben's, and they were rich and influential enough to stay."

Reuben winced. "Sorry."

El held up her hands. "Wait a minute. If it's her—Suzanna—why is she here *now*? After all this time?"

Alex sighed. "Because she's casting the mother of all spells, and to do that you need a lot of magical energy, and guess what's floating over White Haven right now?"

"And she's using it, too," Avery said, realising that she hadn't told them what she'd sensed. "She's drawing on it *right now.* When we released the binding spell she must have known. But why the delay?"

"A spell this big needs preparation," Alex said thoughtfully. "It seems that she's drawing on the power of the Crone and is trying to open a portal to, what?" he hesitated. "The Underworld? The world of the Fey? To allow the Wild Hunt into this reality, to kill, seek vengeance, and generally cause chaos? She's using our own magic against us!"

"It's her magic, too," Reuben pointed out.

Avery rubbed her hands over her face. "Wow. Are we really suggesting that for over two hundred years she has bided her time in order to seek revenge on White Haven?"

"It seems so," El mused.

Alex said, "So, she knows the power of the White Haven witches has been released, and she has to use it as effectively as possible. She waits for the best possible time for her plan—Samhain. And chooses the most affective spot to centre her magic—the Grove. And within two weeks of Samhain, she starts her spell."

Hunter looked at them as if they were mad. "So she makes herself a time-walker, biding her time for revenge, and lucky us, now's the time!"

"And then uses her spare time to target others she considers responsible for Helena's death," Avery said. "Maybe that's why she targeted you, El. Not for trying to stop her spell, but for your family's perceived betrayal of hers."

"And maybe that's why she didn't want to see you at Alex's flat, Avery," El said. "She must know who you are."

"It didn't stop her from trying to kill me though, once she knew I was there," Avery pointed out. "I'm not entirely sure she's rational."

"You were in her way," Hunter said. "At that point, her loyalty to you went out the window."

"Rational or not," Reuben said, "she's powerful, and is prepared to kill to get what she wants. So, let's be logical. We think she killed the tramp to start the spell—the timeframe fits—and she's planning a final human sacrifice to seal the deal—Stan or his niece. How do we stop her?"

Avery became excited. "I've got her blood. I can make a poppet."

"Awesome," El said. "But we need more. We need the Council."

23

Avery walked across Reuben's wide patio enjoying the afternoon sunshine, which had finally triumphed over the clouds, her phoned pressed to her ear.

The sunshine couldn't really be called warm, but it was a bright spot in what was proving to be a dark day. They had talked for a while about whether to involve the other twelve covens of Cornwall. Avery wasn't sure it was worth asking after Genevieve had declined to help with the Mermaids, but Reuben had argued that Suzanna was a much bigger threat to everyone, and she had to try. And he was right.

Genevieve answered the call, her voice bright but abrupt. "Avery, I hope you're not ringing to cancel Samhain."

"Actually, no," Avery said, biting down the urge to tell her to get stuffed. "We have a problem, a big problem, and need your help. We would like to offer Reuben's house as a meeting place for the Samhain celebrations. It's large and private, and everyone could comfortably fit in."

"Why on Earth would we want to change from Rasmus's house?'

"Because we need your help to stop the Wild Hunt from ravaging Cornwall."

There was silence for a moment. "*The what?*"

"The Wild Hunt, which although mythical, does have roots in reality—" she broke off as Genevieve interrupted.

"I know what the bloody Wild Hunt is! Why would it be released on us?"

"We have a rogue witch, who I believe to be a time-walker and one of my ancestors, who is seeking vengeance for Helena's death. We think." Avery went on to explain what was happening, and by the time she'd finishing, Genevieve was spitting.

"You should have told me sooner. This is huge! It has repercussions for all of us."

Avery took a deep breath, reminding herself that they needed the others. "I know, but we didn't fully understand what was happening until today. And quite frankly, Genevieve, you haven't really given much of a crap about our predicaments before."

As usual, the angrier she became, the more the wind was whipping about Avery, and she funnelled it away into the garden, watching it pick up leaves in a whirlwind and carry them across the lawn.

Genevieve's tone was icy. "Well, unlike last time, this situation will affect all of us. The Wild Hunt is deadly and vicious, and once released will be uncontrollable."

"Which is why I'm calling you. We know where it's going to happen. We need to stop the breach between worlds. And if not, we need to form a protective ring around the grove to contain it. And then we have to send it back."

"Can't you seal off your escaped magic?"

"No! You know we can't, or we would have. And besides, she's already using it. But that doesn't mean we can't use it, too."

"And you couldn't feel her using it?" She sounded annoyed. "Don't you have a connection to it?"

"Not 24 hours a day! It's not like a battery we're plugged into! When it was released it flooded into us, but then it was as if our bodies had enough and just—" She struggled to find the right word, "Disconnected! I can't explain it better than that."

Genevieve fell silent for a moment, and Avery could feel her anger crackling down the phone. "I can't come tonight, but I will come tomorrow. And if it's as bad as you say, then yes, I will convene the coven."

She rang off and Avery headed back inside, smiling triumphantly.

"Good news, then?" Alex asked, watching her.

"You could say that. Genevieve's coming to assess the situation, but I know she'll say yes."

"Wow," Reuben said, grinning. "Go Avery. And I get to host the coven. Lucky me."

El came in from the kitchen with bowls of chips and dips. "We need to tell Newton, too."

"Someone else's job," Avery said immediately. "I do not want two people moaning at me today."

Alex rose to his feet. "Fancy another trip, Reuben?"

"Why?"

"We need to ward Stan's house and protect him and Becky. Something to stop Suzanna using either of them as a sacrifice."

"A glamour?" Reuben suggested. "Make them leave for a few days?"

"Brilliant!" Alex looked at him in admiration. "Let's go."

"Can I come?" Hunter asked. "I'd like to pick up her scent again."

"Sure. Road trip! More the merrier."

"Stay here, Piper," Hunter said. "We'll head home once I'm done."

She nodded, watching them silently as they strode out the door, full of energy and intent.

In the silence of their departure, El said, "He's pretty bossy, isn't he?"

Piper met her gaze. "And then some. He's a natural Alpha, which has its pros, but also cons." She stood up and stretched her legs. "I need to run. Okay if I change here?"

"Be my guest. I'm going back to the spell books, and then I'll cook something, enough for everyone." El patted her non-existent stomach and reached for the crisps. "I'm starving. I only had nibbles for lunch."

"And I'm going to go make my poppet," Avery said. "Well, Suzanna's actually."

"There's a sewing room somewhere upstairs," El said, gesturing vaguely. "There'll be plenty of material there, and the herbs are in the attic."

"Laters then," Avery said, and she grabbed her grimoire and swiped some crisps from the bowl before heading for the stairs.

***

After hunting around for a while, which included getting lost in Reuben's vast house, Avery eventually found some material and chose a small square of plain cotton cloth. She'd never made a poppet before, and didn't relish doing one now.

A poppet was a small doll made to resemble the person you wished to cast a spell on. It could be made from cloth, clay, or wax, but using cloth allowed her to fill it with herbs and the tissue with the blood on it, which she'd carefully stored in a small wooden box. Magic should not be about controlling someone's actions, but in this case they had no choice. In order for it to be effective you needed something of the person, like hair, or nail clippings, or blood—so even the tiny drop of blood should make the spell work. There was no way they could get anything else from her.

Avery cut two pieces of fabric out in the shape of a gingerbread man and started to stitch it together, and then added rudimentary eyes, a nose, and mouth. She fashioned some clothes to put on it, to make it look female, and used wool to make long hair. The actions were soothing and contemplative and she focused on Suzanna, envisioning her clearly: her body, her hair, and her face.

When the doll was nearly complete, she took it upstairs into Reuben's attic workshop. Although he lived here alone now—except for El visiting—he still kept most of his magical gear there. She lit candles and incense and then once she'd found the herbs she needed, she mixed them together in a bowl, pounding them down just slightly. Satisfied, she stuffed the doll with the herbs, placing the blood-stained tissue in the centre, then completed the stitching, sealing the ends completely.

Now what? Should she work a spell now, or would that be too soon? Should she try to bind her and weaken her magic, injure her, mute her? Whatever she chose, it had to be effective. If she used it too soon and Suzanna was able to resist it, it would be a valuable resource lost.

Avery closed her eyes, hoping for inspiration. *Was this woman really Suzanna?* It seemed insane.

The warmth of Reuben's attic wrapped around her, folding her within its space that had seen so much magic worked over the years. She inhaled the soothing incense, relaxing her shoulders, the candlelight barely visible through her closed eyelids. She focused only on her breath, and then cast her awareness out, trying to feel Suzanna. She was her blood, like Helena, but she'd got lost somewhere along the way, possessed by revenge and darkness. How would it feel to walk alone through the years with all your loved ones gone? Had she watched them die? Her children and husband? Her friends? Her grandchildren and their grandchildren? She would have had to leave White Haven, she'd have been recognised otherwise, her unnatural lifespan discovered. Perhaps she returned from time to time?

And Helena? Did she know who she was? What she had planned? Did she approve? Avery remembered Helena's sneaky smile. *Yes. She probably did.*

As she sat quietly, listening to the beams creak and settle around her, she became aware of another presence close by, something dark and predatory. She tried not to panic, and kept her eyes closed. It wasn't a physical presence she sensed; it was something else.

A voice rang out suddenly, in her head. *I sensed you earlier, at my grove. You're too late.* The voice was strong, certain of herself. It was the witch.

Suzanna. Is that you? Avery asked, her question silent, in her mind only.

There was moment's hesitation. *I haven't been called that in many years.*

Yes! It was her. Avery desperately squashed her elation, hoping she couldn't sense it, and schooled her mind carefully.

So who are you now?

There is power in a name. You know that, she chided.

But I know your real one, that's powerful enough.

I won't tell you. All knowledge is power.

Yes it is, and we have knowledge, too. We know what you're doing.

I doubt that.

She was so sure of herself, so confident.

Would it hurt to spell it out? Probably not.

You're summoning The Wild Hunt.

More silence followed, and for a second, Avery thought she'd gone. *Well done. You're brighter than I thought. But it matters not. The spell is too far advanced for you to stop it.*

Why are you doing this, Suzanna? These people had nothing to do with Helena's death.

Her voice dripped with scorn. *They are the descendants of those who did. They walk and talk and act as if nothing happened. They celebrate the old ways without fully understanding them. They celebrate their festivals and make their bonfires, but they know nothing.*

They try. Isn't that better than nothing? These are different times.

Suzanna laughed bitterly. *They are no different. People still betray each other out of fear and anger and greed. Trust me. They would betray you in a heartbeat.*

Was she right? Would they? They had told James. Was that a mistake? No.

Your age has corrupted you, Avery said sadly. *You have learnt nothing. You see everything through a veil of the past.*

So would you if you were in my shoes. You, of all people! You only found our grimoires this year! So much secrecy and lying. So much betrayal. You did well to break the spell. I admire you. Her voice dropped, low and seductive. Are you sure you don't want to join me?

Yes. It's pointless to ask.

Then it is pointless to talk to you. You can try to stop me, but you will fail. Our magic will help me, and my spell is too strong. I have prepared for this for a very long time. You should leave now while you have the chance.

I'm not leaving!

Then you will die with everyone else.

And then she was gone.

Avery opened her eyes and looked around the room, and then down at the poppet. She had banished the making of it from her mind, and hopefully Suzanna would not have been able to see it. She wouldn't use it right now. It was too precious. She'd save it and talk to the others first.

Unfortunately, she hadn't seen anything of where Suzanna was living. She had been a voice in the void.

When Avery returned to the snug she found it empty. She could smell cooking; El was in the kitchen.

Audioslave was playing loudly, and El was singing as she chopped and prepared. A glass of wine stood on the counter. She looked up as Avery entered. "You look like you've seen a ghost."

"Heard one, more like. No, not a ghost. Suzanna."

El put the knife down and gaped. "You've spoken to her? How?"

She gestured around her head. "One of those weird head conversations."

"Wow. And what happened?"

"She basically told me I'd die with the rest of White Haven because I wouldn't join her crazy crusade." Avery headed for the wine rack and pulled out a bottle of red wine she'd put there yesterday. "I need this."

"The whole bottle?"

"Eventually," she answered, as she poured a glass.

"Is she Suzanna?"

"Yes. And she's summoning the Wild Hunt. We're right, but it doesn't make me feel any better. And it doesn't make it any easier to try to stop her."

El stirred the pot of whatever she was cooking—something spicy. "Did you make the poppet?"

"Yes. But I don't know what to do with it, or when. I want to use it at the most opportune moment."

El nodded. "Makes sense. We're up against it this time."

"We were last time as well, but we succeeded in the end. Hopefully Genevieve and the coven will help."

***

It was another couple of hours before Alex and the others returned, but when they did, they looked pleased.

"Success?" Avery asked.

"Yes," Alex answered as he headed to the fridge, grabbed three beers, and handed them to Hunter and Rueben. "We successfully glamoured Stan and Becky, and they're heading away for a few days."

"And," Reuben added, "we've added protection to their house with a few well-placed runes around the home."

"That's great news," El said, relieved. "I feel better knowing they'll be away from harm. Will Suzanna be able to find them?"

"Even if she does, we've glamoured Stan enough to resist her charms. Unless, of course, she decides to just grab them and force them against their will, which is highly possible," Alex pointed out.

Avery frowned. "It's great, and I'll sleep easier knowing they're gone, but I can't help but think she'll just use someone else. Did you get her scent again, Hunter?"

"Yeah, it's faint, but there. But of course when she gets in the car, it disappears and I can't track her." He looked frustrated, and the wild power of the wolf hung around him still; his eyes had a strange yellow light to them. "Where's my sister?"

El pointed out to the garden. "Out there, somewhere."

"I'll go and find her, and then we'll head off." He paused for a moment. "I'd still like to help you, so we'll come to the grove for Samhain. I'm calling to get Ollie, Evan, and Tommy to come, too."

"I don't think it's a good idea—you could easily get hurt. We all could, and you don't have magic to protect you," Avery said, frowning. "You don't owe us anything, either."

He gave her a cocky grin. "But I'm a wolf and I hunt. What better help can you get when the Wild Hunt comes to town?"

El agreed with Avery. "You're injured! And you're already in harm's way. We should protect your place, too."

"Already done," Reuben said, sitting down and joining them at the table. "We have been fast, efficient, and effective today!"

El raised an eyebrow. "Go you!"

Hunter headed for the door into the garden. "See you later, guys. And keep me informed!"

24

It was halfway through Monday afternoon when Genevieve strode into Happenstance Books. She looked around imperiously, and when she spotted Avery, she pushed through the customers to get to her.

Genevieve lowered her voice as she approached. "That's a fine mess up there!"

Avery tried to smile, but failed. "How lovely to see you, too."

Genevieve had no time for pleasantries. "You should have told me about this sooner."

"I had no idea how bad it was going to get, or what was going on!"

Customers started to stare, and Avery headed to the back room, Genevieve on her heels. She slammed the door behind her.

"The magic in that grove is very dangerous!"

Avery glared at her. "I know! Why do you think I called? Will you help us?"

"I'll have to. It will need all of us to contain it, and I still think we'll struggle."

Avery sagged into a chair with relief. "Thank you. I really appreciate it. Would you like a drink? Tea, coffee?" Seeing Genevieve's unamused face, she added, "Whiskey?"

"No. I have to get back and start organising things for Samhain. I'll have a think about how we approach this, but essentially I will be the High Priestess leading whatever spell we do. I shall be channelling all of your energies."

"That's fine with me, whatever you need us to do. Do you want to go ahead with our Samhain celebrations at Reuben's before?"

Genevieve shook her head. "No. We'll meet at Reuben's to discuss our plans, and then we'll head straight to the grove. This will be a hell of a way to celebrate." She paused, looking thoughtful. "We haven't performed a spell this big as a coven for many years. Not in my lifetime, anyway."

"Really?"

She sat in the chair opposite Avery, all of her bluster gone. "It will scare some of the witches, the more inexperienced ones. They will need our support. Our strength and our ability to act as one is paramount."

"How many are there in the whole coven?"

She ran through the numbers in her head. "Thirty-seven, I think."

"Quite a few then, really."

"Yes, plenty of energy to draw from, but also a lot to control. And if one person falters…" She trailed off, the implications clear.

Something struck Avery. "Does this mean that you haven't channelled all of our energies before?"

"Not quite so many, and certainly not for an event such as this." If she was worried, she didn't show it.

"I hate to ask, but are you sure you can control all of our power?"

"I was chosen as High Priestess of the Cornish coven for a reason. I am one of only a few who could handle all of that energy, so yes, I can do it. But it will drain me afterwards, for days probably. But that's okay, it needs to be done."

"And who else has the power? I'm just curious," Avery explained.

"Rasmus, Jasper, Claudia, and Caspian. Probably Eve. And in time, maybe you."

Avery couldn't have been more shocked if she'd slapped her. "Me?"

"Surprised?"

"Of course! I'm not strong enough to control the power of so many witches."

Genevieve watched her thoughtfully. "I didn't say now, but you already wield power well, and your focus is good. And importantly, your heart is positive. So yes, I believe one day you could." She rose to her feet, ready to leave. "The road you travel on is long, and the knowledge we gather is never-ending. As long as you're open to that journey, you will always be in a position of power, Avery. I'll be in touch."

She smiled and left, shutting the door behind her softly.

It was almost five when Caspian came in. He glanced around and then headed to the counter. Avery sat behind it on her own, counting down to closing time. The shop had been busy, and she couldn't wait to go home. Well, to Reuben's.

"I didn't think you could get many more Halloween decorations in here, and yet you've managed it," he smirked.

"It's festive. I like it. Have you just come to criticise?"

"No. I've heard from Gen," he said.

Avery looked shocked. "I've never heard anyone call her that before."

"I'm not sure she has, either," he said, winking. "Anyway, she's told me about the grove and the need for a collective spell. All of my family will be present."

"Really?" She squirmed, not really comfortable at feeling she owed so many people her thanks, especially the Favershams.

"They have no choice. Gen orders it, and I endorse it. Besides, we all know of the danger of the Wild Hunt."

"It sounds crazy," Avery confessed.

"It will be. Everyone will be affected, everyone in danger. And besides, it's not your fault."

"Well, actually it is. Our rapidly diminishing cloud of magic over White Haven has given Suzanna the power to do this. So it is my fault."

"You're not responsible for a mad woman's desires. Anyway, that's all I wanted to say. I shall see you on Thursday."

"Before you go, I have a question. I forgot to ask Gen earlier."

"Sure, ask away."

"I've made a poppet with her blood in it. When's the best time to use it?"

He looked impressed. "You have her blood?"

"From when we fought."

He nodded. "Probably on the night itself, but ask Gen. As High Priestess, she will now control the how's and when's."

"All right, thanks, I'll ask her."

He smiled and left, and Avery wasn't sure what was the most unnerving. The Caspian she hated, or the Caspian she was beginning to like. How weird was *that*?

***

Before Avery headed back to Reuben's she had one visit planned. She wanted to see James.

His wife, Elise, answered the door for her and narrowed her eyes. "You're back."

"Any chance I can speak to James?"

"He's in the church." She closed the door in her face with a *slam* that made the frame rattle.

Avery realised that James had shared what she was with her, and that she didn't like it one bit. She shrugged and headed up the path to the church's side door, reflecting on the fact that she couldn't please everyone. She just hoped James's wife would be as discrete as James.

The passageway beyond the door was slightly warmer than the chill air outside, but not by much. She shivered and shouted, "James?"

Silence. She headed to the nave, noting low lights in that direction, and saw James kneeling in prayer before the altar. Feeling guilty for disturbing him she turned away, deciding she could speak to him another time, but he lifted his head. "It's all right, Avery. Come in."

He looked drawn, his eyes shadowed.

"Sorry, I didn't mean to disturb you."

He rose to his feet. "I've finished. What can I help you with?" His voice was cool, and overly polite.

"I just wanted to see how you were."

"As you can see, I'm fine."

No, he was far from fine. She felt so awkward. "Good. Have you been to Old Haven over the last few days?"

His expression was hard. "I went there yesterday. It's an abomination. I felt evil, *true* evil there."

"Yes, we feel it, too. But by Friday it will all be over. You need to stay away from the place on Halloween. Well away."

He walked up to her, challenging her. "Why? Have you found out what's going on there?"

Avery wanted to tell him, but feared it would be too much. "We have, and we can stop it." *Or at least try.* "It will be a very dangerous place, so you must promise me you'll stay away."

"It's my church. I should be there."

Avery's blood ran cold. "No. You shouldn't. You won't like what you'll see."

"Why? Do you plan to desecrate the place further?"

"Of course not!" she said, recoiling at his suggestion. "We plan to free it from the magic that possesses it now. Will you stay away?"

"I think I need to understand more about you and magic, and White Haven's weird happenings, not less."

"Not by going there," Avery insisted.

"What are you hiding?" He watched her for a moment as she schooled her expression to neutral. "You said magic was good. That was a lie."

"Like anything, it can be subverted. The person behind all of this has carried revenge with her for a long time. Suspicion and hatred of others who do not understand her and who have betrayed her family have led to this. Don't perpetuate it."

"How can I do anything else when you still keep things hidden from me?"

He was right, and a war raged inside her as to how much to tell him. So far, his knowledge of what they were and what they did was not really working in their favour. "Once this is over, I will share some more. But until then, please listen to me. Stay away from Old Haven."

He shook his head. "I can't promise anything. You should go now, Avery. I'll see you soon. "

She took one long look at him and then turned and left. *Maybe they should glamour him on Thursday, too.*

25

All Hallows' Eve arrived all too quickly. The sky was a brittle blue and a chill wind sliced down the streets, reaching inside coats, slapping cheeks, and biting fingers and noses.

Avery looked out of the window and shivered, despite the warmth of the shop and her cheery surroundings. This should be a day of harmless fun, trick or treating, and scary stories, not worrying about the battle they would face that night.

Sally nudged her. "You're miles away. Cheer up."

Avery hadn't told her much about the threat they faced. She hadn't wanted to scare Sally or Dan. She'd contemplated glamouring them and trying to make them leave, but had decided against it. It wasn't fair to make someone do something against their will. Glamouring Stan had been a last resort because they knew he was directly involved. Sally and Dan were not.

She smiled. "Sorry. Just thinking of tonight."

"Ah. The coven meeting and the grove. I know you're keeping stuff back, Avery."

"Not really. I'm looking forward to meeting the whole coven. It's long overdue."

And it was true. She wasn't lying about that.

"Well, at least you're wearing your costume today. Thank you."

"Of course I am! It is Halloween."

Sally grinned. "I'm making hot chocolate. Want one?"

"Yes. Sounds fantastic." She headed back to the till while Sally went to the back room. Dan was somewhere in the shop, probably setting up for the storytelling event later. There would be two. One in the mid-afternoon, and one at six as it was late-night opening. But not for her. She'd be at Reuben's by six, waiting for the covens to arrive.

Her phone rang—*Alex*. "Hey, how are you?"

"I've got bad news."

Her heart skipped a beat. "What?" When they left the house together this morning, everything was fine.

"I can't get hold of Newton. He's not answering his phone, and he called in sick at work."

Relief rushed through her. "There you are, then. He's probably in bed, sleeping."

"You know Newton. He's reliable, a workhorse. His colleagues are worried, I could tell—although they didn't tell me anything. I just wanted you to know I'm heading round to his place to look for him."

"You shouldn't go alone," she said, immediately worried. "I'll come with you." She looked down at her witch costume and groaned. She'd have to get changed.

"No. Stay there. I'm going with Hunter. I want to know if *she's* been there. And if he answers the door, grumpy, then at least I know he's okay."

Avery's mouth was suddenly dry. "You're kidding me. You think Suzanna has something to do with this?"

Alex's voice was grim. "All morning I've been feeling this creeping dread steal over me. My neck is prickling, and something is happening at the corner of my vision. It's what triggered me to call him in the first place."

"Oh, no." She slumped against the wall, thinking. "Did we protect his place, or him?"

"No—not recently, anyway."

"Bollocks. Let's hope he's sick… As horrible as that is."

He sighed. "I hope so too, but I don't think he will be. I'll let you know, okay?"

"Okay. Stay safe, Alex." It had been on the tip of her tongue to say, *I love you,* but she couldn't. Ever since that journey in the car, she'd been meaning to bring up that conversation with him, but she'd shied away, terrified she'd misunderstood and he'd look at her like she was mad. He hadn't said a word about it, either. Instead, she repeated, "I mean it. Don't do anything stupid. I'm already worried sick."

She heard the smile in his voice. "I'll be fine. Be careful yourself." And then he hung up.

She could feel her nervous energy starting to build and the air began to eddy, teasing her hair. She caught a customer's double-take, and she quickly quelled it, taking deep, calming breaths. Half of her wanted to race through the day so they could get tonight over with, and half of her wanted the day to last forever.

Sally headed over, precariously carrying three cups. She handed one to Avery. "What else has happened?"

"Newton has disappeared."

"That nice policeman?"

"Yes. Crap! We should have protected him. Of course she'd target him!"

"Slow down!" Sally remonstrated. "Explain."

"I can't. I need to speak to Helena."

Avery headed up to her flat, leaving her drink behind. Once inside, she shouted, "Helena! Where are you?"

Silence.

She missed her flat. Reuben's estate was great, and she'd really enjoyed spending more time with the others, especially Alex. But it wasn't home. Tomorrow, all being well, she would be back here.

"Helena!"

Still silence.

She marched up to the attic where Helena was more likely to appear and sent out her magic and a summons. "Helena. I command you to come to me right now! I mean it!"

With a faint stir of air, Helena manifested, a challenge in her eyes.

Avery glared at her. "You know who's behind all this, don't you?"

Helena's gaze was coolly calculating. She was shockingly tangible. Was that Suzanna's doing, or Samhain, or both?

"Helena, I know that what happened to you was terrible, but that was a long time ago, and the people in White Haven now are not responsible. You have to stop Suzanna. You are the only one she will listen to."

Helena's gaze gave nothing away.

"One of my friends, *a very good friend*, is in danger. If you're helping her and he dies, I shall do my utmost to banish you forever!" She stepped closer so that they were almost nose to nose. "I will do it. This freedom to move between planes will go. You will be locked away forever."

Helena leaned forward, her mouth brushing Avery's ear, and she whispered, "Trust me."

Avery stumbled back in shock, but Helena had already vanished. She held her hand to her ear, still feeling Helena's icy touch.

She headed to her table, ready to start a banishing spell straight away, and then she hesitated. *Newton. The grove. The Wild Hunt.* There were so many uncertainties, and Helena's part was not clear. If she banished her now, would that benefit them, or harm them?

Damn it! She had to wait.

***

Avery was on the verge of calling Alex when he finally phoned her. "Have you found him?"

"No. His place is a mess. There was a fight, so he didn't go quietly, but her scent is all over the place, as is the strong stench of magic."

Avery felt tears prick her eyes and headed to a quiet corner of the shop, facing the wall. "We have to find him. If he dies, I will never forgive myself. We should have protected him. He should have been at Reuben's with us."

"We won't find him, you know we won't. Hunter's been all over that place, and there's not one single scent outside of his house."

"There must be something we can do."

"We can do nothing until tonight. She'll keep him alive. He'll be her sacrifice."

"If she kills him, I will kill her."

Alex's voice was grim. "We'll find a way. Stay safe."

As soon as he rang off, Avery called Ben. "I hope you're planning to stay away from Old Haven tonight."

"Actually, we were planning to come. It's Samhain, Avery, and the biggest event in Cornwall will be at Old Haven. Of course we want to be there."

"No. I'm serious. Stay away. All of you. I will tell Gabe to keep you away, and you know he will."

Avery heard resignation in Ben's voice. "From a distance, then?"

"Like the moon?"

"Funny, Avery. All right, we'll avoid Old Haven, but we'll be in the town. Our spookometer's been picking up some enhanced readings over the last couple of days. If we can't be in Old Haven, the town is the next best place."

"Your spookometer? What enhanced readings?"

"My EMF meter, obviously. The town's reading is rising."

She was incredulous. "You've been wafting that thing around town?"

"Discreetly, yes."

She sighed heavily. "Please try not to rile the locals."

"Trust me. We're all about discretion." He paused. "You sound stressed. I've not heard you sound like this before."

"We've not encountered this amount of crazy before. I'll call you tomorrow."

I hope.

***

The White Haven witches were at Reuben's house and pacing the large front sitting room in nervous anticipation by half past five. They were all dressed in black, much as when they broke into The Witch Museum a few months before.

Briar was far more upset than Avery expected. She stood stock-still and glared. "What do you mean? She's kidnapped Newton?"

Alex nodded, watching her carefully. "I'm afraid so. We should have protected him. I've been thinking on it all day long."

Briar's hands shook. "Yes, we should have. But that's our entire fault. I've been so mad with him lately that I…" She broke off. "I should have put it behind me."

"Well, tonight," Alex reassured her, "he's our first priority."

They were interrupted by the arrival of Genevieve, and Reuben escorted her into the room. She looked calm and commanding, far calmer than any of them. She took one look at them and said, "What else?"

They updated her on Newton's disappearance, and she swore profoundly. "It doesn't matter. I knew she'd have someone. I'm just sorry it's him. I've already decided we need two teams. An inner team, and the witches who will form the main outer circle."

"What do you mean?" El asked. "Why two teams?"

"The bulk of the coven will support me. We'll form a circle around the entire grove. I've decided that the simplest option is the best. Our intention tonight, and the one that we will focus on collectively, is to stop the Wild Hunt escaping from the grove and running riot. The spell will be for that alone. Containment, and then sending them back where they came from. "

Avery was horrified. "So you're anticipating that they *will* break through into our reality?"

Genevieve nodded. "Yes, unless we can stop Suzanna. But at this stage, she's far too prepared and clever for that to happen. I'm taking the broad approach."

"But what about her final blood sacrifice?" Briar asked, squaring up to her. "Are you saying we just let her kill Newton? I won't do it!" Her voice rose in fury.

"Of course not!" Genevieve snapped. "The second, smaller team will be in the grove. You will have to rescue him, but as I said, I don't anticipate that saving him will stop the spell. She will spill her own blood, or any other if she has to. It could well be that at midnight the magic is so great that the Wild Hunt can break through on their own. Once you have him, you need to get back to us, on the perimeter. But it won't be easy."

Reuben nodded. "We're the second team, right?"

"Right. Can you handle it?"

"Of course we can," El said, flexing her hands in anticipation. "If the boundaries between worlds fall, how long before the Wild Hunt arrive?"

Genevieve shrugged. "A second? A minute? An hour? I have no idea. No one in our lifetime has seen anything like this, ever! But if they break through quickly, you'll be in there when they arrive. You could all be killed, you must know that."

They fell silent, glancing at each other, and Avery slid her hand into Alex's, squeezing it gently. He squeezed back, and said, "We know. We're prepared to take that risk."

"And where is the poppet, Avery?"

Avery had told her about it after she'd spoken to Caspian, and she pulled it from her jeans pocket and gave it to her. "How do you plan to use it?"

"I have a few options, so I'll see what the occasion needs." She tucked it into her bag.

Briar was still annoyed. "Why don't we use it now? Bind her tongue, paralyse her—kill her, even. She then can't kill Newton, or complete the spell."

Genevieve held Briar's gaze. "Do you know where she lives, or where Newton is?"

Briar faltered. "No."

"If I maim her now, she could kill Newton this instant out of spite. Or she'll be so incapacitated that if Newton is trapped by a spell, or locked somewhere inaccessible, we may never find him, and he'll still die. Is that what you want?"

Briar's shoulders dropped. "No."

Genevieve patted her arm gently. "And that is why I can't use the poppet now. Personally, I find them inaccurate and haphazard to use. I would rather see the effects of my magic firsthand. Now, can someone direct me to the bathroom? I need to change into my ceremonial robes. I always wear them when I lead the coven in magic such as this."

"Sure, follow me," Reuben said, leading her out of the room.

Avery looked at the others. "This is going to be far bigger than facing the Mermaids. Maybe just a couple of us should go in to get Newton. I'll go. Who else?"

"No way," Alex said firmly, hands on his hips. "We all go together. We're a coven now, and we work better together. Don't go all gung-ho on me, Ave!"

"All right." She smiled weakly. "I do feel stronger with you guys around."

Outside, cars were starting to pull up, and she saw the familiar figures of Eve and Nate exit the first one. "Awesome. The troops have arrived. I'll go and get them."

For the next couple of hours witches arrived from all over Cornwall, and as each coven showed up, they filled each other in on the events of the last weeks and the plans for the night. There were young and old witches in the covens, and Avery understood what Genevieve had meant by some of them being nervous. They were eager to help, but Avery sensed their inexperience.

Some of the witches wore formal robes—long-sleeved gowns or cloaks. Others wore their normal clothes, wrapped up in thick coats with sturdy boots and hats. Claudia wore a sweeping gown and cloak, and she looked regal and imposing, her magic rising to the occasion. Eve and Nate wore their usual clothes, and the White Haven group spent time chatting to them privately and filling them in on the details.

Jasper greeted them warmly, a long thick cloak over his jeans and boots, and Avery was pleased to introduce him to Alex, El, and Briar. "You guys are certainly shaking up our quiet existence," he said, smiling.

"I'm sorry," Avery said. "We really didn't mean to."

He reassured her. "As big as tonight will be, and maybe deadly, for us to practise together is a good thing. Other than celebratory rites, we haven't done anything like this for years."

Oswald and Ulysses arrived together, Ulysses dwarfing everyone. He wore combat gear and a thick coat, but Oswald, like Jasper, wore a thick cloak over normal clothes. The last to arrive was Caspian and his family, and they drove up in two cars. Caspian was the only one to greet them; the others ignored their presence, but like them they wore their regular clothes.

Genevieve was undoubtedly the High Priestess. She looked stunning. Her hair was elaborately bound on her head, and she wore a long, dark green dress with a tight bodice and flowing skirt, and a long black cloak over it. All heads naturally gravitated towards her and she walked around the room, having private chats with everyone.

Reuben had organised platters of food that had been dropped off earlier that afternoon, and Avery and El helped bring them in. They all needed to eat, but heavy food was not advised before magic of this magnitude. Some of the witches refused to eat entirely, preferring an empty stomach and purification.

At length Genevieve addressed them all and the room fell silent, the tension palpable. "Tonight will be a test of our strength. We will see something that people have not seen for hundreds of years. Some of you may doubt that this will happen. I do not. The Wild Hunt *will* arrive. I have seen the grove at Old Haven and sensed the blood magic there. It is an old place of worship that sits atop a crossroad of Ley Lines—a gateway to the Other, not used in centuries. The yew tree at its heart guards that gateway, and the power is building. The boundaries between worlds will crack tonight. The Wild Hunt is vicious and bloodthirsty, and I believe that Suzanna Grayling has channelled the Crone to make this spell so effective. As to who will lead the Hunt—" She shrugged. "We will see. The myths suggest many leaders. But if they break free of the grove, many souls will be lost."

A young, male witch who had accompanied Jasper cut in, "Lost as in dead?"

"Lost as in either dead or kidnapped, taken to the lands beyond ours without a choice."

"What land? Where?"

"The lands of the Fey. Tonight you will experience wild magic, terrifying and chaotic. You must hold firm." She looked at each and every one of them. "You will be frightened, but you must concentrate only on them not escaping. It is a simple spell. We will raise a cone of power and build a wall between them and us, and I will make it impenetrable. And when the time is right, I will cast them back from whence they came. The White Haven witches will be in the grove—they have a friend they need to rescue. When that is done they will join us. But *no one* must flee!"

"Will we link hands?" another witch asked.

"No. The area is too large. We will link mentally, not physically, but you know how to do that. You will be in sight of others, though. We will be on the edge of the grove. No one goes in except myself and the White Haven witches. Is that clear?"

They all murmured their assent.

Avery spoke up. "I should warn you that Hunter said he'll turn up tonight with some other Shifters. He wants to help."

Genevieve glared. "If they get in the way, they're on their own. I can't take care of everyone. Understood?"

Avery nodded, hoping that Hunter wouldn't turn up. She didn't want him hurt too.

"One last thing," Genevieve said. "The Nephilim will be there behind us, but they will not take part in the spell. They may, however, have a part to play in this yet. Any other questions?"

The room was silent.

"In that case, let's meet at the grove, and hope Gabe has kept the onlookers away."

26

Old Haven Church squatted like a troll against the night sky. The air was crisp and clear and a sprinkling of stars shone overhead, but already a ground mist was rising, snaking over the paths and gravestones, and winding amongst the trees.

The witches made their way to the grove, witch-lights illuminating the path. Some of the witches had set off in other directions, heading to the fields behind the church at the back of the grove, to encircle it. Genevieve placed them all carefully, leaving Avery, Reuben, Alex, El and Briar to summon their courage at the edge of the trees.

"Bloody Hell," Reuben exclaimed. "I haven't been here in days. This place is vile!"

Briar shuddered. "I can't believe another witch would desecrate the Earth in this way. She's a monster."

Gabe stood at their side. "She is the Carrion Crow, bringer of death and destruction. You are foolish to step in there tonight."

Briar was resolute. "We have no choice. We have to get Newton."

Avery looked at Gabe's strong profile as he gazed into the wood. "Don't let anyone else in. I have told Ben and the others to stay away, and Hunter, too, but I have a feeling he's already in there with the other Shifters."

He nodded. "None will pass."

"Are there any onlookers trying to get in now?" Alex asked.

"No. Although some may come later—it's inevitable. Eli will stand at the end of the lane just in case. The other Nephilim are around the grove." He frowned. "What will you use to protect yourself?"

Avery answered first. "A protection spell, similar to one I used the other day, enough to numb the worst of her spell."

Gabe nodded and headed off to patrol the grounds.

For the next half an hour they waited, shuffling restlessly and discussing tactics, and time crept on as Genevieve prepared the circle. The stronger witches were interspersed with the weaker, and to her right Avery saw Caspian, his face lit from below by the pure white candle he held in his cupped hands. He caught her eye and nodded and she nodded back.

It was now half-past eleven, and finally Genevieve reappeared at their side. "We will start. Good luck."

"You too," they murmured as the larger group stepped within the outer ring of trees.

As soon as they entered the grove, a shudder ran through Avery, and she heard the others gasp.

"By the Goddess," murmured Briar. "The Earth bleeds. I feel it."

"I feel the air tainted with blood," Avery said.

"And the waters are stained with it," Reuben added.

"Fire will cleanse," El said with determination as she pushed through the overhanging branches. She had unsheathed her sword and held it steady, sweeping it before her, a shimmer of white fire running along its blade.

Alex said nothing, silently following.

Ahead of them, luring the group onward, was a yellow glow that got stronger and stronger as they reached the clearing with the yew at its centre. Suzanna had already been here. The place was filled with candles. They were on the ground, hanging from trees, and wedged into branches. One sat in the yew's hollow trunk, and the red wood seemed to bleed in the rosy glow. It looked both beautiful and deadly, and the smell of blood hit them like a wave.

Alex fell to his knees, clutching his head and breathing deeply. Avery dropped down next to him. "Alex, what's wrong?"

He blinked and gathered himself. "I can hear screaming."

She looked around, alarmed. "From where?"

"Everywhere."

Reuben, El, and Briar stood around him, watching the clearing and protecting him while he was weak, but nothing stirred.

Alex took a few deep breaths and leaning on Avery, rose to his feet. "I'm okay. I've blocked it enough so that I can think."

"What is screaming?"

His eyes were dark and troubled. "The Earth and the trees. The spell affects them, too. It violates everything. The animals have fled."

Reuben gripped his shoulder. "I think we should draw back and cloak ourselves, so she won't see us when she arrives."

"She'll know we're here, though," Avery said, feeling despondent. "She's too good."

Reuben tried to cheer her up. "We have a good plan. We'll spread out around the clearing as we planned—she can't attack all of us at once. As soon as she's here, I'll run for Newton, and you have to cover me. Agreed?"

They all nodded. "Agreed."

Before they separated, Avery said to Alex, "If you have another psychic moment, get out of here—don't risk yourself."

"If you think I'm leaving you, you're mad. I'm fine now. It's under control," he reassured her. "Don't you do anything stupid, either."

She nodded and they hunkered down, crouching behind trees and bushes, biding their time.

Suzanna's spell was making Avery's skin crawl. It was as if something evil had burrowed beneath her skin and was wriggling about. Goose bumps had risen on her arms, and she felt as if the blade of a knife was running up and down her spine. She wanted to scream. It must be some kind of repulsion spell on a huge scale. The power to maintain that over days was impressive.

Avery could also feel the power of the coven begin to grow, a subtle awareness that pricked at her consciousness, and it reassured her. Every now and then she caught a glimpse of a distant flame through the trees, marking the spot where a witch stood. So far, so good.

Without warning, the air in the centre of the grove started to whirl, leaves lifting from the ground and flying around like a mini-tornado. They spun in an ever-widening vortex as more leaves were sucked into the maelstrom, blinding the witches to what was happening in the centre. Avery leapt to her feet as every single candle went out, plunging them into darkness. A scream rent the air, and just as Avery was about to hurl a witch-light into the sky, the candles relit in an instantaneous blaze, and she fell back, almost blinded.

Newton was on his knees at the base of the tree, bound and gagged, and next to him stood Suzanna. Her hair was wild, lifting around her, and she wore black trousers, a tight black bodice over a white shirt, knee-length boots, and a cloak. But Avery only briefly took that in, her attention drawn by the long, jagged knife in her hands and the triumphant sneer on her face.

Avery was vaguely aware that several things were happening at the same time. She lunged forward, whipping air like a lasso in an effort to wrench the knife from Suzanna, and she saw Reuben sprint towards her, weapon drawn. Tree roots thrust up beneath Suzanna's feet, trying to throw her off balance, at the same time that a ball of flames hurtled towards her from the trees. But they were all too slow. Suzanna drew her knife along Newton's throat and blood surged out as he fell to the ground, blood pooling around him as she yelled a furious incantation that Avery couldn't understand.

They had all agreed not to blast her with too much power for fear of hurting Newton, but as she saw him fall, Avery sent a bolt of lightning at Suzanna. Alex was beside her as they sprinted into the clearing, but Suzanna was on her feet, deflecting the lightning around the clawing tree roots, and she rolled free.

Alex, El, and Avery continued to throw everything they had at Suzanna forcing her away from Newton, and Reuben and Briar darted forward, reaching Newton's side. But it was as if Suzanna no longer cared about him. She had spilt his blood, lots of it, and that was all that mattered.

She stood at the edge of the clearing, raising a wall of crackling energy in front of her, and then she started to chant again, raising her hands into the air.

Avery began her spell to bind Suzanna's tongue, but the ground beneath them started to buckle and lift and she fell, unable to complete it. She felt Alex grab her around the waist and pull her backwards at the same time as El sank into the earth, waist deep.

Avery struggled against him. "El, go help El!"

Alex let her go, and together they ran to her aid. Behind them, Avery was vaguely aware that Reuben and Briar were at Newton's side, trying to stem the blood flow.

Suddenly, howling snarls filled the air, and Avery looked up to see half a dozen wolves launch themselves at Suzanna from out of the trees behind her. She was caught completely unaware, and she crashed to the ground. The Shifters must have been hiding, biding their time. They all rolled together in a blur of teeth, fur, and skin.

Unfortunately, Avery couldn't help them. El was uttering a spell in a desperate attempt to free herself, and Alex and Avery grabbed her hands, pulling together.

El screamed. "I can't get free. It's like something is biting me!"

"Wait!" Avery shouted. She laid her hands on the ground and sent a pulse of power deep down into the earth, churning it up as her power sank deeper. Alex continued to pull, and with a reluctant pop, Alex hurled her out and then pulled her backwards. El's jeans were torn and her legs were bleeding as she struggled to rise. In the end, Alex picked her up.

He yelled over his shoulder, "Get back beyond the clearing! I feel it. They're coming!"

Avery glanced back at the wolves. Suzanna was already struggling to her feet, the wolves flung from her as if they were toys, but her arms were dripping blood, and blood was smeared across her face. As much as Avery wanted to attack Suzanna, it was pointless. Her shield between them was still strong, and they needed to get out of there. She shouted, "Run!" But they didn't, and instead snarled and snapped at Suzanna as she struggled to fend them off.

Avery dropped to Newton's side next to the other two witches. Briar had her hand over the wound on his neck. She was covered in his blood, her arms and clothes slick with it, but she ignored it, repeating a spell over and over, her concentration absolute.

Avery looked at Reuben. "We need to move him."

"She won't let me."

Avery turned to Briar. "Briar, we have to go, now!"

A wild wind rushed around them, and the candles' flames eddied, throwing shadows across them.

Avery turned to look at the yew. They were only feet away, and she saw a crack of light within its centre, as if reality itself was tearing apart.

"Briar!" she yelled.

Reuben didn't hesitate. He lifted Newton in one monumental effort, and Briar was forced to follow, and then all three ran into the trees, as far from the yew as they could get, following Alex's path with El.

The grove's edge was now glowing with a bright white light, throwing the trees ahead of them into sharp relief. The coven had raised the shield.

At the edge of the clearing, Avery risked a look back and saw the yew tree split in two as light blazed from its trunk. The air was rent with the sound of horses screaming, dogs barking, and the long, haunting bellow of a horn carried across the night.

She turned and ran, fear in her throat, her stomach twisted with panic. Wild magic surged outwards, obliterating the revulsion that had filled the grove, and replacing it with something far scarier.

Thudding hooves filled the night, and Avery staggered and fell. She looked back and saw the light shimmer as a huge, black horse emerged, hounds at its feet, on its back a man with antlers on his head and a bow in his hands.

She froze, filled with a mixture of terror and fascination. The horse cantered into the clearing, and behind him more and more horses emerged, the riders shining with a strange spectral light and mad, wild music surging around them. The horn sounded again, and more dogs ran through, all huge, with gaping jaws dripping with saliva as they snarled and snapped.

Avery shuffled backward, hiding within the darkness of the trees and bushes, well away from the gusting candlelight. Not that it was needed anymore. The Wild Hunt brought their own light.

She watched the figure that had entered first. She knew who he was, from a myth; the partner of the Goddess, Herne the Hunter, come to ride through the night. The figures behind him were not of this world, either. They looked like men, but they weren't. They must be Fey. Even on horseback she could tell they were tall, and they emanated magic. They were bewitchingly beautiful, a mix of masculine and feminine; fierce, strong warriors, dressed in dark mail, with swords in their hands and bows at their backs. Their horses were decorated with feathers and plumes, and the saddles and harnesses jingled with silver.

Herne turned towards Suzanna, who stood triumphantly watching. Her face was transformed. She was no longer Suzanna; she was the Crone, bringer of death.

In a voice that transcended time, Herne said, "Ride with me, my queen!" He held his hand out and as she took it, he pulled her up behind him.

His horse whinnied and pawed the ground, and he turned and stared right at where Avery crouched in the undergrowth. He threw back his head and laughed. It echoed over the grove and the ground trembled beneath her feet, and then he pointed at her, and the hounds at his feet raced towards her, teeth barred.

Suddenly, Alex was at her side, and pulled her upright. "Avery, run!"

As she turned, she saw Hunter the wolf launch himself at the hound, and they rolled into the undergrowth. Then all hell broke loose as the Hunt reared on their horses as one and raced out of the clearing in all directions, charging through the trees towards the edge of the grove.

The wolves emerged from their hiding spaces and attacked.

Alex and Avery ran, pursued by Herne himself. They scrambled, half falling and mad with fear, the hounds howling. Together they turned, and while Alex hurled balls of fire and energy at their pursuers, Avery lifted the leaves up to form a wall and sent it rushing towards Herne, buying themselves seconds only.

The grove was alive with the thunder of hooves, the bark of dogs, the howl of the wolves, and the frustrated shouts of the Hunt as they pulled up against the circle of protection the witches had created. A couple of Fey charged at the perimeter, but were thrown backwards by the projected force of the coven.

The wolves continued to attack the dogs and horses as they raced through the grove, but they were horribly outnumbered, and the Fey slashed at them with their swords.

Avery and Alex stumbled to the edge of the woods, seeing Genevieve ahead of them. She stood a few feet clear of the wall of light. Behind her Newton was prone on the ground, Briar next to him, desperately trying to heal him as his life ebbed away. Reuben and El stood next to Genevieve, ready to fight.

Genevieve looked as spectral as the riders. She was bathed in the pure white light of the protection spell, her arms outstretched. She called to Alex and Avery. "Join me, now!"

They stood next to her, raised their energy and joined it to hers, backs to the circle, facing the Hunt, and Avery felt the protection spell envelop her, too, wrapping her in its warm embrace.

Herne came to a halt, a few of his riders spread behind him, each one eager to probe the spell that sealed them inside. Herne's horse pawed the ground in fury, desperate to start the true hunt, but Herne laughed.

Avery tried to focus on his face, but it was hard. His features almost repelled memory. He was handsome, cruel, dark-eyed, long-haired, and broad-shouldered, his feet ended in hooves, and his many-tined antlers rose several feet above his head. His eyes seemed to glow with a feral light.

His deep voice rattled the earth. "You seek to stop me, witch?"

Genevieve's face was fierce. "I seek to send you back from whence you came."

"It is our time now, leave while you still can."

"You underestimate my power, old one. Your time has long gone. You have new hunting grounds now. This place is not for you."

He threw back his head and laughed again as if they were a joke, and the riders behind him laughed too. "You challenge the immortals?"

"I do." Genevieve took a pace forward and pushed her power out towards him. The circle stepped forward, too, and she continued to advance on him, one step at a time, and against his will, he was forced back, the circling tightening continuously.

Herne pulled his bow free, raised it, and fired an arrow at Genevieve.

Avery's heart faltered in fear, but she kept her magic raised, feeling the coven's powers surge with hers, as Genevieve swatted the arrow away like a fly.

Suzanna leapt from behind Herne, her face contorted with fury. She pointed at Genevieve, releasing a stream of fire at her, but it was pointless, as Genevieve deflected it easily.

Avery had experienced the joined power of witches before, but nothing compared to this. She felt it lift her hair, and elemental air lifted her off the ground as magic swelled through everyone.

Herne lost patience. He raised his bow, aimed at Genevieve, and released another arrow at her, but again, she batted it away, her concentration absolute. She stepped forward again, and Herne raised his hand for a moment. Every single rider raised their bow and the air crackled with tension. And then Herne dropped his hand again and the air was alive with flaming arrows, all desperate to penetrate the shield. They failed, and the arrows fell uselessly to the ground.

Avery heard a scream to her right. A young, unknown witch stood the other side of Caspian; she looked terrified. She sank to her knees and the wall wavered. A rider immediately spurred his horse and charged at the weakened spot, punching through it as his horse left the ground, leaping over the fallen witch and escaping into the night, closely followed by a few others.

Genevieve didn't falter, she strengthened the wall, sealing the breach, and Avery heard the riders engage with the Nephilim beyond them, their cries piercing the night.

Genevieve kept advancing and the coven followed her, moving ever forward as they tightened the circle. She paused momentarily as they stepped over Briar, leaving her and Newton behind, and then they pressed on.

As they advanced the wolves attacked again and again, snapping at the legs of the horses, dodging swords and arrows, and harassing the dogs so that they howled with frustration and pain. Herne turned and raced back towards the yew tree.

The coven was advancing quickly now as they reached the clearing around the yew, and soon they were within feet of each other. The wolves paced before them, many of them bleeding and limping as they watched Herne and his Wild Hunt forced back to the gateway between worlds.

Suzanna was spitting with fury. She launched many spells at the coven, but none of them worked. She screamed, "You cannot end this! I will not allow it!"

Genevieve pulled the poppet from one pocket and a knife from another. Her voice boomed out, "You have no choice, Suzanna. You, like Herne, are out of your time. There is no place for you here. I banish you from this world forever." She plunged the knife into the heart of the poppet and Suzanna staggered back, her hand to her breast.

Half of the Hunt had already retreated back through the open doorway to the land beyond. As Suzanna stumbled, Herne's horse reared up, Herne's wild eyes furious in defeat as he glared at them, the only part of his face visible with the light behind him. Then he whirled around straight into the light, the remainder of his Hunt following him with a jangle of spurs, the flashing of silver, and malevolent stares of regret.

Genevieve threw the poppet in after him and in the blink of an eye Suzanna disappeared. With an almighty rumbling sound the light between worlds shrank and then closed with a deafening crack, and the grove was once more filled with silence.

Genevieve slowly lowered her hands, releasing the power of the coven back to the witches, and with it, the bright white light of the protection spell.

With a word, the remaining candles flared into life.

Most of the coven collapsed on the ground, Avery one of them. She felt so weak; she could hardly lift her head. She held her hand out and felt for Alex's, grasping it firmly. He squeezed back. But Genevieve didn't stop. She turned and raced back towards the edge of the grove.

Newton.

Alex pulled her to her feet. "Come on."

El and Reuben had risen too, and together they ran, finding Briar still crouched next to a barely alive Newton, Gabe on the other side, and now Genevieve, as well. She placed her hand over Briar's and sent her the last of the coven's power she still carried.

The blood flow had stopped, though Newton was horribly pale. But at Genevieve's touch, his eyes fluttered and he groaned. Avery sighed in relief, unaware she'd been holding her breath. But it wasn't over yet. He was still just clinging on to life.

Briar was crying, tears streaming down her face. "I wasn't good enough," she said, her voice cracking.

"Oh yes, you were," Genevieve reassured her, "or he'd already be dead." She turned at the sound of someone approaching, and saw Caspian had arrived. "Caspian, take Briar and Newton to the hospital. Do whatever you need to do."

Caspian looked as cool, calm, and collected as always. He crouched down, a hand on Newton's shoulder, and then extended his hand to Briar. In seconds they disappeared.

Genevieve looked at others, clearly exhausted. "I think I'm going to sleep for a week. That's the most magic I've drawn on for some time."

Avery felt a rush of guilt as she remembered how snappy she had been with Genevieve at times. "You were amazing. We couldn't have done it without you."

She smiled weakly. "It's okay. I understand. Life gets frustrating sometimes." She gathered herself with determination. "Come on, we're not done yet. We need to cleanse the grove, tend the injured witch, and ensure that doorway is closed forever." She looked at Gabe. "Did you catch the escaped Hunters?"

He nodded grimly, and Avery realised he was holding his shoulder stiffly. "You've been injured," she said.

"I will live, and the Fey are dead. But you need to go into White Haven."

Avery looked at him and then the other witches, confused. "What do you mean? We need to cleanse the grove."

"Ben has phoned. The spirits have risen. They walk the streets of White Haven, your Helena among them."

She looked at Alex, Reuben, and El in shock, speechless.

Alex gathered himself first. "When did this happen?"

"Before midnight." He gestured around him. "They rose from here and other places as you started to battle with the Hunt. Go, now!"

They looked at Genevieve, but she only shooed them on. "Go. We will finish here, and then we'll talk later."

***

As Reuben drove recklessly into town, Avery called Ben, and it took him a while to answer.

"How bad is it?" she asked, finally connecting.

"Pretty bad from your point of view, but great from ours!"

"What do you mean?"

"There are ghosts flitting all over the town and we've got some great footage—I hope. You survived the Hunt, then?"

"Only just." She looked around her at the exhausted faces of El, Reuben, and Alex. They were streaked with dirt and blood, and were covered in bruises and cuts from their pursuit through the woods. Reuben was driving with fierce concentration, taking corners way too fast, and Avery bounced around in the backseat. "We're almost there now. Where are you?"

"Bottom of High Street. Prepare yourselves, because—"

Ben's voice crackled, and the line was broken.

Avery looked at the others. "I think this is going to be big."

Reuben turned onto the main street and continued to race down the road. It was now almost two in the morning and the roads should have been deserted and dark, but instead lights were on in upstairs windows, front doors were wide open, and a few people were running down the street, pulling on clothes as they ran.

"This is not good," El said, worriedly.

They were close to the bottom of the town now, and as Reuben rounded a corner, he mounted the pavement and screeched to a halt, and they were all thrown forward. El's hands slapped the dashboard. "Bloody hell, Reuben—" she started but didn't finish, because in front of them was utter chaos.

In the middle of the road was a procession of ghosts, their spectral forms giving off a pale blue light, and what looked like half the town watching with shocked faces, some at the edge of the main street, some down side streets and others half hanging out of upstairs windows. All of them had phones in their hands, recording and snapping frantically. Shop windows were lit up, displays of pumpkins, jack-o-lanterns, and strings of lights a backdrop to the craziness of the spirits.

And there was a lot of screaming.

While some of the spirits were walking slowly, seemingly oblivious to their onlookers, others raced around, disappearing and re-appearing in the blink of an eye, running down streets, appearing on roofs, and manifesting in the middle of huddles of people who then scattered and ran away screaming, only to turn around and run the other way as spirits raced towards them.

"Holy shit!" Reuben exclaimed, and he started to laugh.

Alex groaned. "How the hell can I banish ghosts with half the town watching?"

Reuben laughed again. "There is bugger all that we can do about this! And look, no one's getting hurt!"

He was right. The spirits were like naughty children. They pulled hair, baited people, ran around, ransacked rubbish bins, and actually seemed to be having fun. And despite the palpable fear, sometimes terror, and general excitement of the crowd, Avery had to agree and she turned to the others, grinning. "Wow! This is mad!"

The witches moved in, circling slowly, and now that they were closer, they could see the ghosts' old-fashioned dress and their strange hairstyles as they progressed their mad carnival march towards the harbour.

And then Avery saw her—Helena. She led the procession, a look of delight on her face, as her spectral being gave off reams of smoke that billowed around her. She looked around and saw Avery watching. For a brief second their eyes met as Helena grinned in triumph, and maybe a look of relief, too, at seeing Avery unharmed after their battle at Old Haven. And then she turned away, leading the mad carnival onward.

As they reached the harbour, the crowds were swelling, and Avery saw Ben, Cassie, and Dylan perched on the harbour wall. Dylan was filming, while Ben and Cassie were fiddling with their other equipment. A short distance away, Avery saw Sarah Rutherford and Steve the cameraman.

Avery pointed them out to the others. "Crap. This is going to be all over the news!"

Reuben was still laughing. "This is going to be all over the Internet, all over the world!"

El was giggling, too. "This is awesome!" She turned to Avery. "This is what Helena's been up to. You suspected she was up to something!"

Alex snaked his arm around Avery's waist. "Maybe this was her way of keeping people from Old Haven."

"Maybe it was," Avery said, watching the spirits enjoying their freedom. It was infectious, and she felt like running with them. Some people actually were. It was like a collective madness had infected the town. She starting laughing, too, feeling her tension ebb away. Helena never ceased to amaze her. "You know what? I'm going to call Genevieve. I think the coven would enjoy this."

"So would Briar and Newton," Alex said sadly.

"No, he would not," El corrected them. "He would be furious with the publicity and the paranormal tag the town will get." And then her voice trembled. "If he survives."

"He'll be okay," Avery said resolutely. "He has to be."

27

At dawn, after no sleep at all, Avery and the others went to Truro Hospital.

The mad rabble of spirits had finally disappeared as the night edged to a close, by which time Avery was convinced most of White Haven and the surrounding countryside had flocked to the town.

When they were convinced it was safe to leave and that nothing more sinister was going to happen, Avery and the others left the scene and drove straight to the hospital, still in their dark clothing and filthy with dirt, but they didn't care. They wanted to see Newton and Briar.

Newton looked awful, and Briar didn't look much better. He was in a side room, hooked up to drips giving him fluids and a blood transfusion, and a large dressing was on his neck. He was pale and sleeping, but he was alive. Briar was sitting next to him, half asleep in a large chair next to the bed. She had washed the blood off her hands, but her clothes were stiff with it. She stirred as they entered, and El and Avery rushed over to hug her.

"How are you?" Avery asked.

At the same time, El cut in, "How's Newton?"

Briar nodded as tears welled up again. "He's okay, I'm okay. He'll make it."

Alex came over and enveloped her in a huge hug, and Reuben gave her a squeeze of the shoulders as they all crowded into the small room.

Alex smiled. "You did good."

She shook her head, doubting herself again. "Not good enough."

"Briar, none us were that great," Avery said regretfully. "We were there to stop Newton from being hurt, and we failed. Suzanna was too quick, and in the end we weren't prepared enough. But if we hadn't have been there, he'd have bled out. So…" She shrugged.

El sat on the edge of the bed, trying not to disturb Newton. "What happened last night with Caspian?"

Briar rubbed her eyes and sat up. "He was amazing—hard to believe, I know. First he saves you, El, and now Newton. He brought us to the doors of the accident department, using witch-flight obviously, and then ran in for help. He said he'd found Newton on the street close by and just brought him here." She shook her head again, clearly stunned by the events. "No one questioned him. They just whisked us in, and it was fine. The police came and took statements, but we said we hadn't seen anything. If I'm honest, it sounds completely implausible, but Caspian was together enough to use some glamour, and well, here we are."

"Damn it," Reuben exclaimed. "I should like the guy, but I'm still struggling, to be honest."

Avery felt the need to defend him a little. "We have to give him a break, despite what happened to Gil. He's clearly trying to make amends." She felt Alex watching her, and she smiled. "Right?"

He nodded silently, and Avery had the horrible feeling he was mulling something over. She reached forward and squeezed his hand and he gripped hers back, fiercely possessive all of a sudden.

"What happened after I left?" Briar asked, breaking into Avery's thoughts.

Reuben answered. "Unfortunately, the young witch who had collapsed and let the wall break was trampled by one of the riders. She's in a pretty bad way. She's also here, on another ward. Gabe brought her in—once he and the other Nephilim had stopped the riders from escaping the grounds."

Briar's face fell and she sat up. "No! That's terrible. Will she be okay?"

El nodded. "We think so. We looked in on her before we came here. Broken bones, internal injuries, and a fair degree of shock. She's from Jasper's coven, and he was there with her. Her name is Mina."

"Did the riders cause any more problems?"

Reuben grunted. "Depends what you mean by problems. They fought viciously. Eli was injured. He ended up with a spear through his wings, and cuts down his arm, but he'll heal. One of the advantages of being a half-angel is that you have great healing powers apparently, as well as being supernaturally strong."

"Zee, too," Alex added. "A sword almost took his eye. Now he has a scar down his cheek."

"And Hunter and the Shifters?"

"A few injuries there, too. Mainly bites and mauling. They're at Hunter's house now, but they'll be heading back to Cumbria later today. We'll catch up with Hunter later."

"He's okay?"

Alex laughed. "No. But he'll survive. He was worried about you."

Briar dropped her eyes. "Tell him I'm fine."

"You can tell him yourself, he'll be visiting later."

Avery noticed Briar's constant checks on Newton, and how close she sat to the bed. She was pretty sure Hunter wasn't going to like what he was going to see or hear. But it really came down to Newton. What did he want from Briar? Avery was pretty sure her feelings hadn't changed for him at all.

"Something else happened, too," Reuben said, a wicked glint in his eye. "Something big!"

"Wasn't the Wild Hunt big enough?" Briar asked, looking worried.

He laughed. "There was a mad carnival of spirits in White Haven!" And then he started to describe what happened.

At that moment, Newton stirred in his bed. He peeled an eye open and grimaced. "You lot make such a racket."

"Hey, Newton!" Alex grinned. "You must be better, you grumpy git."

"Sod off, Bonneville. I better have drinks on the house for a year."

"Maybe a month! Don't push it."

Avery sighed with relief. He was going to be okay.

***

After visiting the hospital, Avery collected her gear from Reuben's house and took everything back to her flat, including the cats. It was great to be home, and she turned up the heat, relishing a night in front of the TV, doing nothing.

There was no sign of Helena after her antics of the night before, so trying to convince herself she didn't need to sleep, Avery headed into work to reassure Sally and Dan that everything was fine. To make up for the crazy week, she bought coffees and pastries, and spent time catching up with them—mostly gossiping about the night before, which they had witnessed, too. In fact, it was all the town could talk about. The story was on the news, on the radio, and all over the net. There was a stream of people in the shop all day long, and they didn't want books.

By the time Avery and Alex got to Hunter's house it was late afternoon. Hunter opened the door, once again covered in fresh bruises and with another black eye, and now bite marks scored his arms.

"Wow. You look terrible," Alex greeted him.

Hunter grinned and let them in. His grin split his lip, and it started bleeding again. "Ouch. Thanks. Don't make me laugh. Why aren't you battered and bruised like me and Piper?"

"We have mental scarring, as well as plenty of cuts, scratches, and bruises, thanks."

Avery added, "And enough memories to give me nightmares for a lifetime."

"True that!" He led them into the kitchen. "Beer or tea?"

Alex snorted. "Beer! It's almost five."

He handed them a bottle each and cracked one open for himself. "That was probably the weirdest night of my life. And that says something, after what happened at Castlerigg."

Piper joined them, her hair now a violent crimson, which matched the long cut running down her arm. "Last night was insane! My skin is still tingling with all that magic." She pinched her arm. "It's right here! And those spirits in the town! I still can't believe it."

Avery agreed. "You're not the only one. There was too much magic everywhere. Ours, Suzanna's, the magic of the Wild Hunt… Who cut you?"

Piper shook her head. "Some rider guy with a huge sword. I managed to bite his ankle. Hard."

Avery looked around. "Where's the rest of your crew?"

"Headed back at dawn. They didn't want to stay away too long, in case of insurrection," Hunter explained. He leaned against the counter, thoughtful. "Were they Faeries in the grove? Fey? And who was the guy with the antlers?"

Avery answered. "It was Herne the Hunter. The God of the Hunt, the partner of the Goddess. And yes, they were Fey with him, and yes, they brought a wild, chaotic magic all of their own."

Alex agreed. "Too wild. It was unpredictable, uncontrollable for us."

"I could feel it here." Hunter tapped his chest and his head. "Took all of my strength to resist running."

"It's easy to understand why normal people would have no chance when faced with the Wild Hunt tearing through the countryside and streets," Alex said. "They'd go mad, die of terror, or simply become frozen in fear waiting to be cut down or carried away. Without our own magic and supernatural abilities, we'd have stood no chance." He exhaled heavily. "The more I think about it, the luckier I realise we were."

"Don't you guys worship Herne and the Goddess?" Piper asked.

Alex groaned. "Worship is an interesting word. Sometimes we appeal to them to aid our magic, but not worship. Witchcraft does not involve bowing to gods. Magic works all on its own."

Avery agreed. "We possess and wield elemental magic, no gods needed, but we sometimes like to satisfy the gods. They're out there—in everything, if you adhere to pagan beliefs. But they have their own agendas, as you saw last night."

Piper was still confused. "So, Suzanna became the Crone?"

"She had taken on the Crone aspect of the Triple Goddess, but subverted it for her own ends, and yes, Herne recognised the Goddess in her. Gods have many faces. And I probably won't ever appeal to Herne again," Avery said with certainty. "It's easy to give them human emotions, but they're not human, and last night was a good reminder of that. They can be cruel and indifferent to our brief lives."

Piper said, "Your High Priestess, she made all the difference. And the Nephilim. Otherwise, those escaped Hunters would have caused enough chaos on their own."

They all fell silent for a moment, contemplating their great escape, and then Hunter laughed. "But what a thing to see! It was insane, but amazing—something out of a storybook! Definitely something to tell the pack about over drinks and a fire. At least that hasn't made it on to the news."

Avery had to agree. "True. It's better to have ghosts on the news than a huge coven of witches spelling away the Wild Hunt."

Alex gestured to the boxes in the room. "So, you're going, then?"

"Seems so."

"We'll keep in touch, though," Piper said, smiling. "If you ever need a pack, just call."

"Same goes," Avery said, smiling back. Despite her snark, Piper had grown on her, and she'd actually quite miss seeing them around. "You're not taking Briar with you?" she asked, half wondering if she'd go.

Hunter shook his head sadly. "I know when I'm beat. That sodding Newton guy just had to get injured, didn't he? She's all cut up about him."

"Hunter!" Piper was outraged. "He's their friend and he almost died!"

"Don't get me wrong, I'm glad he's okay, but well, you know." He shrugged and then grinned. "All's fair in love and war. He better treat her right or I'm coming back to try again."

As Avery watched him, with a wolfish glint in his eyes and Alpha swagger on display, she knew he meant it. *Newton better sort his feelings out, or he'd lose Briar forever.*

***

On Saturday night, Avery was at a very different Halloween celebration. It was the night of the town's bonfire, and she was in the crowd at the castle grounds, waiting for Stan to begin the ceremony.

She leaned into Alex's side, her arm wrapped around his waist, and pulled him so close he complained. "I can't breathe, you crazy woman." He kissed the top of her head.

She looked up at him, admiring his smile, his dark eyes, and gentleness. "Sorry. I can't help it."

"Hugs are good, but breathing's important."

She laughed and nuzzled into him again. Ever since the other night, when they'd all almost died, she felt she was so lucky to have him as her partner. It was only really four months since they'd got together, but it felt like a lifetime, and she meant that in a good way. He made her laugh, looked after her, and kept her grounded. He had simply changed her life. She kept thinking about the conversation in the car when they drove to Cumbria, and was annoyed with herself that she still hadn't brought it up. What was she so scared of?

Avery was disturbed by a shout from the front, and then she saw Stan stand on the small raised platform that served as a stage. He and Becky had returned from their short trip, slightly confused as to why they had gone away in the first place, and also wondering why Suzanna was no longer answering his calls. He was also utterly disappointed he'd missed the ghosts. She and Alex had been around to see him, just to check that they were okay, and offered lame excuses on behalf of Suzanna. Now, however, he was again dressed in his Druid robes, and after he'd made his speech and performed his libations, the fire was lit, and the party got underway.

They wandered through the crowds and visited a few stalls that were offering apple bobbing competitions, hot food, donuts, and mulled wine, and then found a good spot to watch the fireworks. Halfway through the oohs and ahhs, Avery summoned her courage and turned to Alex.

"Did you mean what you said in the car the other day?"

He looked at her thoughtfully. "What did I say? When?"

"You said to Hunter that you would move anywhere and do anything if it saved me or anyone else you loved."

He gave her a half smile. "Yes, I did mean that."

She swallowed. "You love me?"

He pulled her to him and looked down into her eyes, his hand stroking her cheek. "So you heard that? I wondered, because you didn't say anything, and I thought maybe you didn't care." He looked troubled. "But of course I love you. I'd do anything for you."

All of a sudden, Avery was flooded with overwhelming joy. She beamed at him. "I was terrified I'd misheard and didn't want to make a fool of myself. I love you, too. So much." She laid her hand over his, and then rose on tiptoes to kiss him, the noise of the crowd disappearing as she savoured his heat and his kiss.

When he finally released her, he was grinning. "I thought you were planning on letting me down gently, like some hideous 'we're just friends' crap."

She punched him on the arm. "Idiot."

"So no second thoughts about Caspian? He's obviously just waiting for the right opportunity."

And then she realised why he'd been looking worried lately. "No! He'll never have the right opportunity with me, Alex Bonneville!"

He grinned again. "Awesome. Let's talk about a trip I want to take you on." And then he nuzzled her neck and started whispering in her ear, and Avery couldn't stop giggling.

End of Book 4 of the White Haven Witches.
White Haven Witches Book 5 will be out in 2020.

Thank you for reading *All Hallows' Magic*. All authors love reviews. They're important because they help drive sales and promotions, so I'd love it if you would leave a review. Scroll down the page to where it says, 'Write a customer review' and click. Thank you—your review is much appreciated.

Author's Note

Thank you for reading *All Hallows' Magic*, the fourth book in the White Haven Witches series. I love Halloween and the magical lore that surrounds the night. I thought it would be a great subject for my series. It was fun reading up on druids, yew trees, the Wild Hunt, and ley lines.

Thanks again to Fiona Jayde Media for my awesome cover, and thanks to Kyla Stein at Missed Period Editing for applying her fabulous editing skills.

Thanks also to my beta readers, glad you enjoyed it; your feedback, as always, is very helpful!

Thanks also to my launch team, who give valuable feedback on typos and are happy to review on release. Once again, they were fantastic. It's lovely to hear from them—you know who you are! You're amazing! I love hearing from all my readers, so I welcome you to get in touch.

If you'd like to read a bit more background to the stories, please head to my website - tjgreen.nz, where I'll be blogging about the books I've read and the research I've done on the series—in fact, there's lots of stuff on there about my other series, Tom's Arthurian Legacy, too.

If you'd like to read more of my writing, please join my mailing list at www.tjgreen.nz. You can get a free short story called *Jack's Encounter*, describing how Jack met Fahey—a longer version of the prologue in *Tom's Inheritance*—by subscribing to my newsletter. You'll also get a FREE copy of *Excalibur Rises*, a short story prequel.

You will also receive free character sheets on all of my main characters in White Haven Witches—exclusive to my email list!

By staying on my mailing list you'll receive free excerpts of my new books, as well as short stories and news of giveaways. I'll also be sharing information about other books in this genre you might enjoy.

I look forward to you joining my readers' group.

About the Author

I grew up in England and now live in the Hutt Valley, near Wellington, New Zealand, with my partner Jason, and my cats Sacha and Leia. When I'm not writing, you'll find me with my head in a book, gardening, or doing yoga. And maybe getting some retail therapy!

In a previous life I've been a singer in a band, and have done some acting with a theatre company – both of which were lots of fun. On occasions I make short films with a few friends, which begs the question, where are the book trailers? Thinking on it ...

I'm currently working on more books in the White Haven Witches series, musing on a prequel, and planning for a fourth book in Tom's Arthurian Legacy series.

Please follow me on social media to keep up to date with my news, or join my mailing list - I promise I don't spam! Join my mailing list by visiting www.tjgreen.nz.

You can follow me on social media –

Website: http://www.tjgreen.nz
Facebook: https://www.facebook.com/tjgreenauthor/
Twitter: https://twitter.com/tjay_green
Pinterest:

https://nz.pinterest.com/mount0live/my-books-and-writing/
Goodreads:
https://www.goodreads.com/author/show/15099365.T_J_Green
Instagram:
https://www.instagram.com/mountolivepublishing/
BookBub: https://www.bookbub.com/authors/tj-green
Amazon:
https://www.amazon.com/TJ-Green/e/B01D7V8LJK/

Printed in Great Britain
by Amazon